Happy C
M

with lots of love from Juliet,
Alwin & Sarah xxx

SCARFE

by *Scarfe*

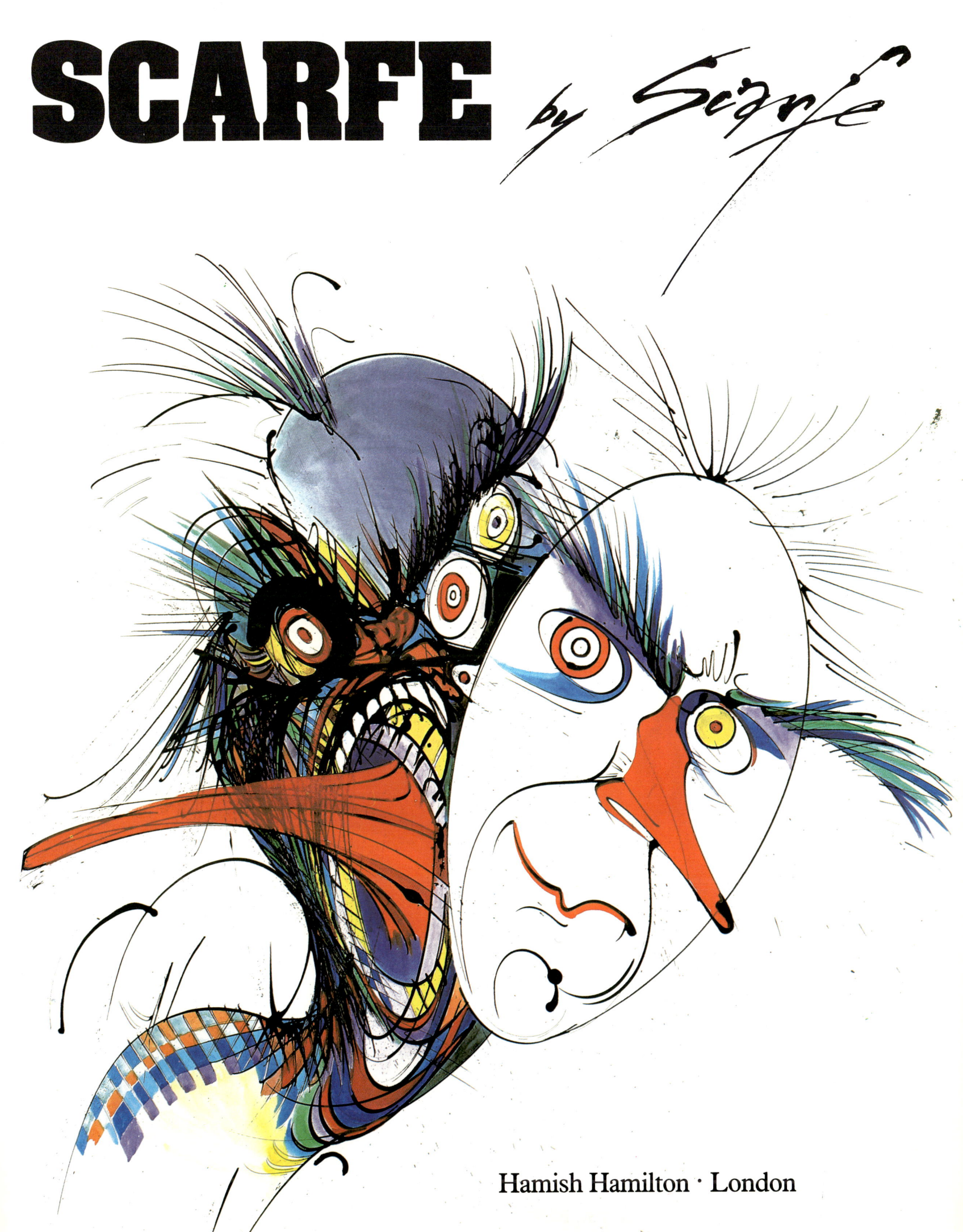

Hamish Hamilton · London

This book is dedicated with all my love to Jane, Rory, Alexander, Katy, Araminta and Rupert.

Book design by Craig Dodd

First published in Great Britain 1986
by Hamish Hamilton Ltd
27 Wrights Lane London W8 5TZ

Copyright © 1986 by Gerald Scarfe

British Library Cataloguing in Publication Data

Scarfe, Gerald
    Scarfe by Scarfe : an autobiography in
    pictures.
    I. Scarfe, Gerald   2. Cartoonists — Great
    Britain — Biography — Pictorial works
    I. Title
    741.5′092′4   NC1479.S33

ISBN 0-241-11959-6

Typeset by Rowland Phototypesetting (London) Ltd
Reproduction by Keene Engraving Co Ltd, London
Printed and bound in Spain by
Graficas Estella, S.A.

Photographs are by:
Catherine Ashmore
David Bailey
Zöe Dominic
Terence Donovan
Patrick Eager
Mark Fisher
Adrian Flowers
Manchester Guardian
Don McCullin
Gordon Scarfe
Bryan Wharton

FOREWORD

I keep no diaries and these memories are assembled by filtering through what press cuttings, articles and catalogues I have. But the strongest source of material is the drawings themselves. Each one triggers the memory of when it was drawn and why.

I do not intend this to be a complete autobiography. A lot has had to be left out because of the restrictions of space, but I have tried to cover the main artistic directions I have explored: Journalism, Reportage, Sculpture, Exhibitions, Films, Documentaries, Animation, Theatre, Costume, Rock and Roll and Opera Design.

My great thanks to those who have helped me realise the work in this book: my wife Jane Scarfe, Gordon Scarfe, Leslie Richardson, Kenneth Mahood, Norman Swallow, Mike Whittaker, Marcia Williams, Vin Burnham, Ray Scott, Mark Fisher, Harold Evans, Alan Thomson; the costume and prop departments of the English National Opera and of the Manchester Royal Exchange.

Gerald Scarfe

When I was a child I had terrible nightmares. I felt that my hands were swelling to enormous proportions and I would strike out at anyone within distance.

I would lie awake in my sick bed, listening to stories of the ghostly
monks in the marshes on Children's Hour while I waited for my mother
to return from shopping.

I was born in St. John's Wood, London in 1936. My mother was from Radnorshire and had been a schoolteacher before her marriage. My father, a Londoner, spent all of his civilian life in banking. From the age of one I suffered from chronic asthma. I was three when the war broke out and my father joined the Royal Air Force.

We were living in Goldhurst Terrace when the air raids started on London and when the siren went and the bombs began to fall we sat in the cellar. I was frightened of the wolf I knew was hiding down there and I was frightened of the claustrophobic Mickey Mouse gas mask I sometimes had to wear.

My father was posted to Shaftesbury within a year and my mother and I followed to the comparative safety and bliss of the Dorset countryside. I have memories of walking with my mother down golden brown country lanes in the Autumn sunshine collecting acorns for pigs as part of the war effort and eating dried eggs and dried bananas. My mother saved me all the family butter ration to 'build me up'. I hated it. I preferred margarine.

I remember watching my father playing the violin in the R.A.F. band at a Christmas dance and afterwards waiting for my turn to get a present from the Christmas tree only to find I was the one child who had been forgotten. My father was posted to Penarth. I suffered from terrible asthma and had to go to hospital. There would be lots of toys, coaxed my parents.

Hospital was frightening. Visiting hours were short. Sometimes my parents would walk across fields to wave to me from behind a wire fence. Misery! The cleaning lady was a witch, I had to humour her. The man in the bed opposite threw me a slab of toffee because I was crying. It missed the bed and slid into the fluff underneath. The witch gave it to me. I smiled at her.

I remember walking under the belly of a horse time and time again as a dare set by myself, fear and excitement pricking the back of my neck; finding a beautiful horse-shoe and having it taken away by a bigger boy.

When I was five, we moved to Cardiff. On the first day of school my mother dressed me on the kitchen table by candlelight because of the black-out. Then my father took me on the crossbar of his bicycle downhill through the dark streets. I was miserable. I had not thought that I would ever have to leave home. My one distinction at that school was that I was renowned for drawing the Welsh dragon.

Thereafter followed a succession of schools as we moved around the country. My parents put me into the nearest one regardless of quality so that, should I get an asthma attack, they were near at hand. I was ashamed of my illness because it made me feel different. During mild attacks I tried to pretend that I was breathing normally.

Any friends that I made lost interest because I was never at school and all found it boring to visit a friend who was bedridden. I had always been 'good at drawing' and so, in my isolation, I took to it more and more and it became my method of communication with the world. I could spend hours engrossed in a drawing and not notice the time pass by.

When I was six we moved to Ludlow in Shropshire. I remember everyone singing "Bless them all, the long and the

This drawing of an iris was made at the age of ten.

short and the tall" as my father, the only man in uniform, carried me into an air raid shelter as the siren went. My mother and I felt very proud.

I watched an army exercise on the wooded banks of the river in the shadow of Ludlow castle: a mock battle with Tommies versus Tommies dressed up as Germans. A German fell off the bridge into the water. The Tommies won.

I played mothers and fathers with the girl next door amongst some bales of straw in the barn and afterwards let her have a go on my tricycle.

When I was seven I went to stay with my grandfather and grandmother in Kidderminster. My grandfather, white-haired and stern, a retired headmaster, would not let my grandmother water the garden. Waste of water. She had to do it during his afternoon nap. I remember watching boys pulling the legs off spiders in the school playground, burning my hand on my father's cigarette and walking home tearful and soggy in dripping grey flannel trousers after falling in the river while tadpoling. I see myself trying to pluck up courage to ask a Yank "Have you got any gum, chum?" and plucking up even more courage to ask an Italian prisoner of war to give me a torch. All the other boys had. He passed it through the wire mesh of his 'open prison'. "Escapa, escapa," he said.

In 1945 when I was nine the war ended. V.E. day celebrations. Long tables with cakes and jellies down the centre of the streets. Union Jacks and bunting flying in the sunshine. We returned to London.

So many doctors, so many different theories. One thought I wasn't swallowing properly. Another punched me on the neck knocking me unconscious. During one bad attack my parents, on doctor's orders, thrust a walking stick between my elbows and my back to make me sit up straight. It was unbelievable torture. The next day the doctor said, "Oh my God, not during an attack!"

Another bad attack. My father rang Harley Street. "Put him in a taxi and bring him here," the doctor said. "But he can barely breathe, let alone move," said my father. "He'll manage it," said the specialist. We arrived in Harley Street to find that the doctor had moved on purpose to the top floor. I struggled upstairs and was near to collapse at the top. "Lie down," said the doctor. I fought for every breath. I lay down with difficulty. "In a minute you'll feel better," he said, and miraculously the asthma began to lift almost immediately. There were no drugs. Maybe he hypnotised me but fifteen minutes later I left his house feeling perfectly normal. No sign of asthma. It's a strange disease. It

didn't stay away long. So many nights were spent dark-eyed and haunted, my chest heaving, propped up on rigid arms to ease the breathing. Waiting for the night to end.

It was a relief when daylight came and still gasping for breath I could draw and read, listen to the radio, or watch the occasional bird through the window. "I don't know what's the matter with you, Scarfe," said one teacher. "Why are you always drawing disasters?" During this period my fascination with puppets, toy theatres and working models began. I made umpteen hand puppets, string puppets, plasticine figures and scenery, and gave shows for myself. I'm doing the same thing now but the puppets are thirty feet high and the theatres and the actors are real.

I drew constantly. My uncle was incensed when I didn't win first prize – any prize – in an art competition for schoolchildren held at Finchley Road Baths. He went and complained and the organisers said, "Yes, his drawing was the best, but the judges just didn't believe that a nine-year-old could have drawn it."

Although Walt Disney was my biggest hero at that age and I waited with excitement for any of his films to appear, my first artistic influence was my paternal grandfather. In the holidays I "Scarfe, why do you always draw disasters?" I was always painting mines collapsing, volcanoes erupting, natives uprising, ships going down at sea.

went to stay with him and my grandmother in Twyford, near Reading. He was a magician with wood, he could transform it into anything he wished. His workshop in the garage was a child's delight, racks of chisels, bradawls, planes and saws. Shelves with brightly coloured pots of paint, half-finished toys and the floor covered with ankle-deep wood shavings. He made all his grandchildren's toys. Best of all I admired his model soldiers, some were mounted and some were on foot. Hussars, Lancers, Horse Guards and Coldstream Guards – every detail carved and painted to perfection. I made some myself.

They were happy days in Twyford. My youngest uncle who was an officer in the army, and the most fun because he was the most irresponsible, visited often. He would take me into Henley for an afternoon at the pictures, driving too fast through the leafy lanes around Marlow in his open Riley sportscar.

Happy summer holidays were also spent in Kington, Herefordshire, with my Uncle and Aunt. They had a riding school and I learned to ride. I remember driving sheep through the narrow lanes while standing on the running board of an old Austin Seven and riding the horses back at dusk through the dark and mysterious trees. Fish and chips afterwards bought from the shop. I was allowed to stay up late. There were visits to the local flea pit: farm boys with their boots up on the stove while Hopalong Cassidy galloped to the rescue. Then there was the Horse Show at the Recreation Ground; Colonel Harry Llewellyn and Foxhunter were coming. Good days.

Back in London things were dull. I argued with my mother. School was impossible and asthma was worse. Every school report said, 'Tries hard but due to unavoidable illness' . . . 'due to great absence . . .' 'due to ill health . . .' etc. etc. I would arrive back at school and find they had started algebra. No idea what they were talking about. My teacher knew it wasn't worth bothering to coach me: I would be absent again in another week. So I took more and more to expressing my hopes and fears through my drawing.

By the age of fifteen I had passed through that difficult period in a child's artistic development when he wants to draw 'properly' or realistically and scorns the charming, naive and direct drawings of early childhood, the simplicity of which so many artists have tried to recapture in their later life.

I had taught myself to do realistic watercolours and shaded drawings by looking at 'real' artists. My Headmaster thought that I was exceptional and should start at St. Martin's School of Art although I was just fifteen, so I duly went with my father for an interview.

"Where are your drawings?" said the Principal of St. Martin's. "I haven't brought them," I said. "Ah!" he said. "Well, I think you are a bit young for us anyway", and that was that. My Headmaster was furious. "Remember," he said, "you are an artist. You never go anywhere from now on without your portfolio."

My parents, though proud of my ability, never for one moment took art seriously as a possible career; they regarded it, quite rightly, as a shaky profession and wanted me to have a proper job.

The author with his brother Gordon on an elephant 1945
'Unfortunately' 'Absence' and 'Illness', were words used constantly in all my school reports.

BENNETT STREET J.E. SCHOOL.
KIDDERMINSTER.

Report for term ending..Midsummer..1945....

Name..Gerald..Scarfe........ Class..II...

Subject	Maximum.	Obtained	Remarks.
Recitation.	10.	9½	V. Good
Reading.	10.	9½	V. Good
Writing.	10.	8	Good
English.	35.	33	V. Good
Composition.	35.	33	V. Good
Arith. Mech. Problems.	100.	70	Fairly Gd.
Arith. Mental Mech.& Ml.	100.	75	" "
Geography.	100.	65	Fair
History.	100.	92½	V. Good
Drawing. Art	100.	90	V. Good indeed
Total.	600	485½	

Punctuality..V. Good

Number in class...46.

Remarks:-

Attendance..Fairly Gd.

Position in class...10...

Conduct..Very Good....

Considering Gerald has been absent so much during the year – he has done remarkably well.

....F.R. Davies, Head Teacher.

"Draw an advertisement for Ingersol watches and win a grand prize," said the competition. I did and won first prize. I was delighted. I felt my first glow of recognition. I won a grand prize – a sweater, a shirt, a Dan Dare watch, a boomerang, etc. All useful stuff. I thought I'd like to carry on winning grand prizes. It felt good.

I sent a drawing to EAGLE comic called 'Eagle Artists Nightmare' and to my excitement they used it. I loved seeing my work in print. I knew there was something here, but I had no idea how I could make a living by selling my drawings. I had always admired and collected the work of Ronald Searle and thought he might know what I should do. I wrote him many letters but didn't dare send them. I even cycled to his house in Bayswater but didn't dare ring. It was wonderful to read in an article about Ronald Searle in the SUNDAY TIMES in 1982 that "Among younger contemporaries, he most admires Gerald Scarfe, in Searle's opinion a more direct descendant than himself from the bloody quilled age of Cruikshank."

The doctor stood over my bed looking anxious. He went in and out of focus. "He'll be all right," he said. He had just given me an adrenalin injection. He picked up my hands – the fingernails were blue. He had given me too much.

"Perhaps we'd better get him to hospital."

They called the ambulance. I could tell they were panicking. It was a long time coming. My parents didn't come in the ambulance.

Please note "Hearty congratulations" to David Hockney of Bradford.

The doctor gave the ambulance man a letter saying explicitly, "On no account give this boy any adrenalin."

I remember being shown into an arrival room. The nurse asked me umpteen questions. I could hardly breathe.

"How old was my father?" I could not remember.

"I'm just going to give you an injection," she said.

"What is it?" I asked.

"Adrenalin," she said.

"I mustn't have it," I gasped. "Didn't you get the doctor's note the ambulance man had?"

"No," she said. "I didn't."

I've always been frightened and intolerant of incompetence since then.

At the age of sixteen I was sent to the French spa town of La Bouboule in the Auvergne. The water there had arsenic qualities which were supposed to be good for asthmatics. I drank the water, bathed in the water, douched in the water and shivered in the water. I had needle-sharp jets from narrow hosepipes played all over my body – very painful and very useless. In a dark brown consulting room behind heavy net curtains, through which no sunlight ever penetrated, I sat on a stool before an enormously fat and pompous French doctor. He whirled me around on the stool and put the fear of God into me by telling me I had a weak heart, that I needed 'cupping', and that on no account should I go out into the sunlight.

'Cupping' was the almost mediaeval French custom of placing glass jars with burning candles in them on the skin. As the candle burns up the oxygen, the flesh is drawn by suction up into the glass jar. There one lies with great red mounds of sucked flesh all over the body. Fortunately they'd given up leeches.

The main benefit of these visits (I went twice) was that away from home I felt a wonderful freedom and independence. This, in its turn, benefited my asthma.

The time came for me to find a job. A proper job.

My parents sent me for an interview with the Commonwealth Bank of Australia. I didn't try very hard and they decided I was not worth training, with my record of ill health and absenteeism. I must be the only person to fail a bank on medical grounds. I didn't care. My mother always used to say "Don't care was hanged". I never understood that.

My parents were convinced that I would be dependent on them for all their lives, but I had other ideas.

The main hall of the spa, La Bouboule, drawn aged sixteen.

Fortunately there was one other artist in the family: an uncle who ran an advertising studio at the Elephant & Castle in South London. He took this bank reject on at thirty shillings a week as a junior.

It was an old Dickensian building and my first chore in the morning was to bring buckets of coal from a filthy back shed and light the antiquated stoves with newspaper and wood. Then, to further my talent, I had to clean the artists' water-pots, sweep the floor and make the morning tea. I also had to run errands and make deliveries all over London. I remember thinking, if I ever make it from here it will have been the perfect traditional deprived beginning.

As time went on and I proved that I could draw, I spent more and more time at the drawing board. In a very short time I was doing some of the main work in the studio. It was excruciatingly tedious work. Some artists spent all day painting stitching, one stitch at a time, onto drawings of shoes. Retouchers spent hours putting highlights onto photographs of saucepans, sometimes adding unnecessary work so that the client would think he had got his money's worth.

At least I was drawing. I drew everything from bedroom suites to Humpty Dumpty. I made flat pieces of flannel look like deep fluffy blankets, sad pieces of rag like crisp linen tea towels: glasses sparkled, furniture gleamed, shoes shone. The world was one wonderful big highlight and I was bored stiff. I could not stand it; I could not wait to get out. I knew I was misusing my talent. I felt the whole point of being an artist was to use my craft to tell what I see as the truth. This advertising was lies. I am sure my later work was a strong reaction to all this. An effort to put down on paper what I really felt in an emphatic way.

Any opportunity I had, I dropped my mindless commercial work and drew whatever I could see outside the studio window. I filled sketch books with people, animals and buildings. At weekends and evenings I had taken to sketching in coffee bars and on Hampstead Heath. I had several of my paintings in the open air exhibition in Heath Street but nobody bought them.

It was decided that I would make a fashion artist, one of the gifted élite in Advertising at the time, who earned big fees. So, to this end, I was sent to St Martin's School of Art for life drawing two evenings a week. It was a different world and I felt at home at last. Here I was mixing with other artists but, paradoxically, their aims seemed to be totally different. They seemed to have all the time in the world and produced very messy drawings covered in charcoal and fingerprints. I had been taught to clean up every drawing and do it quickly. If they had a new folder they would drop it in the mud and jump on it until it looked old and used. Instant experience was what they sought.

With my indifferent education I also sought instant experiences, academic as well as artistic. I taught myself French and started German. I studied Greek art and became obsessed with the beautiful simplicity of archaic sculpture and I spent hours at the British Museum. I went to the theatre and struggled with Shakespeare.

Self-portrait, 1957.

Andy Warhol's Campbell's soup cans became famous, but I'm afraid my Robertson's marmalade pot fell into obscurity. However it became useful later to frighten Enoch (see page 123).

Austrian Mountain Scene, aged 21.

When I dug this advertising drawing out of the attic Katy, my twelve-year-old daughter, said, "Dad! That's brilliant!" I found it difficult to explain to her why I thought it was far from brilliant. Like most children and many adults she admires representational art and finds Picasso's work meaningless. I tried to explain that these drawings carry no feelings, they were empty representations.

I continued sketching from life, but, lacking guidance, I was producing realistic, representational scenes in the style of my commercial drawings. An example of this is the Austrian alpine scene above. My drawing for the advertising studio had been bland and anonymous and had thrown my work off course. I now had to start again and find myself.

"MOTHER."

He wants to know if he can borrow the bike, 1961.

My first published cartoon in PUNCH, 1960.

Is this the second syllable they're acting, or the whole word?

*H*umour had become the mainstay of my life. From an early age I had listened to every radio comedy programme on my crystal set, from ITMA to the Goons. Certainly making jokes about 'the awful' seemed to dispel my anxiety. I had always made little cartoon drawings to amuse myself, and in 1957, while still working in the studio, I sent my first cartoons to the DAILY SKETCH and to my excitement they accepted one and paid me three guineas. It seemed like money for old rope, and so I became a joke factory, churning out batch after batch every week. It came easily to me and I was soon selling a great quantity. Many were based on the macabre, like 'Mother', published in 1957. It all gave me enough confidence to leave the studio, and at the same time I left home and took a room in Parliament Hill Fields, Hampstead. For a while I continued advertising on a freelance basis, and worked night and day, non-stop. I made a great deal of money, felt a lot better, and my asthma began to improve. Meanwhile, the cartooning took off. I was selling five or six a week to the EVENING STANDARD and for the first time, in 1960, PUNCH accepted one of my cartoons.

Once a week I would gather with a group of other cartoonists in a Hampstead coffee bar for an ideas session – a kind of luke-warm Bohemia. We would sit over cups of espresso discussing desert islands, mothers-in-law, burglars with swag, policemen with trousers down, hypnotists and drunks with lamp-posts. It began to get me down; surely there was more? My black humour had begun to creep into my work, as you see in the PUNCH covers, and in the soldier building a snowman on the retreat from Moscow. They show individuals trying to make the best of a bad situation, as I had during my bed-ridden days.

My natural approach to life was beginning to show in my drawings. My style, like handwriting, arrived on its own, in its own time, as a direct result of my feelings, which were aching for an outlet. My cynical attitude to life which was to fuel this style had evolved over the years, and is more or less the same today as it was then. Jokes came easily to me, but I soon tired of churning them out. I wanted to draw something with more point than desert islands, because they were not 'real' situations. They seemed as endless and meaningless as the blankets and shoes I had drawn in the studio and I had the continual urgent feeling that I was a late beginner who had taken a seriously wrong turning and had to make up a lot of wasted time. I felt a desperate need to make drawings that had some purpose, that expressed my hopes and fears. I felt above all the need to capture on paper some sort of social comment. I wanted to use my pen to speak. The pressure was enormous.

Black humour had already started to creep into my work, as you see in these PUNCH covers.

THE PLEASURE SEEKERS

By Scarfe

Suddenly the dam broke. I found a way of expressing myself. The first drawing in this new direction was 'The Pleasure Seekers' in 1963. Simple though this drawing was, it was a bridge. I was expressing people's emotions: pleasure, pain, terror, etc. I realised that humour, properly used, is a devastating weapon. I had found a new direction.

PUNCH encouraged me and I produced a long series of double-page spreads with satirical undertones and stories about human nature with cynical and ironic twists like: 'Miss Public Taste', and 'The Fad'. Sometimes I took directly from my experiences in life and produced drawings like 'The Officials' and 'The Vigil'. PUNCH also sent me on my first assignment as a visual reporter to draw three pages on the newly-built Coventry cathedral in May, 1962. Most of my original drawings from this period were destroyed in a fire at Liverpool St. station while returning from an exhibition.

I was flattered to be working for PUNCH, but I was continually getting notes from the art editor saying "this nose is too big" or "these feet are too large". I think in those days PUNCH thought of itself as the ultimate arbiter of humour. The following conversation that I had with Bernard Hollowood, the editor, about political cartoons, which was printed in KING magazine, gives some idea of PUNCH's feudal attitude to its artists:
Scarfe: "Couldn't you have a cartoonist with a view of his own?"
Hollowood: "I don't see much point in letting a cartoonist have his own say if one doesn't think much of his views anyway. Obviously people buy a newspaper or magazine because they find its views stimulating. And the best way we can guarantee interest among our readers is by recruiting a group of competent artists who can translate ideas into drawings under editorial guidance."

I can count myself lucky that apart from the noses being too big I didn't get any of this 'editorial guidance'. I continued commenting on things in general – education, architecture, health care, etc. but I still felt I had more to offer.

OFFICIALS by GERALD SCARFE

A Top Official at Work

DO NOT THINK

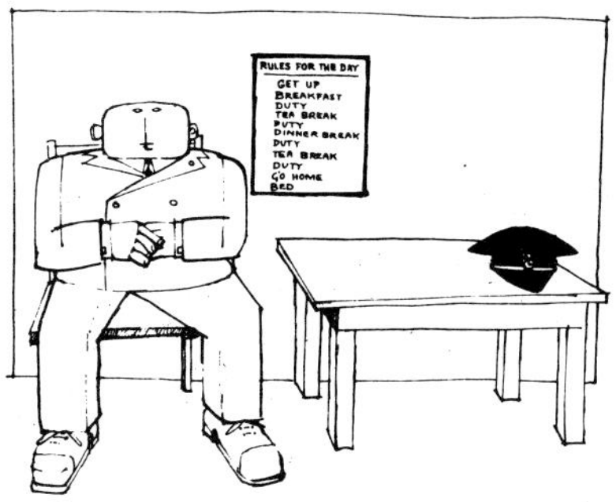

An Off-Duty Official at Home

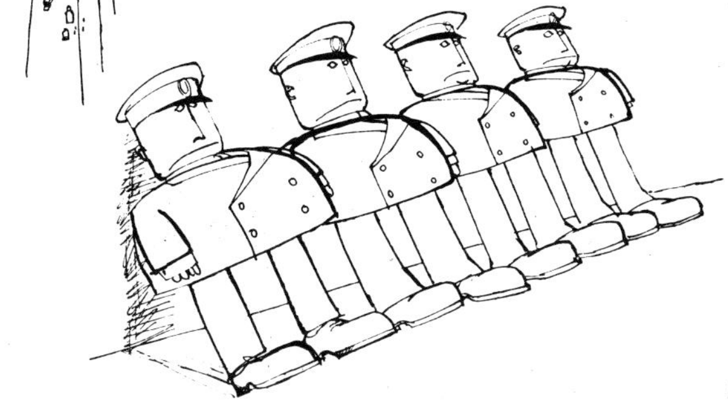

"No! If I let you do it, they'll all want to do it."

Off-Duty Officials Stacked for Immediate Use

An Official Thinking up a Swift and Cutting Reply to a Tentative Inquiry

---

The Fad

I hope you'll excuse me asking — but why are you dressed in Louis XIV attire, with your finger up your nose? It looks a bit silly to me!

It may look silly but it's the latest thing. Anyway, striped shirts are out!

I hope I'm doing it correctly — I don't want to look foolish.

Serf!

Poor fool, he must be a bit simple.

Look out! He's not even trying.

You're good at it!

What about this then? — Rather overdoing it I feel! It looks vulgar.

Never has it been practised with the taste and décorum I'm showing.

These people are ill! — unbalanced with the excitement and ecstasy that follows enthusing over the very newest and latest thing.

Which dress are considered acceptable?

The previous fad being mangled underfoot.

Gibbering and chattering a crowd surges forward bearing aloft the latest fad.

Safe and secure in their numbers, they tumble into 'Trend' boats. The helmsman sets the course and away they go — comfy in the knowledge that they are doing what everybody is doing. Unfortunately unscrupulous types have taken advantage of these good simple folk, and not only suggest the next trend but try to make hard cash out of it! Despicable!

Is it true news cottages with coach lamps are in/out

I'm anxious to discover which painter, actor, writer is fashionable

oo I'm the latest dog — I don't like it much

This is marvellous — All doing the same thing

Yes then you can be sure it's right.

WARNING!
Be sure you are doing the latest thing like everybody else — otherwise you will certainly look a booby.

Gerald Scarfe

I was taking lessons in 'General Drawing' at the London School of Printing when I met the only man who has ever taught me anything about art. His name was Leslie Richardson and I owe him a great debt of thanks. He simply taught me to think of myself as an artist by encouraging and bringing out what I had to offer. He didn't give me examples, he just talked to me.

Such was Leslie Richardson's faith in my work that he encouraged me to apply for the Royal College of Art and I was accepted.

My first day at the Royal College made me feel as though I had received a card saying 'Return to Go'. My tutor made me carry his books upstairs for him; he was going to show me that I may have made my name in the outside world but in the RCA I was just another student. That was bearable but when he talked about the world outside the Royal College I knew he'd never been there. He was a student who had become a teacher and never applied a theory in his life. "When you leave here and receive your first commission," he said, "it won't be easy, you may have to finish the rough design in two weeks and may not get more than another two weeks for the finished artwork." I knew from experience that this was nonsense, two hours was more probable.

Sadly it was too late for me; I was no longer a virgin; I was not innocent enough. Three weeks later I left the Royal College.

I had become the new face of PUNCH – the old one had a hooked nose and a hunchback.

450

MISS PUBLIC TASTE

PUNCH, September 26 1962

This delectable lady is Miss Public Taste. She is rich and capricious and to many extremely attractive. As you can well imagine she has numerous suitors. They all dance attendance on her, for she can bring fame and prosperity—and they need it

As for humour, here it is personified—star of TV, film and everything else, master of falling trousers and double meanings The sight of the underwear alone will give her a paralytic fit

Combinations? An hilarious alternative

Dirge about white-haired mothers, teen-age love and my old home town: Nasty!

The gentleman in the sequined sharkskin suit is sincere in his wooing. (He is assisted by three banshees who give a yeh yeh! backing)

These heart-tugging pets are paraded to bring a lump to her throat. A big tough boxer (or something) looking after a tiny budgie . . .

. . . a mummy pussy-cat with some weeny kittens (as seen in boots) . . . a lost wet doggie with sad eyes —ahhh!

PUNCH, September 26 1962

451

This superb piece of design is made with her in mind. Finished in chrome, glass, tin, and synthetic plastic

This artist knows how to please her by painting properly just like a lovely photograph

Her literature must not tire or tax her mind, pictures where possible

The producer above has found he can curry favour with her by presenting smashing, real people plus real sincerity, in real everyday situations

So you see, with a little simpering and grovelling her whims can be met. But, sometimes, even she is nauseated by the antics of these suitors. Then she turns on them.

Incidentally—at the top of the page is a strange group of idiots who please themselves and care nought for her

Gerald Scarfe

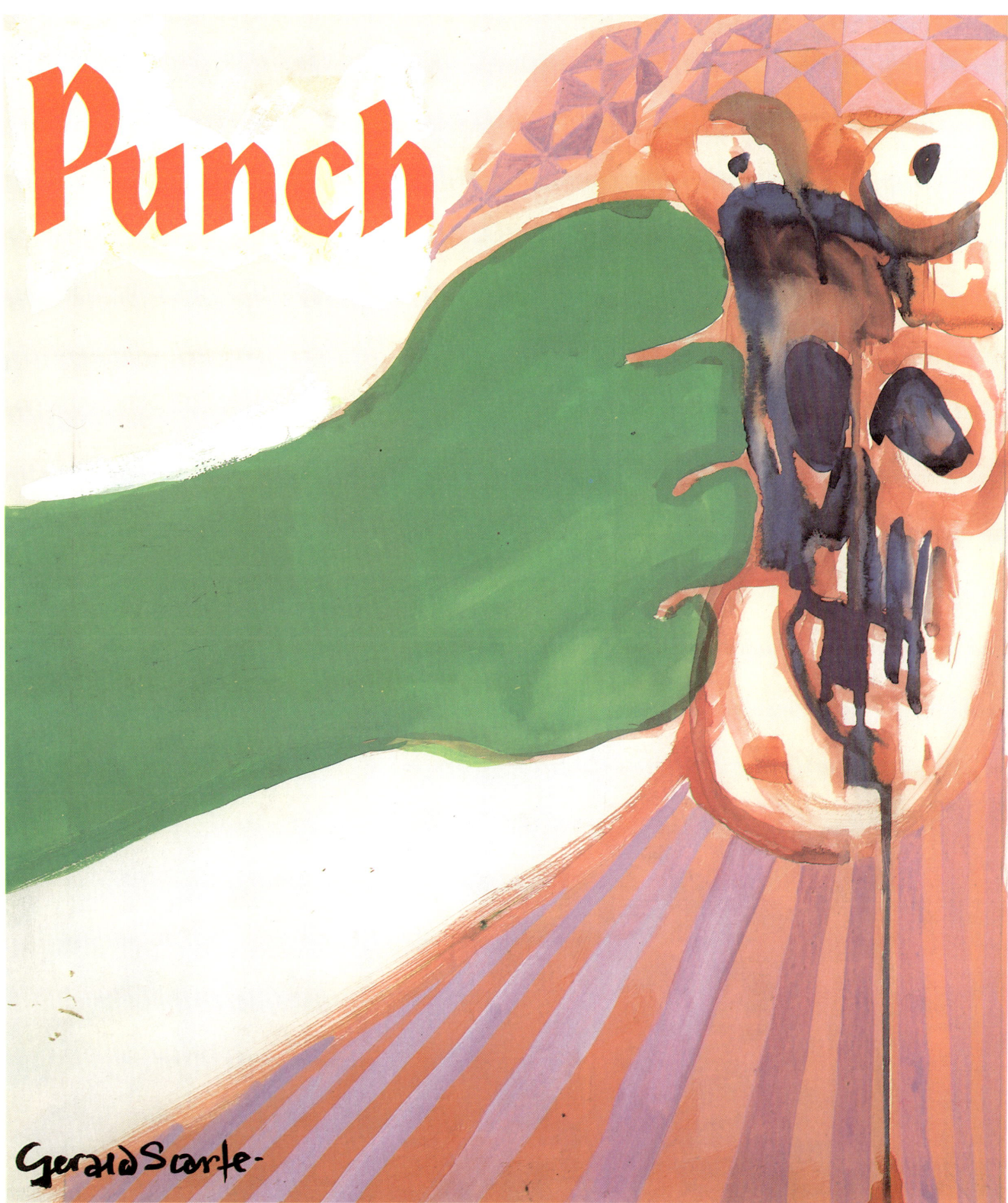

PUNCH cover 1961 – rejected.

and so on....

The Vigil

Here, sitting knee-deep in the lush grass, the hush of expectancy hanging over them, are several thousand ordinary swine like you and me (not me really).
I can't draw them all, but this will·give you a rough idea.

Trained men, every man-jack of them—they wait . . . For what are they waiting?—you may ask. Ah, we shall soon see, for from the left of the page sweeps a beautiful hand-fashioned bandwagon.

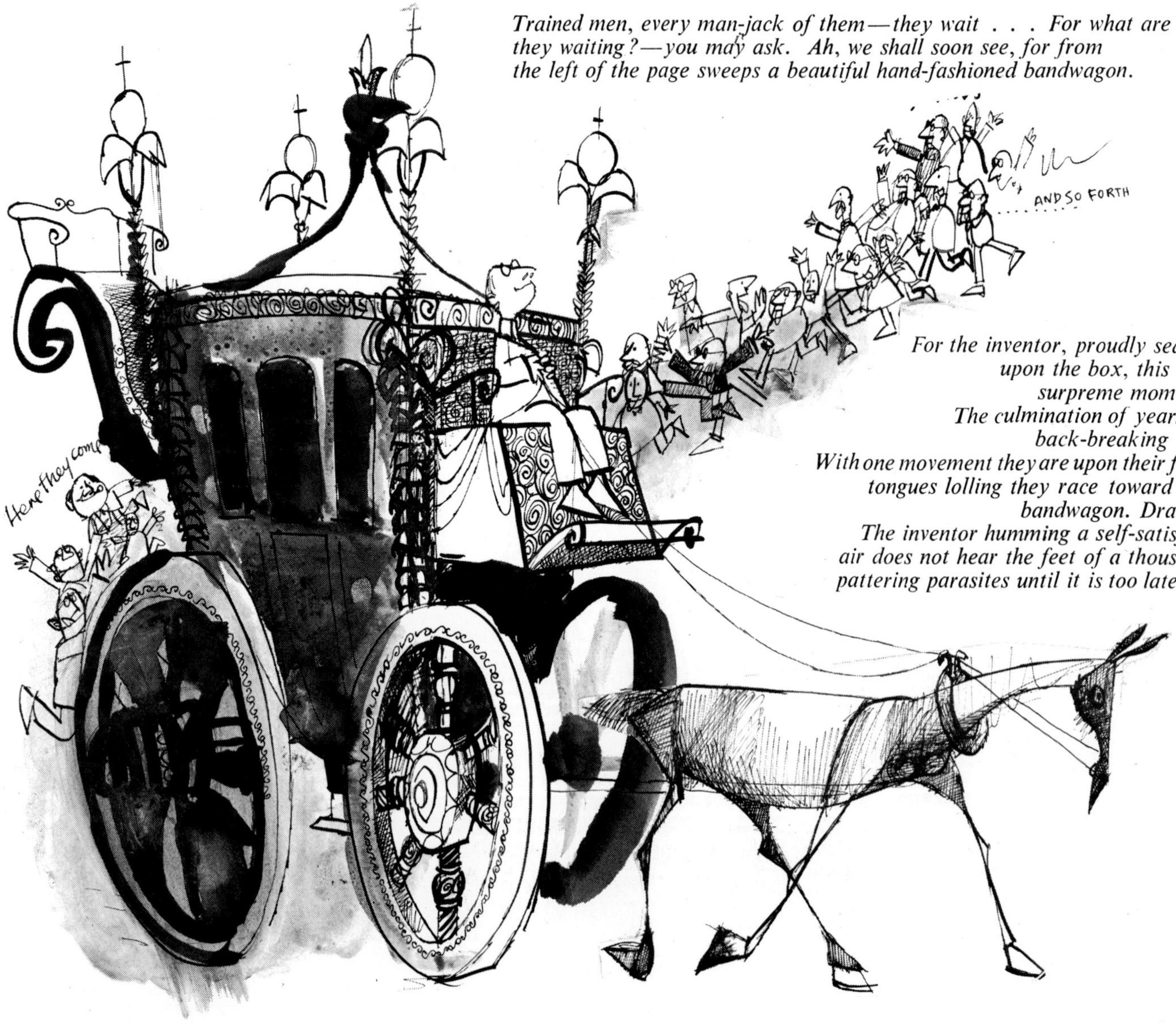

AND SO FORTH

Here they come

For the inventor, proudly seated upon the box, this is a supreme moment.
The culmination of years of back-breaking toil.
With one movement they are upon their feet, tongues lolling they race toward the bandwagon. Drama.
The inventor humming a self-satisfied air does not hear the feet of a thousand pattering parasites until it is too late . . .

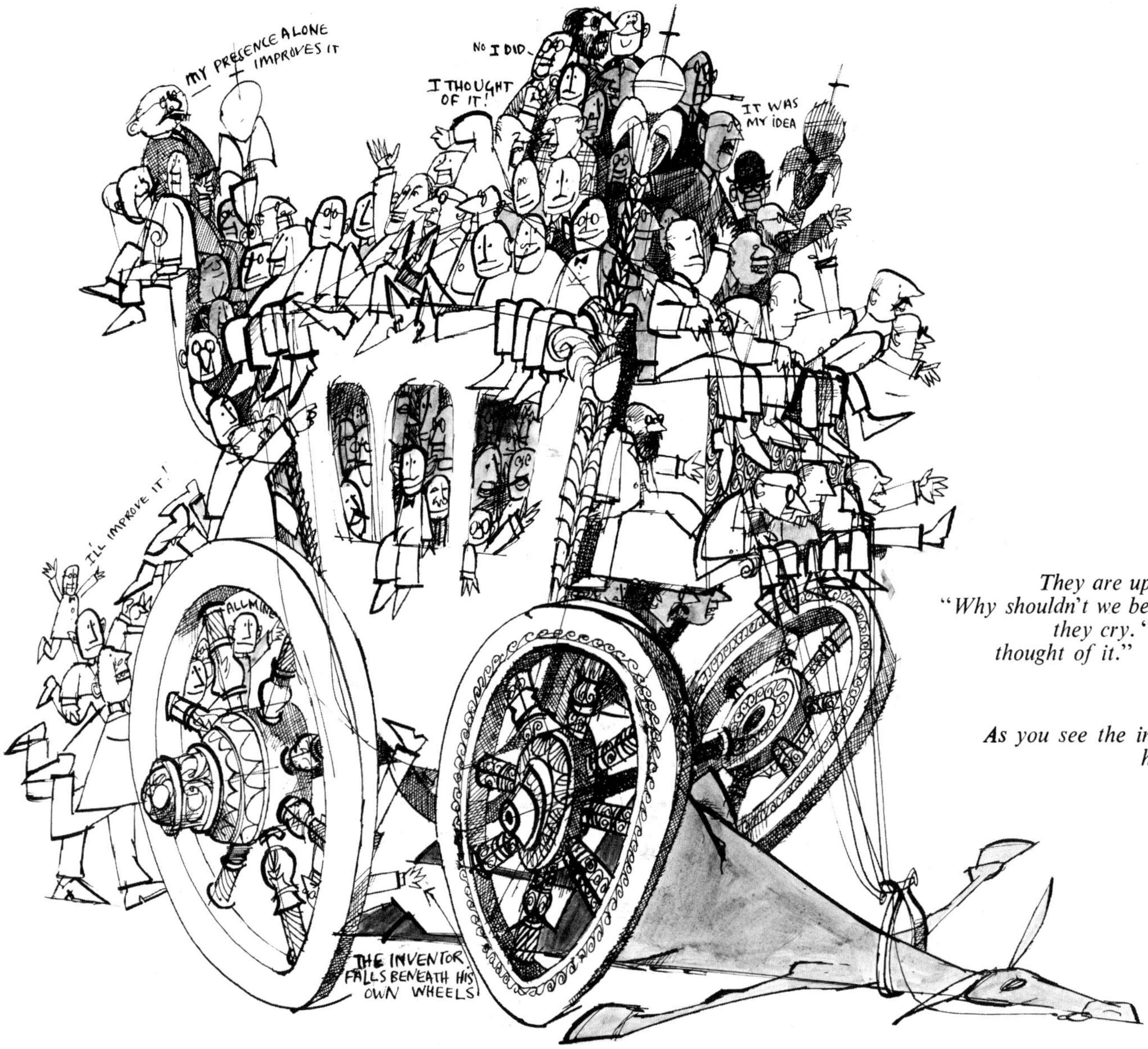

They are upon him!
"Why shouldn't we be in on it?"
they cry. "We almost
thought of it."

As you see the inevitable
happens!

A sad moment.

A spokesman stands up midst
the debris with a few words
of comfort. "Gentlemen," he cries,
fighting back the tears.
"Somewhere, some idiot is working
his knuckles to the bone
in order to provide us with an
even better bandwagon —

we must prepare ourselves for the **vigil.**"

Fairy Story

One day, while I was driving in Richmond Park, I saw to my astonishment a Good Fairy flying overhead. "I grant you three wishes, she bawled," as she passed above.

Three wishes! Naturally I was delighted and gave it a great deal of thought as I circled the park.

What an opportunity this was to right the wrongs of the world!

"HAPPY BIRTHDAY GREAT GREAT GREAT GRANDAD"

My mind dwelt upon disease and malnutrition. If only the doctors had power to cure all ills! So I decided for my first wish on "A LONG AND HEALTHY LIFE."

My mind now turned to the millions without protection from the elements. So for my second wish I chose "A ROOF OVER MY HEAD."

My last wish was the most precious of all. Here was the chance to fulfil my ambition. How wonderful if the brotherhood of man could be united, without jealousy or envy of each other's material welfare. So I chose "WEALTH."

After all, other people have an equal chance to meet the fairy!

Gerald Scarfe

Spring, the sweet Spring . . .

. . . is the year's pleasant king;
Then blooms each thing, then maids dance in a ring,
Cold doth not sting, the pretty birds do sing—
Cuckoo, jug-jug, pu-we, to-witta-woo!

Because of the direction my work was taking in PRIVATE EYE, PUNCH gave me a series of articles to illustrate, called Private Affluence and Public Squalor. In these, my last and perhaps best drawings for PUNCH, I explored the possibility of expressing myself without drawing funny little men.   This drawing was about the state of television watching in the 1960s. The man in the grave screams as endless trivial images whirl around him, 1964.

This drawing shows the state of housing, 1964.

After my days in advertising I came to a subject close to my heart – the
poor quality of mass commercial design, 1964.

Saying:
"All men are born —

Two more subjects very close to my heart. Education – it shows one system encouraging brains/minds to develop and the other restricting them and nurturing the physical side to produce a work force. Opposite – the overworked National Health doctor and the affluent Private doctor, 1964.

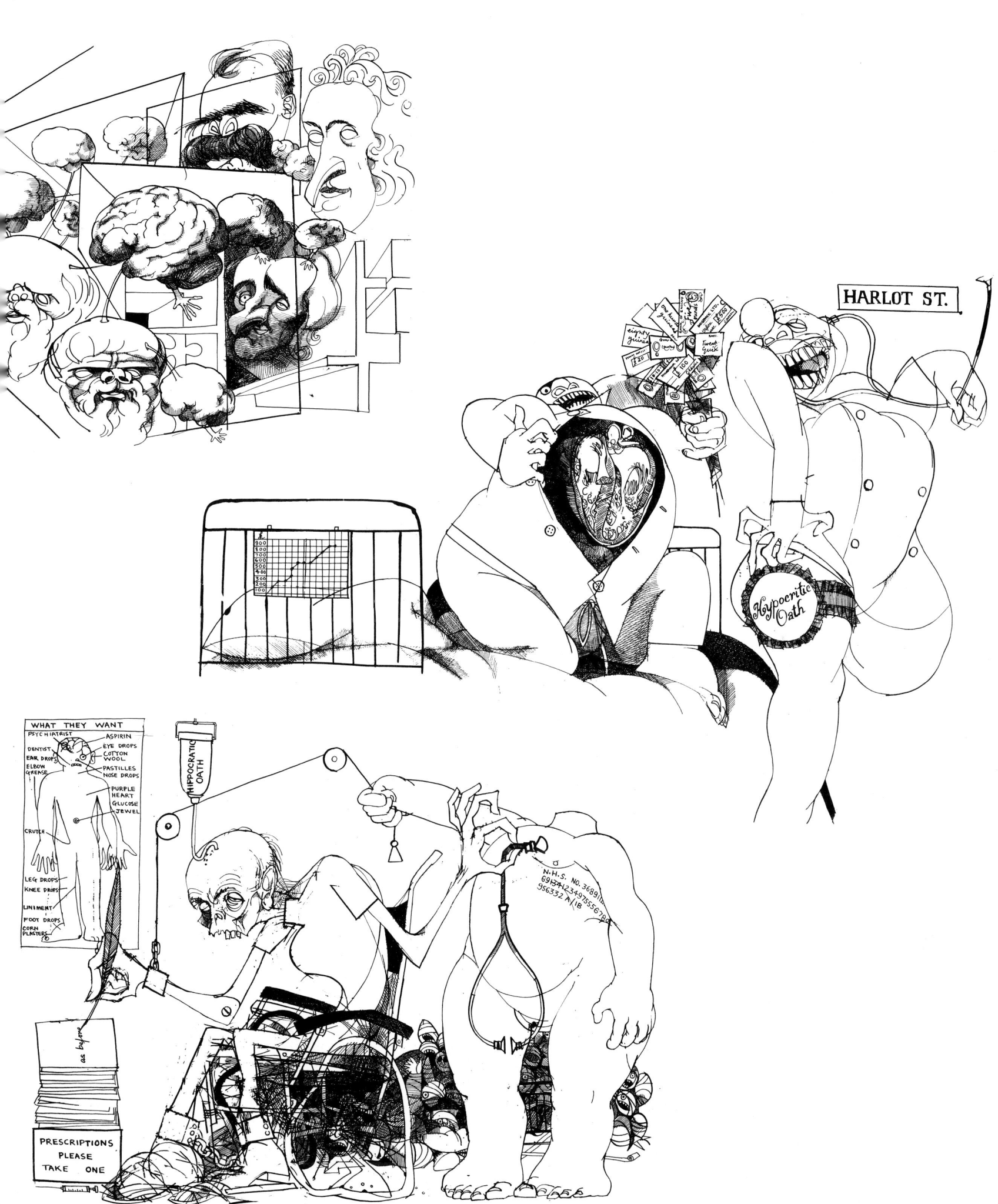

Gerald Scarfe Exhibition at the Tib Lane Gallery, Manchester.

'Gerald Scarfe insults royalty visually yet, two days ago, people were being turned away by the dozen from Tib Lane Gallery because his exhibition there does not open until today.

For the power of Scarfe is the power to touch the public nerve. He reacts to the same things as us, but with a violence unequalled since Gillray.

Gillray was anti-evolutionary, but his political sympathies are less important to us now than his overwhelming contempt for men's illusions. This is what Scarfe has in common with him: and with Gillray, Bosch-Goya, and Luis Buñuel. He shares his obsession with one creature devouring another, his fascination with nightmarish anatomy.'

M.G. McMay *Manchester Guardian* January 4 1967

I continued my exploration of 'man's inhumanity' with these anonymous abstract creatures. They represent Everyman.

Left: 'Setting Them On' prompted by employers encouraging workers to vie with each other for promotion, 1963.

Bottom left: 'Plagiarism', a subject I felt strongly about, 1961.

Bottom right: 'Vanity', a drawing designed to go with John Berger's article about me in the OBSERVER, 1963. The OBSERVER refused to print it and John Berger resigned.

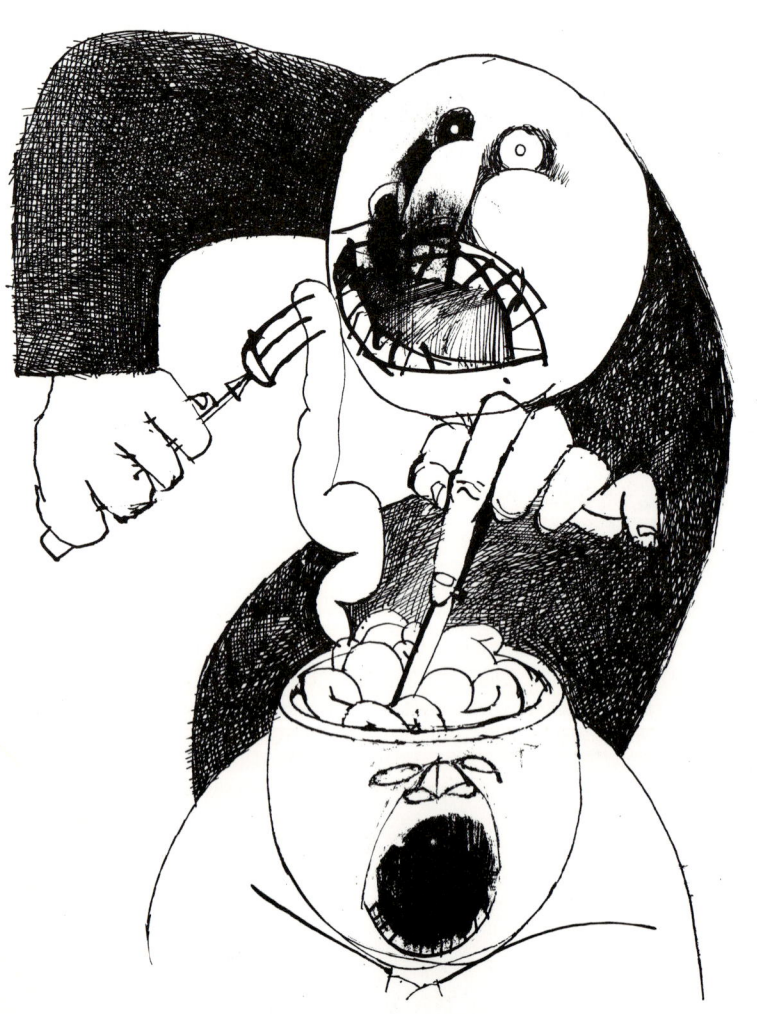

PRIVATE EYE

No. 88
Friday
30 April 65

1/6

Private Eye Jamboree, St. Pancras
Town Hall, May 4th - see page 11.

I'VE HEARD OF A SPECIAL RELATIONSHIP, BUT THIS IS RIDICULOUS

VIETNAM
WILSON
RIGHT
BEHIND
JOHNSON

It was amongst the sex shops and the strippers of Soho that I found my release. Over a betting shop the magazine PRIVATE EYE was born, and it was a breath of fresh air for me. The bottled-up feelings of my frustrated, bed-ridden childhood found the perfect vehicle, the perfect compost for my particular talents, and I very quickly began to flower. PRIVATE EYE was run by people about my age who encouraged me to develop and push my drawings even further. They suggested subjects and accepted everything that I drew. They encouraged me to turn my pen towards the art of caricature and I was able to attack the sources of so many troubles: the powerful, the leaders, the politicians who think they know what is best for us all. I focussed my attention away from the victims of society onto those who created and ran that society.

It's difficult today to describe the repressive moral climate of the early sixties. 'Lady Chatterley's Lover' was prosecuted and the world was shocked by the revelations of Christine Keeler and Mandy Rice Davis. Harold Macmillan became my first real target and when I drew him as Christine Keeler for the cover of the PRIVATE EYE annual bookshops refused to stock it. I lashed out in every direction, sometimes flailing wildly and hitting my targets by a combination of luck and instinct. I drew every politician under the sun – as libertines, vultures, philanderers, dogs and pigs. I really enjoyed myself.

I also satirised the leaders of the social scene – Mick Jagger, David Frost, David Bailey and so on. They too had the power to influence society and were worthy of attack. Alan Coren, the present editor of PUNCH, tells me I had the ability to capture a personality in such a way that you could not remember the original person. He could not recall what Jean Shrimpton looked like, but he could picture my caricature of her.

I have good memories of those days. While the strippers scurried business-like from club to club to take off their clothes, upstairs in the tiny PRIVATE EYE office I struggled to finish my work, Peter Cook pushing past knocking over the ink, while tea-making debs showered my drawing with sugar. I always thought that when I got a proper job in Fleet Street it would be different; things would be organised, not so haphazard. I was wrong. The only difference was it was not so much fun.

Because of my lack of training in Art, I taught myself anatomy from medical books. My efforts to draw anatomically led to caricatures that showed the workings of the body, the bones, sinews, muscles, skin, bulging flesh and veins and sometimes the innards: the intestines, the heart, the lungs. Through these drawings perhaps I unconsciously expressed the frailty of life which had been instilled into me by my hospitalised childhood.

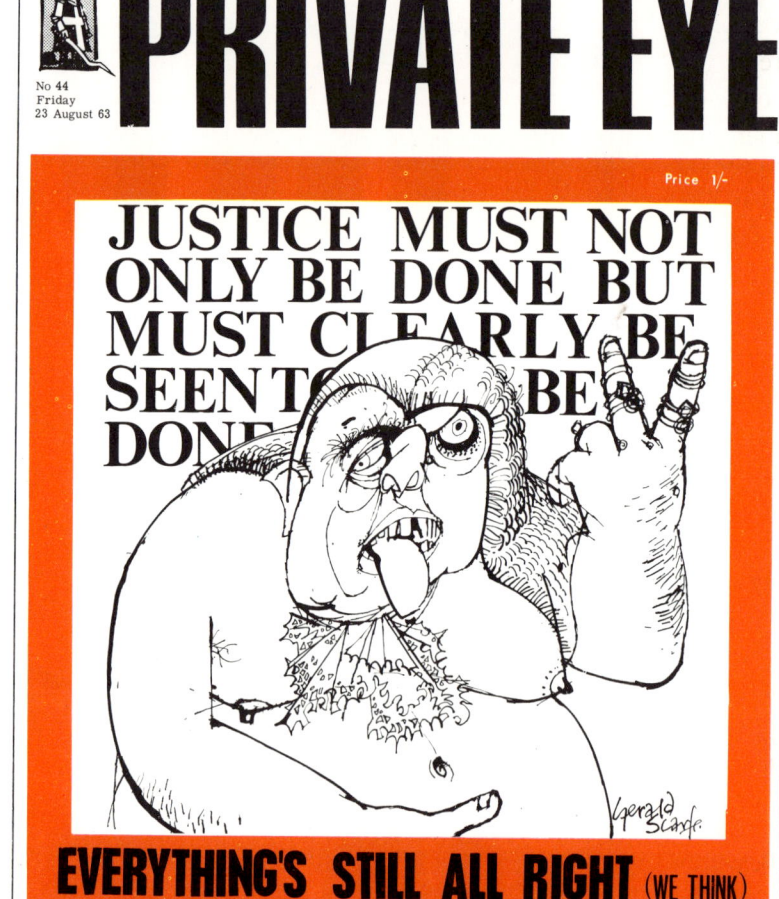

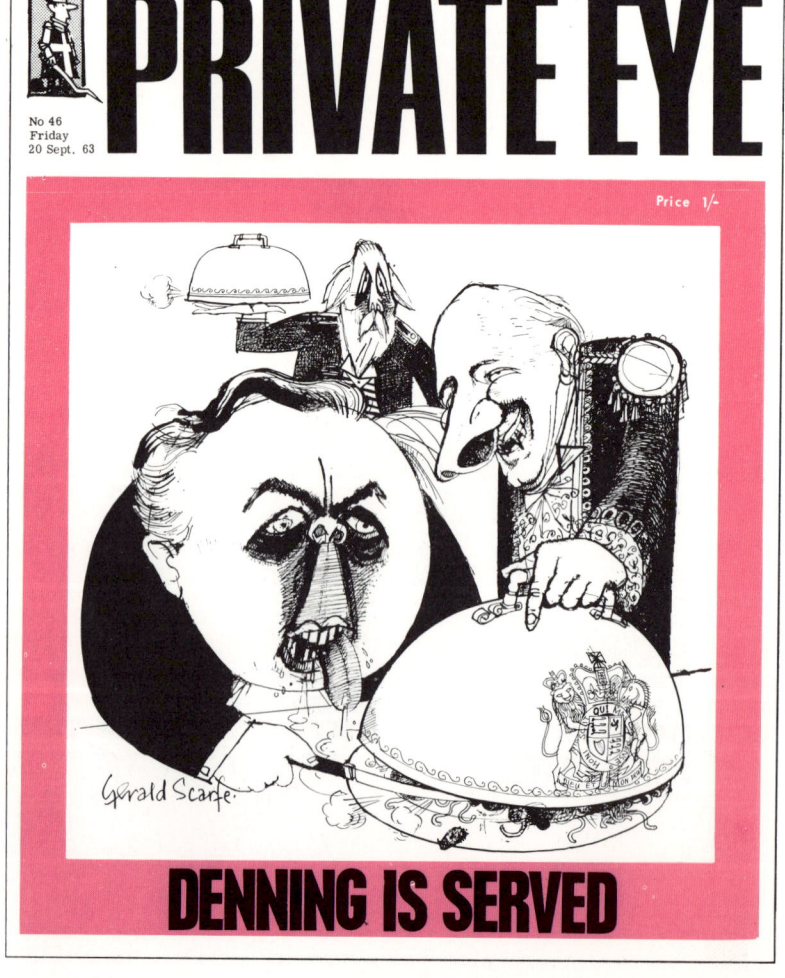

On the lighter side I found I could draw who I liked and what I liked, warts, nipples and pubic hair. I had not known I had wanted to draw these things but I had a great feeling of childish release when I did, like shouting 'bum' at the vicar's tea party. I soon got it out of my system. I have always had an urge to mention the unmentionable, to make jokes about the taboo. Nothing was sacred for me – I had no heroes. All was grist to the mill.

This brought about a reaction that my work was cruel and grotesque – I was genuinely surprised by this, since it was the way I drew naturally. I became known, not for inventing a cartoon character like Mickey Mouse or Charlie Brown, but for a view of life and attitude of mind. I was flattered by imitators. "I always wanted to do that," said one fellow cartoonist, "it's just that you showed me the way."

Left to right: Christopher Logue, Peter Cook, Christopher Booker, John Wells, Claude Cockburn, Richard Ingrams, Gerald Scarfe and Tony Rushton.

Below, left to right: Christopher Booker, Richard Ingrams, Nigel Dempster, Peter Cook, Auberon Waugh, Peter McKay and Paul Foot.

PRIVATE EYE brought me to prominence – I was deluged with commissions, offered books, interviewed on television, given exhibitions, won awards and critics took me seriously – it was bewildering. I almost began to believe it… the SUNDAY TIMES called me the only real satirist to appear from the whole movement and I was flattered when the art critic John Berger wrote, "Scarfe is that very rare thing, a natural satirical draughtsman. Gillray was one, Rowlandson wasn't. George Grosz was one but Low isn't. The supreme examples are Goya and Daumier… what is essential to them is that they draw faithfully – and with pain – the ghosts that crowd in upon them. He seems to me to belong to the proper and rare tradition. Certainly I can think of no other draughtsman in Britain who, since the war, has shown more promise in this genre." I was fast becoming one of those figures I was so fond of attacking. I had never heard of Rowlandson and Gillray and had arrived at this point by instinct. It was a great time and I have PRIVATE EYE to thank for it.

I have another thing to thank them for; travelling down to Brighton on the last trip of the Brighton Belle for a party to celebrate PRIVATE EYE's tenth anniversary I met Jane Asher, who became my wife.

Opposite: Harold Macmillan at the time of the Profumo Scandal, 1963.

'Don't Drink and Drive', left to right, Harvey Orkin, David Frost, Norman St. John Stevas and Anon, 1963.

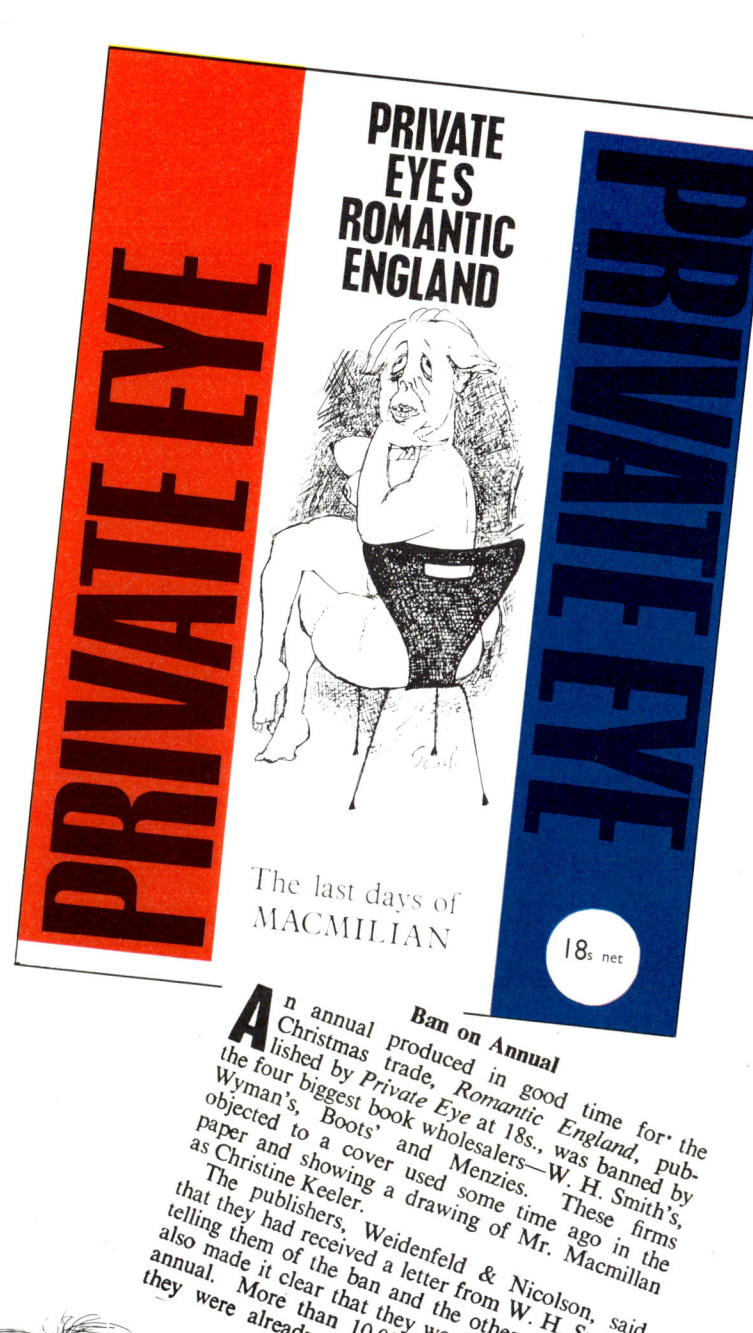

PRIVATE EYES ROMANTIC ENGLAND

PRIVATE EYE

PRIVATE EYE

The last days of MACMILLIAN

18s net

Ban on Annual

An annual produced in good time for the Christmas trade, *Romantic England*, published by *Private Eye* at 18s., was banned by the four biggest book wholesalers—W. H. Smith's, Wyman's, Boots' and Menzies. These firms objected to a cover used some time ago in the paper and showing a drawing of Mr. Macmillan as Christine Keeler.

The publishers, Weidenfeld & Nicolson, said that they had received a letter from W. H. Smith's telling them of the ban and the other wholesalers also made it clear that they would not handle the annual. More than 10,000 copies were printed: they were already on sale through independent

Auberon Waugh's Diary

TUESDAY

THE MORNING is spent sitting for my portrait by Gerald Scarfe, the cartoonist. This may seem a curious thing to do, but I am persuaded that it is one's duty to leave posterity such a memorial, showing warts and all.

Scarfe's problem is one which has confronted all the caricaturists who have ever faced the task of making something ugly or grotesque out of my bland, symmetrical features: there are simply no warts to show. Many have been driven to suicide, and Mark Boxer, sent by the small but resourceful Dame Harold Evans to mock me, had to be led away after quietly inanely, swallowing mothballs for a week.

As I watch Scarfe wrestling with the problem of finding ugliness where there is only refinement, stupidity out of high intelligence, spite out of good humour, affectation out of manliness, a strange transformation comes over him.

First, I notice a wild, frustrated look in his eyes, then his lip begins to curl like a cabbage leaf, ending up as a sort of jam-and-chocolate swiss roll; next his tongue elongates like a snake until it lies ten feet long, red and glistening on my carpet. His eyes pop out on curious antennae and his penis. . . but then, perhaps I had better not say what happens to his penis, as this is a family magazine read by many impressionable young people.

PRIVATE EYE

No. 175
Friday
30 Aug. '68

1/6

STALIN:
New Heart

PUNCH IN THE

PRIVATE EYE

1/6

No 69   Friday   7 August 64

GOYA
SCARFE
AND THEIR TIMES

Published by Pressdram Ltd., 22 Greek Street, London. W. 1 GERrard 4018-9
Printed by Leo Thorpe Ltd., 215a East Lane, Wembley, Middlesex. ARNold 6009
Distributed by Moore's General Distribution Agency, 135a Goswell Road. London. E.C.1. CLE 4882

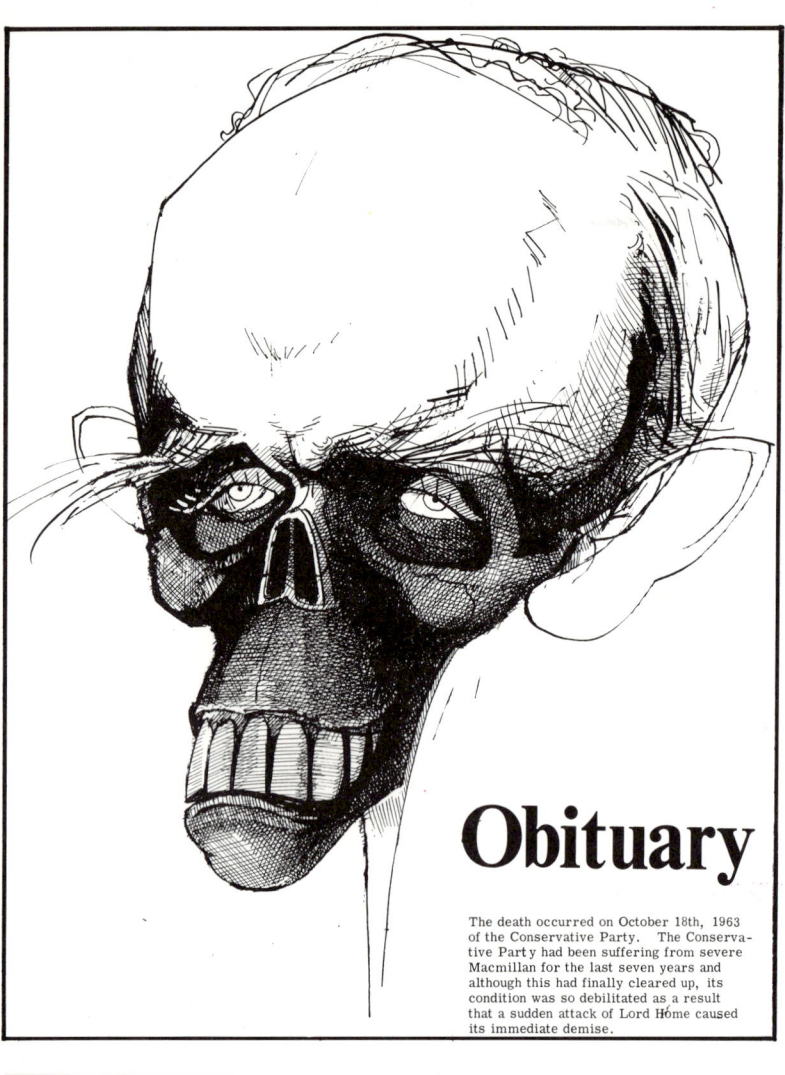

Obituary

The death occurred on October 18th, 1963 of the Conservative Party. The Conservative Party had been suffering from severe Macmillan for the last seven years and although this had finally cleared up, its condition was so debilitated as a result that a sudden attack of Lord Home caused its immediate demise.

Dr Christiaan Barnard, 1967.

Gerald Scarfe's Box of Throwups

Gerald Scarfe is fascinated by the brittle, gay, tinsel world of fashion and trends.
His heroes are ephemeral - but heroic, invulnerable and grotesque. FRANCIS WYNDHAM

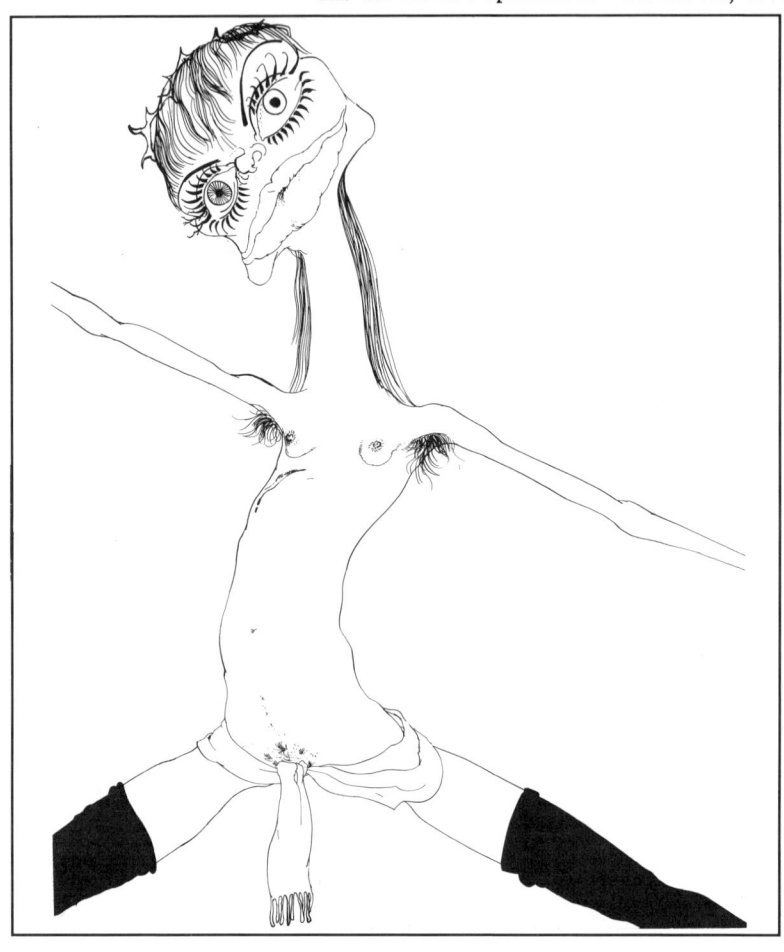

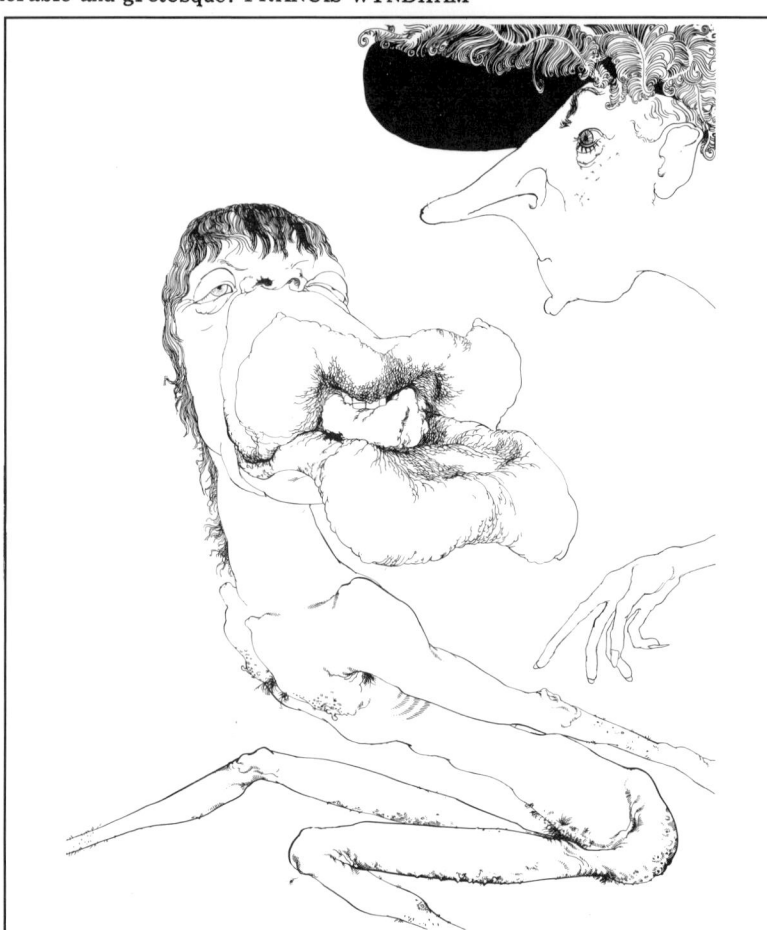

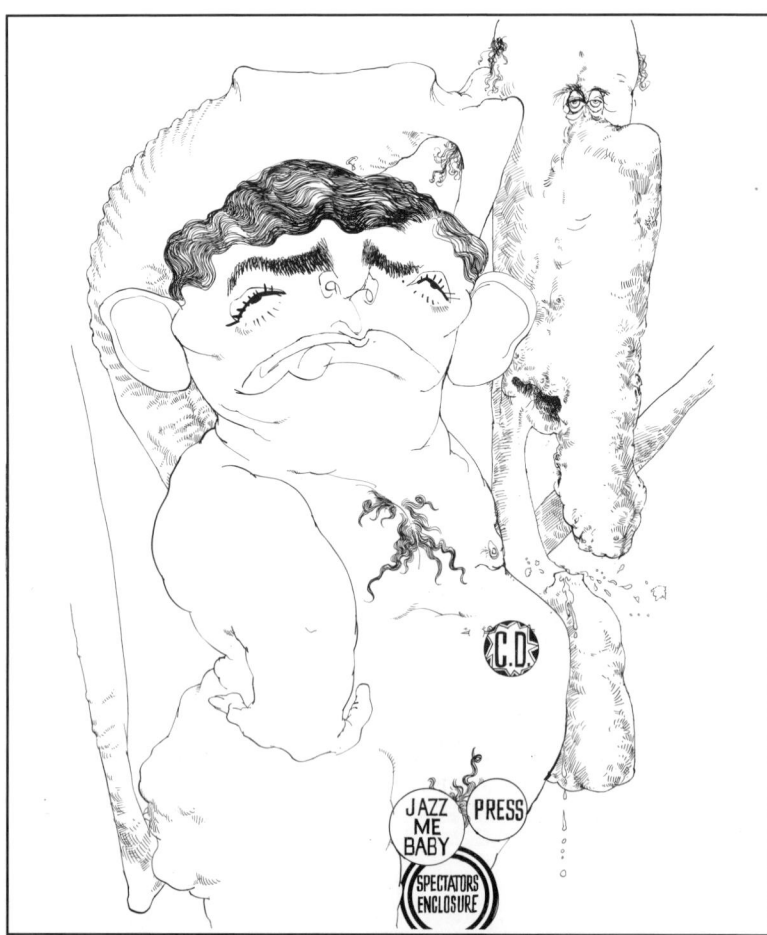

Top: Jean Shrimpton. Above: Nigel Lawson and Patrick Campbell.

Top: Mick Jagger and Cecil Beaton. Above: Lord Snowdon.

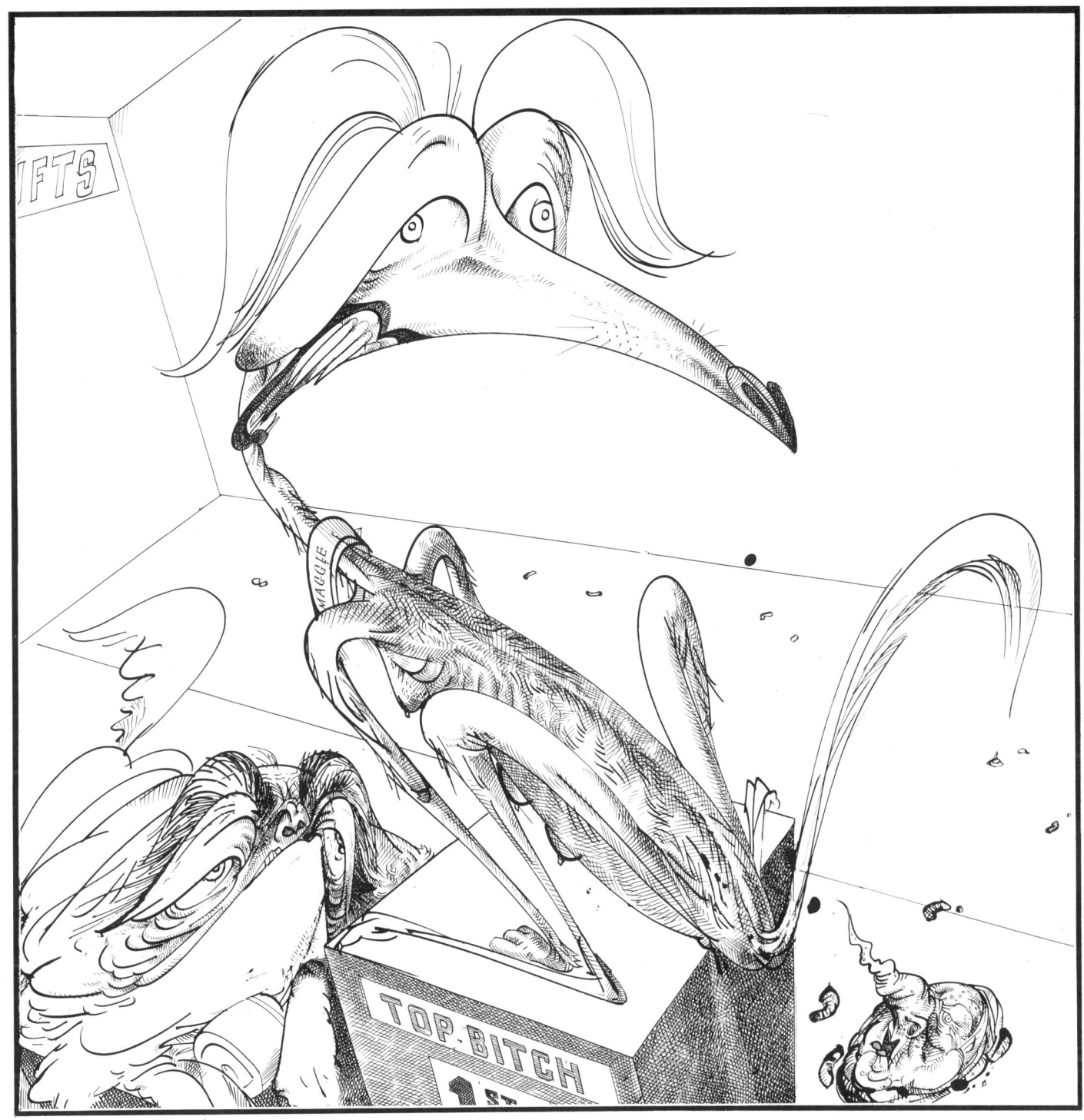

TOP BITCH

THE JUDGES were unanimous. "Thatcher", the bright-eyed, shrill-yelping little number from Grantham, Lincs, was voted outright winner of this year's Crusts with the biggest roar of acclamation ever. Owned by proud, quiet-spoken Mr and Mrs Airey Knees, "Thatcher" delighted the judges and a thousand "fanciers" with her clever tricks, which included sitting up and begging, rolling over on her back for the cameras, and leading the blind. Top marks were also awarded for her freshly shampooed coat and well-turned-out appearance. Second place was won by "Willie", a flea-infested, malodorous elderly Old English Vicar Dog. Said his owner Mrs Whitelaw from London: "I had high hopes for my Willie, many of the judges fancied his chances. But he has a nasty habit of falling over when asked to perform."

Drawings made for Christopher Logue's stories in PRIVATE EYE of man's
inhumanity to man – and animal, 1964.

Right: A Gaggle of 'Swinging London' Folk, 1966.

Some people who make London swing group around a modern piece of sculpture, 'Box' 1965 by David Hall at the Arts Council in St. James's Square. Top (l. to r.): Jan Blake—figure maker, Maureen Cleave—journalist, Gerald Scarfe—cartoonist, John Michael—men's wear designer, Barbara Hulanicki—dress designer–artist, David Bailey —photographer. Middle: Pauline Fordham—designer, Peter Blake—painter, Celia Hammond—model, David Hockney—painter, Rose Evansky—hair stylist. Bottom: Susan Murray—model, Mary Quant—dress designer, Kasmin—gallery owner, Caroline Charles—dress designer, Susan Hampshire—actress, Paul Clark—graphic designer

Above: Mick Jagger and Keith Richard 1967.
Right: Twiggy 1967.

Opposite: The characters on this once-only magazine SWILL include: Harold Wilson, Joe Grimond, Lord Home, George Brown, Rab Butler, Lord Hailsham, Selwyn Lloyd and Reginald Maudling, 1964.

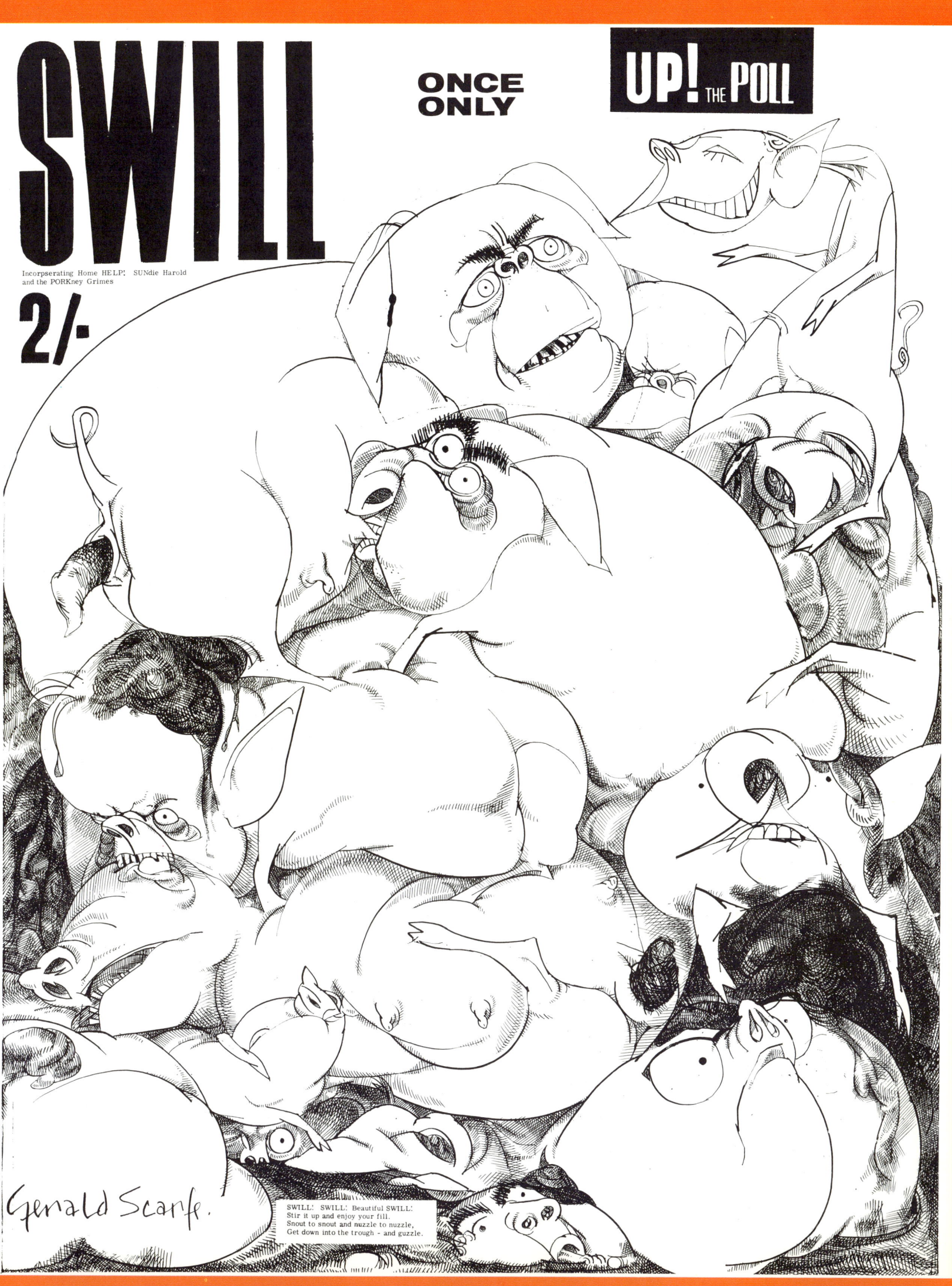

This drawing of Winston Churchill, made during his last days in the House of Commons, was commissioned by THE TIMES in 1964.

I sketched from the Public Gallery and was shocked to see how much he had deteriorated. We, the public, had only been shown the British Bulldog image of Churchill – cigar clenched between teeth, steely eyes and upheld two-fingered victory salute.

THE TIMES refused to print my drawing, saying that Churchill's wife Clemmie would be upset when the paper came through the letterbox in the morning. Later PRIVATE EYE used it on one of their covers. No sentiment there. Quite right.

It led to another commission from the SUNDAY TIMES.

I was given special dispensation by the Sergeant at Arms of the Houses of Parliament to sketch from the Public Gallery again if I were discreet. I went day after day and drew every member of the House present during those weeks. I learnt to sketch on my knee without looking down and, using the hundreds of drawings, made the eight feet by four oil painting you see overleaf.

Previous pages: The House of Commons in session. I have forgotten the names of some members.
Left hand side. 2nd Row includes *left to right* Christopher Soames, Julian Amery, Ernest Marples, Enoch Powell, Jo Grimmond, Jeremy Thorpe, Eldon Griffiths, Christopher Chataway.
1st Row *left to right* Duncan Sandys, Peter Thorneycroft, John Boyd-Carpenter, ? , Iain Macleod, Quintin Hogg, Reginald Maudling, Edward Heath, Alec Home, Selwyn Lloyd; *standing centre* William Whitelaw.
Right hand side. 2nd Row *right to left* Ray Gunter, Frank Cousins, ? , Christopher Mayhew.
1st Row *right to left* Richard Crossman, Michael Stewart, Roy Jenkins, Kenneth Robinson, Frank Soskice, James Callaghan, Denis Healey, Harold Wilson, George Brown at dispatch box, Herbert Bowden, Michael Foot.
Back benches left Ian Gilmour, Peter Walker.

Six prime ministers I have drawn…
the old showman, Harold Macmillan…
the unsuitable Lord Home…
the avuncular wheeler-dealer James Callaghan,
the two-faced Wilson,
the pompous Edward Heath
and the truly, truly dreadful Margaret Thatcher.

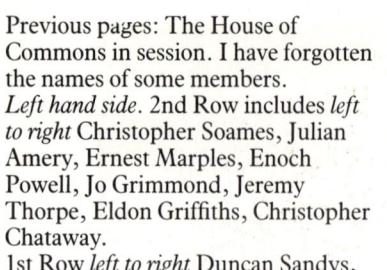

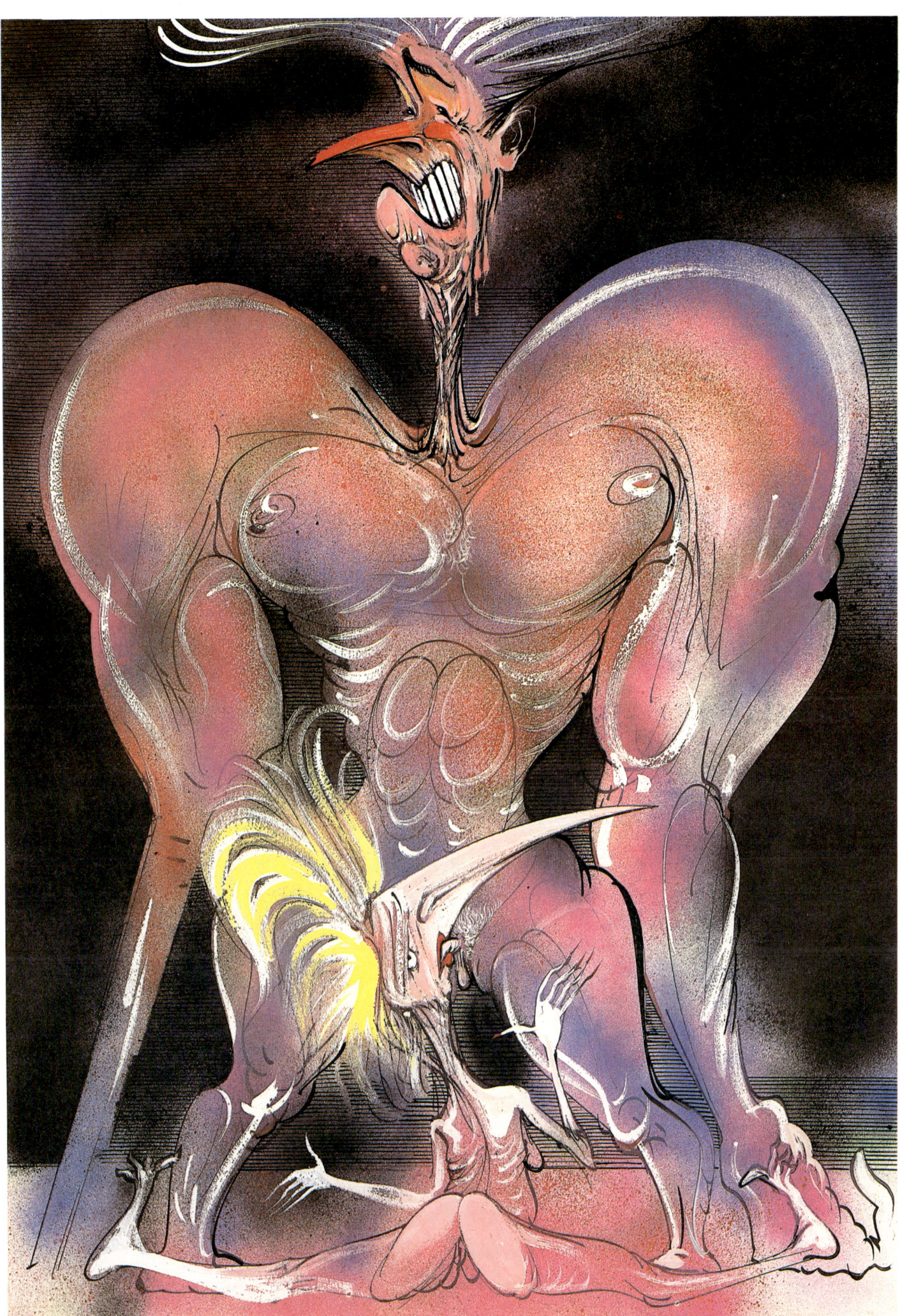

As reporters scrambled to their seats, the jet with its screaming engines, silencers removed for extra power, took off at an impossibly steep angle. I clung to my seat as a typewriter and briefcases bounced down the gangway. We were on our way to Indianapolis on a whistle-stop tour with President Johnson.

Three days before, a trip to America had been no more than a wild dream. Then one night the telephone rang. Could I leave tomorrow for New York to report on the Presidential election and have drawings back by the end of the week? "Certainly," I said. "No problem!" "Good," the SUNDAY TIMES said. American correspondent Henry Brandon would set it up for me – just ring him when I got to New York.

I arrived in New York and rang Brandon. He didn't seem to know anything about it. I said, "I must travel on the Presidential plane and get a signed portrait of President Johnson and hopefully travel with Senator Goldwater and get a signed portrait of him." "Forget it!" said Brandon. "You haven't got a hope in hell. These campaign planes have been booked up for months." He gave me the name of the Press Agent and rang off.

If I heard that today, I would return to the hotel for a sleep and a short holiday then return home . . . . but in 1964 I was all fired up and desperate. The SUNDAY TIMES had spent all that money, first class fare because economy was full. I mustn't fail them. I rang the Press Agent and pleaded.

"Not a chance, buddy," he said.

"What if I fly to Peoria, Illinois, maybe someone may get off," I said.

"Not a chance!" he said.

I pleaded once more.

"Listen," he said. "Fly to O'Hare airport and meet me in the lobby of the O'Hare Inn. Remember, I'm promising you nothing." And he rang off.

The next day I flew and found him. I was in luck. He let me board the reporters' jet to Gary, Indiana and I found myself in the thick of the impossible, exciting, hurly-burly of an American whistle-stop election campaign.

The President's Jet climbs into the sky, levels out and dives to next town, Indianapolis. It disgorges President, aides, reporters, et al. Motorcade to town, same speech, different place name, back in cars, airfield, take off, climb, dive, motorcade, same speech, different name, Cleveland, motorcade, airfield, climb, dive, motorcade, same speech, Louisville.

The further south we went the deeper became the President's drawl. I drew him while he drawled, and decided to ask him to sign the drawing at a Press Conference, later.

I rolled up my drawing, which was about two feet long, and waited for him to enter the Press Conference room. Immediately he came in I took my chance and stepped forward holding my rolled drawing. The President flinched and I was pinioned against a wall by two bodyguards with dark glasses and walkie-talkies. "What the hell are you doing?" they asked. I explained and finally convinced them that this was not the first assassination attempt with a rolled up drawing. I got my signature.

Mission half accomplished.

I was almost sad when the President's jet roared into the distance at Tennessee airport, leaving me to wait for a plane for New York.

In New York I showed my signed portrait to Senator Goldwater's press agent. "O.K." he said, and allowed me to sit with Goldwater in his private jet flying to Atlantic City.

I drew him as we flew over New Jersey. An aide asked to see it. "Excuse me," he said, pointing to the line that runs from the side of the nostril to the corner of the mouth on my drawing: "That is definitely an anti-Goldwater line!"

The Senator however was much more pleasant.

"Sure, I'll sign it," he said. "I've got a sense of humour."

New York fascinated and hypnotised me like a great, glittering snake. I had never seen so much excess, such violence, rudeness, inhumanity, such vulgarity, such energy, such riches, such poverty, and such a voracious appetite for getting to the top of the

heap. I was frightened and horrified the first day I switched on the multi-channel television in my hotel room: it told me of a human head that had been found wrapped in newspaper in a trash can. After the explanatory nature of my reportage drawings I felt a strong need to draw what I saw and felt expressively. I made drawing after drawing of the American way of life. My first drawing was 'Gorillas in the Streets' which told of the menace and fear I felt on the streets of New York in 1964.

I took the controls of a private plane as it flew over Palm Springs.

"Yeah, I used to be a cartoonist," said the pilot and owner. "Mug's game.

"You don't want to waste those brilliant ideas of yours on paper, you want to put them into harness. I marketed mine. I patented a remote control camera that films operations. Sell them to medical schools. I'm a millionaire several times over now – keep the nose up."

I have returned many times to America and I am still fascinated but not so alarmed, as I have grown used to their ways.

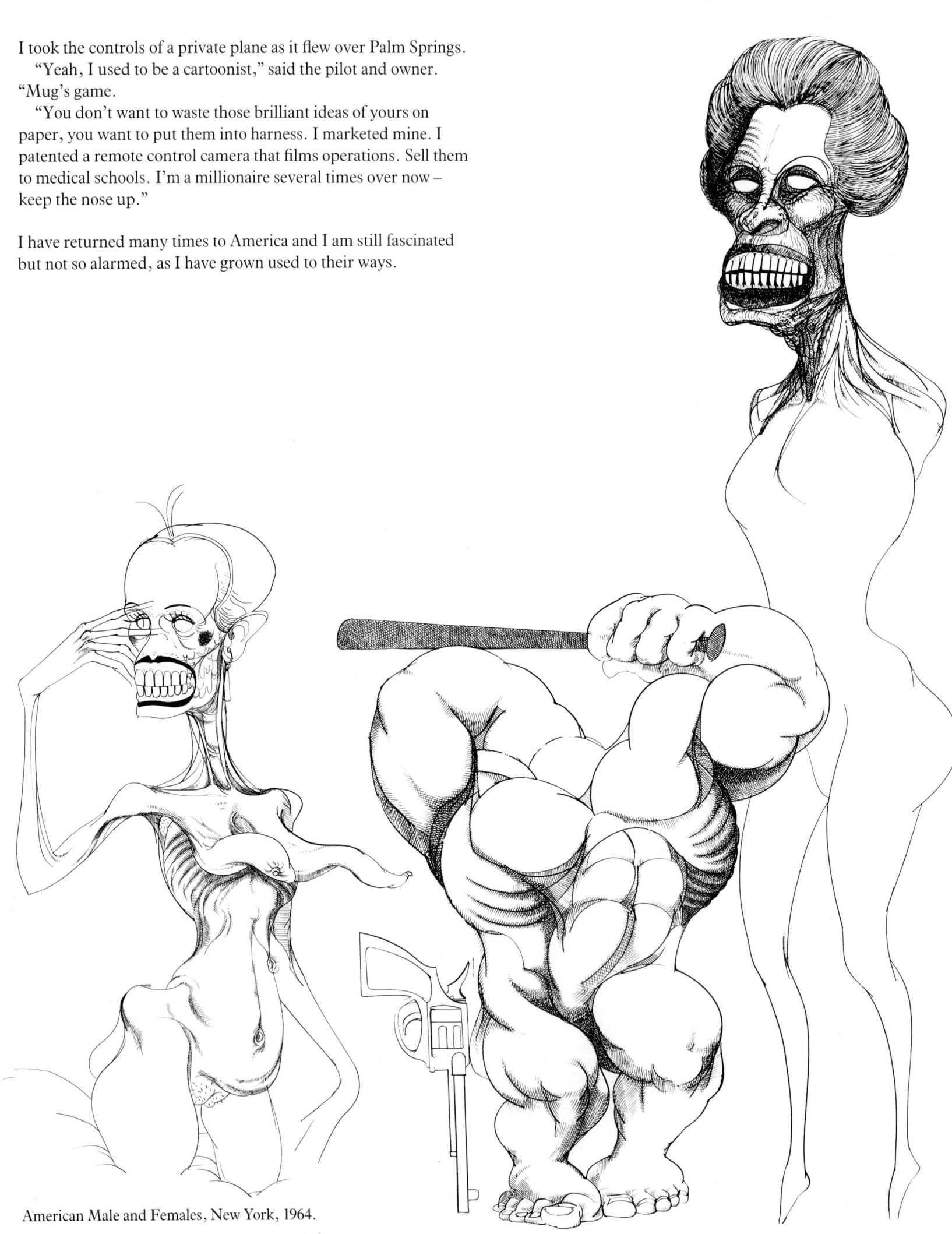

American Male and Females, New York, 1964.

Below: 'Dog Eat Dog'.

Robert Oppenheimer, 1964.

Sitting with Stephen Spender on the bed in the Iroquois Hotel in New York, while he writes letters to his intellectual friends: "This is to introduce a young artist friend of mine from ENCOUNTER magazine. Please allow him to sketch you."

I don't know how to draw these famous people. Sitters always inhibit me. I try to make the portraits more acceptable, not too caricatured – I know they will ask to see them afterwards.

I sketched Stravinsky rehearsing his orchestra. "Would you sign it?" I asked. "Why should I?" he said. "I did not draw it!"

"Please sign it for Stephen Spender," I said. He wrote, "A good drawing by Gerald Scarfe."

Robert Oppenheimer, the man who developed the bomb in Los Alamos, sat staring into space while I drew. Mel Lasky liked it and said, "He looks like a man who's wondering what he has done."

I drew Leonard Bernstein during rehearsals. I was astounded when the orchestra broke for lunch in the middle of a phrase. "Please, gentlemen," said Bernstein, "give me five more minutes to finish the movement." They ignored him.

Robert Motherwell liked his and rang up Mark Rothko, so I went to Rothko's house to draw him. He hated it and told me it was awful. It was . . . Press on. Next to Adolph Gottlieb, Robert Lowell and Barnett Newman. Larry Rivers helped me draw his nose. Aaron Copland, Alan Ginsberg, Elia Kazan. Arthur Miller said, "Pity Marilyn's not here, you could sketch her." Norman Mailer said, "I look like a punched up Beethoven."

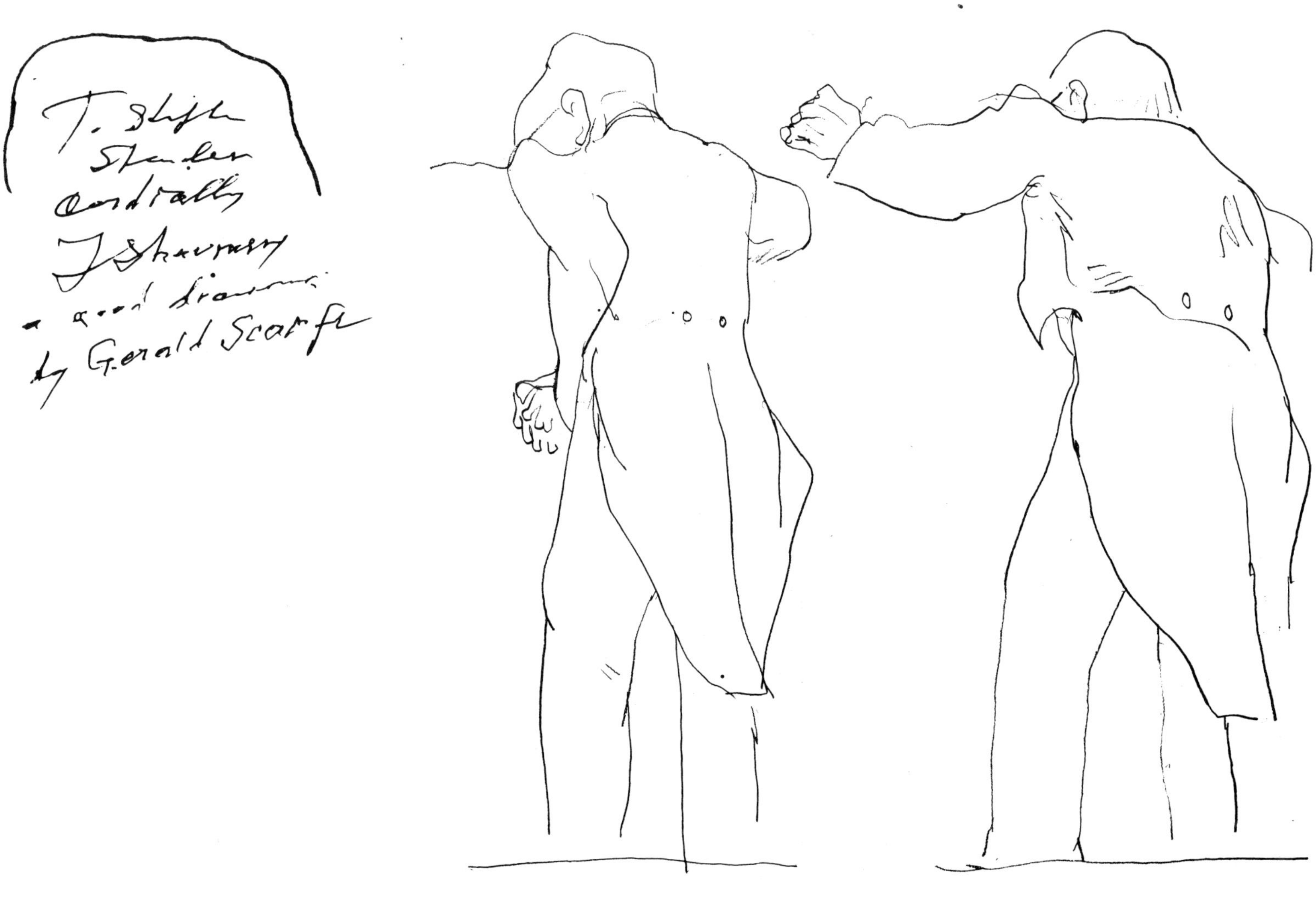

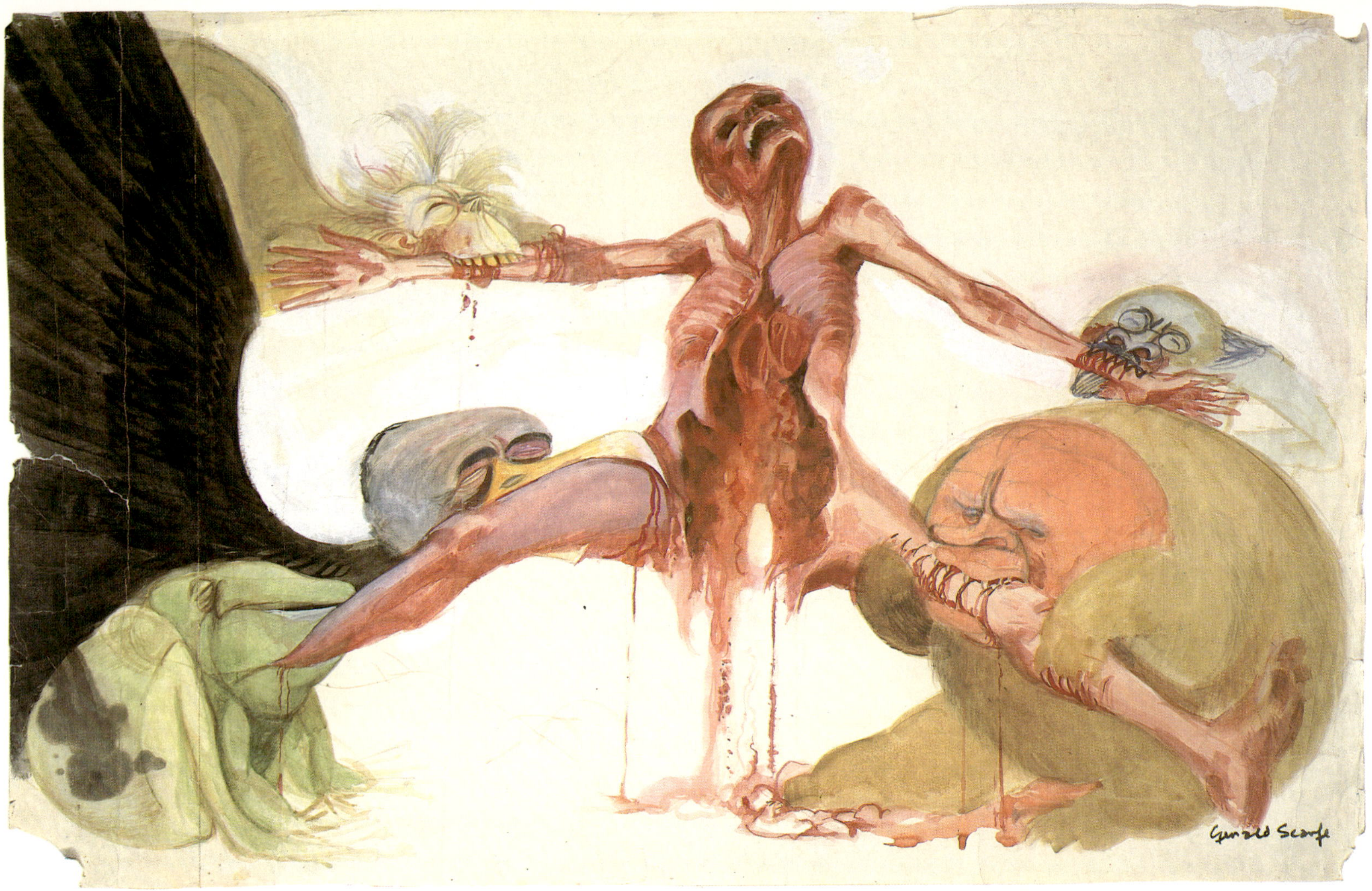
Gerald Scarfe

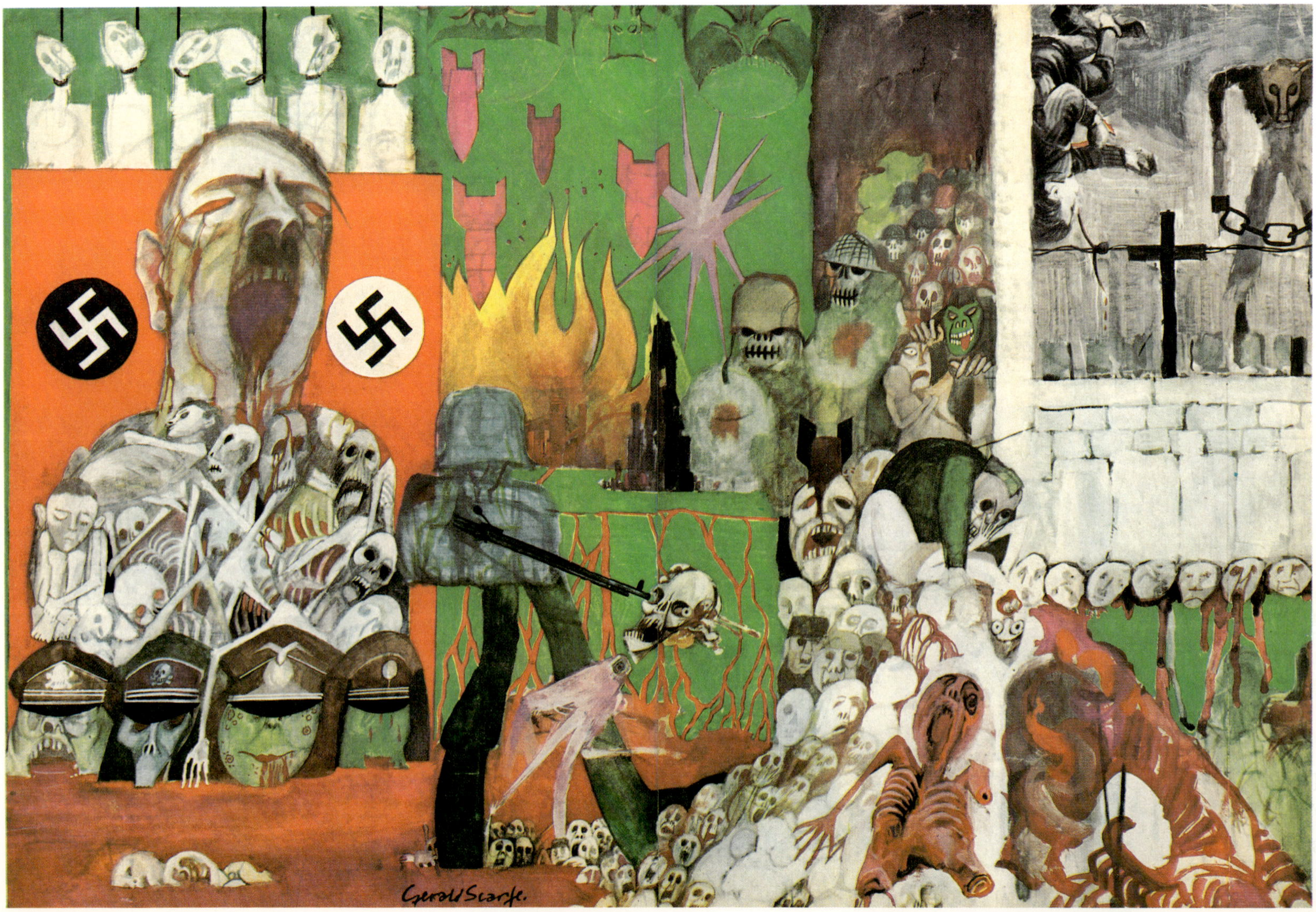
Gerald Scarfe.

I was asked to draw the Berlin Wall by ESQUIRE magazine in America. The tragic stupidity of the wall is symbolised by the sixteen-year-old boy Peter Fechter who was shot crossing from one side to the other and callously allowed to lie bleeding for two hours at the foot of the Wall. He died. The drawing above shows his grave.

In 1965, the DAILY EXPRESS ran a large article on me. "Just you wait," said a Fleet Street friend. "They'll all start trying to buy you up now."

Sure enough the DAILY EXPRESS editor rang. Would I like to come for lunch on Thursday? "Wonderful, yes please," I said.

The next day the DAILY MAIL rang. Would I like to come and have lunch on Tuesday? "Wonderful, yes please." "Now!" I thought, being young and zealous. "I'm determined to go to these meetings and make clear that I will not work for them without complete assurance of my political freedom. Yes, absolutely!"

With this resolve I went for my lunch with the editor of the DAILY EXPRESS, Derek Marks. "Well," he said, "you won't want a big lunch today. What say we pop over to El Vino's for a sandwich. They do a damned good sandwich over there!"

He offered me £5,000 a year and a Rover. I forgot to mention political freedom.

The DAILY MAIL did better. The Editor and the owner, Vere Harmsworth, took me to the Caprice. "Now, what car have you offered Gerald," said Harmsworth, after a couple of glasses of white wine. "Well," said the Editor, Mike Randall, "we thought of giving him a Rover 2000!"

I tried to explain about the political freedom I hoped for. "Nonsense," said Harmsworth. "Give him £6,000 a year and an E-Type. Ha!" he said, slapping the table. "Let him have a short life and a merry one."

"It's not really the issue," I said lamely. "I've already got a car." But they were busy paying the bill.

I joined the MAIL and I did have a clause in my contract saying that I would not be censored for political reasons.

Vere Harmsworth

Sketching a Buddhist fast at the An Quang pagoda, Vietnam.

This soldier has a gun in my back. He didn't like me drawing in the street.

The DAILY MAIL decided that, as I was a brutal artist, they should send me to a brutal situation – the war in Vietnam. They failed to understand that the brutality in my drawings comes from things that I fear, not things that I advocate. I hate violence.

However, off to Vietnam I went. Until my visit, Vietnam was a word on a map or film of marines jumping out of a helicopter on the television news. I felt sympathy but only saw it symbolically and made symbolic drawings.

The reality was far different. Vietnam is a beautiful country with gentle people who, like most civilians in wartime, were confused and frightened. They did not want to die. They did not want a war and I realised, for the first time that, apart from the tough professionals, most of the soldiers did not want one either. Most of them seemed to be young college kids, hoiked out of their studies, flown to some strange jungle, given guns and told to go out and kill 'gooks', as they contemptuously called the Vietnamese.

The way to travel in Vietnam was to hitch a lift from an aircraft going towards your destination. Wherever it landed, you hoped that another aircraft would turn up in which you could continue your journey, leapfrogging across the country. Many hours were spent in some jungle clearing desperately hoping that something would turn up, and many more bouncing about in the sky in strange craft.

The helicopters were the worst. Occasionally brought down by a lucky shot from a Vietcong rifle, they were most at risk on takeoff and landing. I hated travelling in them. The passenger seats were facing the side of the helicopter, the huge doors were open on both sides, and the pilot continually banked left and right so that the two machine-gunmen could fire at the puffs of smoke from the countryside below which told if the Vietcong were shooting at us.

I continually found myself staring at the sky and then suddenly at the jungle below, over which I was suspended like a sitting duck held in by a simple belt around my waist.

I arrived at a camp in the jungle. Everything was in disarray. I was told by a tough sergeant that the previous day a platoon far from camp had been surrounded by the Vietcong. They had radioed for help and were told that a napalm air strike would be carried out if they gave the precise position of the Vietcong. The surrounded soldiers radioed that they were pinned down in a circle about a quarter of a mile wide, gave their position, and asked that the airforce strike should be outside that circle. The pilot had misheard this instruction and dropped napalm inside the circle, killing and maiming his own men.

As the sergeant told me this story, a few bewildered survivors of the disaster were still wandering back. Others had deserted. Rain spattered off the tin roof as I made this drawing of one of those young soldiers, who sat silently on his bunk and stared at the gun and the boots of his dead buddy.

The little boy had stepped on a land mine and lost his foot. The surgeon sent me a photograph in England to show me that he had recovered. But the old man looked as though he was in a bad way.

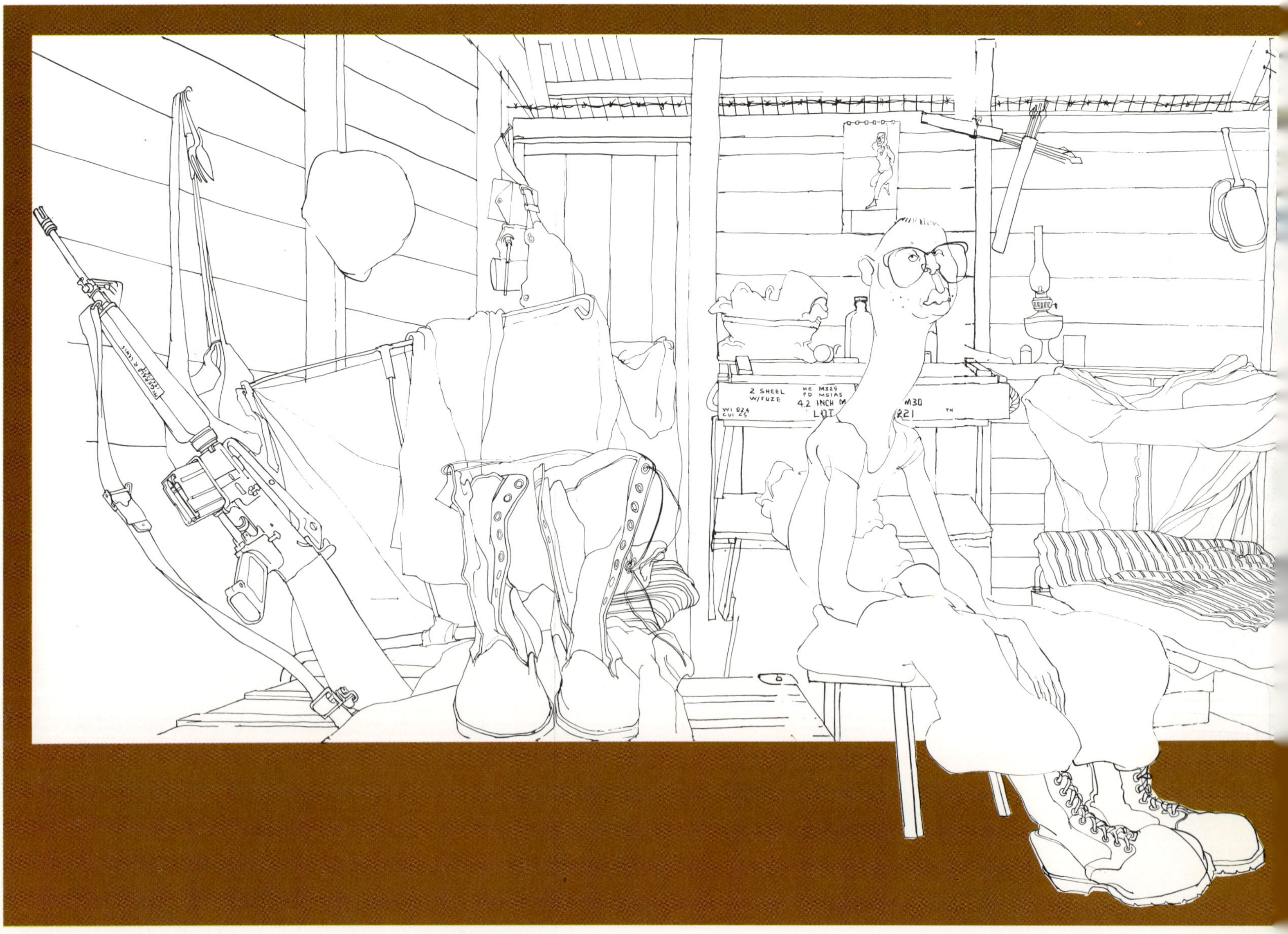

ZCZC OT P361 AU873 TLB1668
LONDON 148/144 7 1345

PRESS
GERALD SCARFE HOTEL ROYAL SAIGON

41320 CONGRATULATIONS ON BRILLIANT DRAWINGS ETEXCELLENT
PIECES STOP BLURB READS QUOTE A BRILLIANT ARTIST STOP
AYE REALITY THE CAMERA CAN NEVER QUITE CAPTURE
MULTIDOTS GERALD SCARFE IN VIETNAM STOP SEE TOMORROWS
DAILY MAIL UNQUOTE PUBLISHING VISIONWISE DRAWING
ETSTORY OF SOLDIER TOMORROW STOP VISIONISING DALAT

AU873 PAGE TWO

DRAWING FRIDAY STOP WELLINGTON
REFUSAL ON THIS STOP HOLDING
NEXT BATCH ARRIVES STOP WEST
CHILDREN ETCIVILIANS SOUNDS
STOP PLEASE SEND DRAWINGS
DRAWINGS STOP COULDST EXCL
EXYOUR EXCELLENT LIST AS
INSURANCEWISE STOP

AU873 PAGE THREE

IMPERATIVE YOU UNGO FIGHTING AREAS
WITHOUT SPECIFIC PERMISSION STOP INDIRECT IDEAS BESTEST
ANYWAY STOP CABLE IMMEDIATELY IF THIS WRECKS PLANS
STOP WILL CONTEMPLATE DRAWINGS EXJAPAN ETAMERICA BUT
URGE UNDALLY LONG THESE PARTS AS POLITICAL SITUATION
HERE NEEDS SCARFE COMMENTS STOP MANY THANKS
MIKE RANDALL

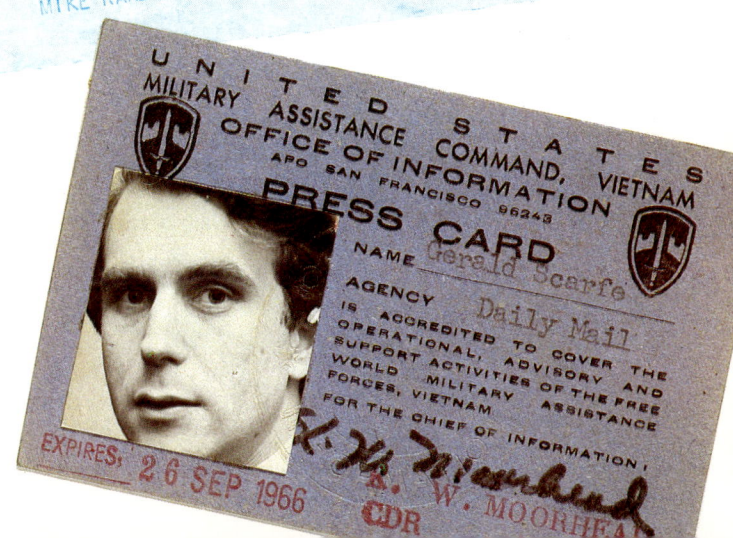

UNITED STATES
MILITARY ASSISTANCE COMMAND, VIETNAM
OFFICE OF INFORMATION
APO SAN FRANCISCO 96243

PRESS
CARD

NAME Gerald Scarfe

AGENCY Daily Mail

IS ACCREDITED TO COVER THE
OPERATIONAL, ADVISORY AND
SUPPORT ACTIVITIES OF THE FREE
WORLD MILITARY ASSISTANCE
FORCES, VIETNAM
FOR THE CHIEF OF INFORMATION,

EXPIRES 26 SEP 1966   W. MOORHEAD
CDR

Vietnam,
'Dalat'
1966

I took a plane to the highlands of Dalat, about 150 miles from Saigon. Unlike the wet, humid air of Saigon Dalat's was cool and fresh at 4,500 feet. I felt a million miles away from the war and yet Vietcong strongholds were only fifty miles away.

Pine trees and oaks grew alongside lush tropical plants and banana trees. Giant grasshoppers and other large insects hid amongst the exotic flowers that covered the hills and grew along the lakes. It was here that I made the drawing above.

I stayed in a baronial hotel with stuffed animal heads on the oak panelling and a duck press on the sideboard. For my first peaceful night in Vietnam I slept in a cool room covered in a white mosquito net, and when I woke to birdsong in the

In the bars and dives in Saigon, sad, swaying, drunken war veterans and iron-muscled, foul-mouthed construction men hug and crush the beautiful, tiny Vietnamese girls. These girls can hold their own. In one bar I saw a giant of a man driven out by a minute, furious girl, spitting fire.

As I said, flying in Vietnam was not a pleasant experience. I found myself either in a flimsy plane, being thrown around like a piece of tissue paper in the cloudy sky or shut in a windowless, monstrous transport plane (used for tanks, etc.). Like flying blind in the Albert Hall. In the drawing above I was flying with a dejected platoon to some god-forsaken spot in the jungle.

morning, it was raining. During breakfast the rain cleared to a fine drizzle, and several Vietnamese left the hotel for a round of golf. It is extraordinary how in times of stress we all revert to the normal.

In Saigon, I stayed at the Hotel Royal. It wasn't the best hotel in town, but it didn't invite the unwelcome attention of the Vietcong who attacked the Americanised Intercontinental across the square.

Monsieur Octavj, a world-weary French Colonial, was the owner and could occasionally be seen in the bar. The bar was run by his Vietnamese staff, one of whom would frequently slip photographs of war atrocities to you as you sipped your beer. As I sat there, cockroaches with inquiring feelers would wander around the metal top.

A huge lone cockroach lived in my room on the first floor. I didn't like him much because he kept surprising me but, although I bought a spray can of insect killer, I could not bring myself to kill him. When I returned each evening from my day's travels, I would lay the sketches I'd made across the floor like a carpet so that I could look at them all from the bed – and there they stayed. At night when I put out the light, I could hear the progress of my room-mate as he scuttled across the dry surface of my sketches.

One evening, Monsieur Octavj took me to an opium den, a small room in a back street in Saigon. Several figures sat or lay blissfully around a bare room while the pipe was lit by an emaciated man with greying hair. He handed me the pipe. I am not a smoker and inhaled tentatively. I can't remember how long

I was there but that night, when I returned to the Royal, I made a very careful drawing from memory. I was hours on it, drawing each line very, very slowly – it seemed wonderful at the time. It was only when I looked at it later that I could see it was rubbish.

Two days later I had a fever. I don't think it was the opium, more probably something I had picked up on my travels. I felt slightly delirious. Monsieur Octavj invited me to a 'special' lunch in the dark shuttered dining room of the Royal. A long table with twelve chairs either side was set with a white cloth. Only half the guests seemed to have arrived and I sat with them on one side of the table but, although places were set, the other side remained empty. The first course arrived, a watery soup, and twelve bowls were set at the empty places. Octavj explained that this was the 'Feast of the Dead' and that opposite us sat the souls of twelve dead relatives.

In my heightened delirious state and, under the nervous strain of all that I had seen, I believed that the dead were there. I could barely face the rest of the meal. Course after course arrived and I struggled to eat under the invisible scrutiny of the dead.

As soon as I could, I excused myself. I went up to my room and lay on the bed staring at the ceiling. I turned on to my side and almost crushed the giant cockroach with my head as it sat alongside me on my pillow. I leapt out of bed and seized the can of insect killer and sprayed it all over. The force of it blew him off

the bed. I gave him several more squirts, blowing him around the room, but suddenly he was up and running. He looked bigger than ever. I leapt back on the bed and watched his mad agonising progress as he tore round the room, his dry legs clattering across the surface of my dusty sketches.

It seemed as though he took an hour to die, scuttling blindly and noisily around the room. Eventually he was quiet and I fell into a disturbed sleep.

The next morning I felt better and carefully set about picking up my sketches, expecting to see his huge corpse any moment.

But I never did find him.

As part of my self-imposed duties I felt it right that I should draw some of the Vietnam wounded. I was given permission by a Vietnamese surgeon to be present at a small operation on a wounded man. His hand and arm had been lacerated when a mine exploded and he was going to have to lose several fingers. I steeled myself for the scene and entered a rudimentary operating theatre – an operating table with patient lying on his side, a trolley of instruments, a nurse and very little else. The window onto a courtyard was open and a crowd of curious onlookers gazed in, impressed by the fact that there was an artist present.

They found me a chair to sit on whilst the patient squirmed in agony. I was upset that they should pay me any attention while there were far more important matters in hand – and set about making myself as inconspicuous as possible.

"Ah, yes," said the Surgeon, as he picked up the surgical scissors, "I was a student at the Ecole Française de . . ." He took up the patient's hand and cut off one of the damaged fingers. "But I was no good as an artist." Snip, snip, off came another finger. The patient writhed in pain.

"Keep still!" said the crowd of onlookers ouside the window. "There is an artist here trying to draw you."

"Oh, no!" I said. "Please, please!" But the patient stiffened into a pose.

I felt obliged to sketch life and death whilst I was in Vietnam, so I screwed up courage and asked for permission to visit the morgue at Tan Son Nhut airport in Saigon. Permission was granted and I arrived at a concrete and corrugated iron building in the airport complex. I was met by a black Sergeant who asked me if I really wanted to do this. It made me even more apprehensive but I said yes and we walked across a sluiced concrete yard channelled by rivulets of water. The Sergeant opened the door of the shed. I will never forget the sight as I walked inside.

The whole area had a workmanlike atmosphere, medics in white coats were whistling as they worked methodically and efficiently. The Sergeant explained that the platoon had been ambushed the day before and most of them had been massacred. The remains of the platoon lay in front of me and I remember thinking, as the Sergeant took me on a guided tour, that it had never struck me before that when people died in war they did not fall over in one piece like American film stars. There were bodies without heads, half-bodies, one-eighth-bodies, all being neatly tidied up to send back to the USA by the automaton-like medics.

I remember clutching my armpits and sweating in fear. I told the Sergeant I had made a terrible mistake, I could not draw a line. I stumbled out of the shed in panic.

Vietnam Veteran 1971

Believe it or not this is a dog, a bitch to be exact. I designed the costume for a production at the Royal Court, London, but it didn't come on heat.
A drawing is an illusion, created on a flat surface; an illusion designed to give a feeling it is a three-dimensional object or a living creature. As I draw I imagine and feel the softness of the flesh on a cheek, or my pen explores the hardness of a shin bone. My creations can never come to life like Pygmalion's but I have a damn good try. I have animated them for films, put electric motors in them for exhibitions and inflated them to thirty feet high for rock shows, but taking into account my desire to be a showman, give good value and play to an audience the nearest I come to it is when some poor unfortunate actor is staggering around under one of my creations, transforming him into a god or a hamburger.

I have not actually exhibited in the National Gallery but I have had a big show on the pavement outside.

These giant cut-out puppets of Harold Wilson, Ian Smith and President Lyndon B. Johnson were heavily guarded by police – note helmets – they were part of a C.N.D. show held in Trafalgar Square in 1966.

Traverse backs down on erotic costumes

Ubu in Chains: Traverse Theatre Company, Barrie Halls

THE TRAVERSE did a quick last-minute about face and refused to display Gerald Scarfe's controversial costumes in this play — because of the "present climate of opinion in Edinburgh."

A man and woman were to have appeared in costumes depicting sexual organs. Instead two actors appeared with symbolic and slightly erotic drawings on their costumes. An after-curtain statement by the Traverse revealed they had had second thoughts.

Off-beat

The statement said: "Undue emphasis has been placed on supposedly scandalous aspects of recent Traverse productions" a reference to the controversial *Futz*, in which a man has relations with a pig.

"The public would be unable to see the costumes in the context visualised by Gerald Scarfe."

Scarfe still managed hilarious and off-beat effects with a 6ft.-plus actor in suspenders, Britannia's shield advertising teas at 5s. a time and soldiers with umbrellas and pantaloons. Other effects include a psychedelic beat group, colour slides which disappear in flames and Ubu at one stage eating a spider.

It's a pity the whole character has to be wasted on a plot so inconsequential and meaningless.

— I. W.

Visiting Edinburgh to see my costumes in a production of 'Ubu in Chains' at the Traverse Theatre, I was amazed to find the press out in full force – must be because the word SEX had been mentioned.

The fact that I had designed the two leading costumes as genitalia probably had something to do with it. I was even more amazed to find the Traverse had censored these two costumes without a word to me and designed two of their own "because of the present climate of opinion in Edinburgh".

The Gentlemen of the Press were very disgruntled. Edinburgh is a long way to go to see no scandal.

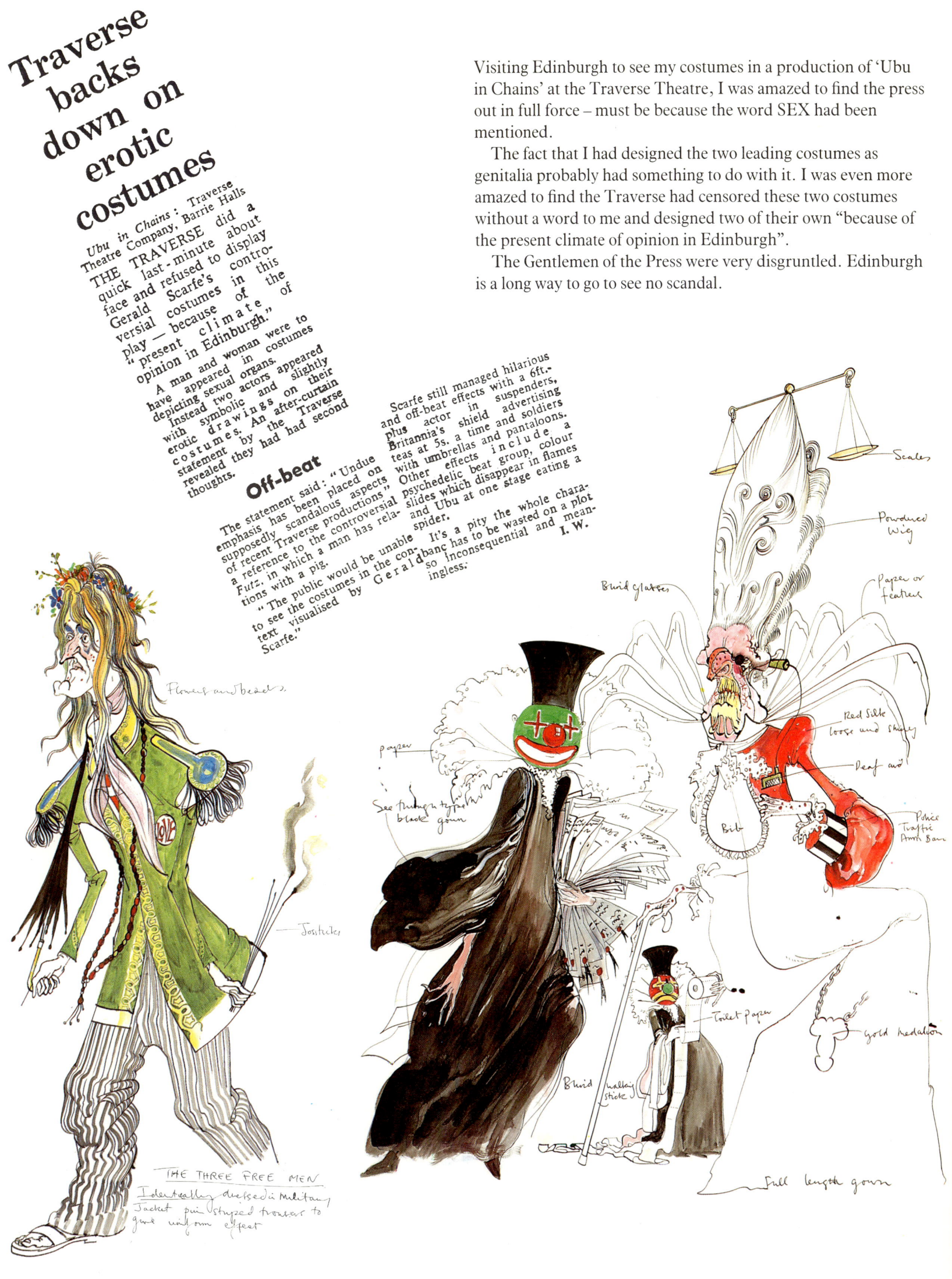

Flowers and beads.

Josticks

THE THREE FREE MEN
Identically dressed in military jacket pin-striped trousers to give uniform effect

Scales

Powdered Wig

Paper or feathers

Burd glasses

See through typ ? ? black gown

Paper

Red Silk loose and shiny

Deaf aid

Bib

Police Traffic Arm Band

Toilet paper

Burd walking stick

Gold Medallion

Full length gown

drawing for the SUNDAY TIMES at Crockford's, the gambling establishment. Nervous manager hovering: I won't identify any of the gamblers, will I?

"No, these are just sketches and caricatures from which I'll make the finished drawing," I say.

"Ah," he says, unconvinced. Hover, hover.

I sketch away in a corner. After an hour or so I decide I have had enough and start to leave. I'm stopped by two heavies, and the manager.

"May I see your drawings please?"

"Yes, of course," I say, handing them over.

He flicks through them. "Ah, non," he splutters. "Ah, non! C'est monsieur . . ." He runs into his office and, when I follow, I find him feverishly rubbing out my pencil sketches.

I am appalled. "What are you doing?" I say.

"Ah, non," he says. "I cannot allow it. I will be sued. They are all recognisable. This man here, he owes us a fortune. I'll never get it if you publish this." He continues frantically rubbing the drawings out.

"Listen," I say. "You cannot do that. They are my drawings, my property. You understand, you can't do that." "I can." "You can't," and with that I tear them into tiny pieces and throw them all over his office.

"Ah non," he says. "This is not necessary."

I had hidden some of the sketches and published them immediately afterwards.

THE SUNDAY TIMES
200, GRAY'S INN ROAD, LONDON WC1

The holder of this card

M. GERALD SCARFE

whose photograph and signature are attached is an accredited staff

(REPORTER, PHOTOGRAPHER, WRITER)
of the Sunday Times. It is requested that all facilities may be accorded to the holder whilst on Sunday Times business

W Harland
NEWS EDITOR/PICTURE EDITOR

VALID UNTIL

Signature

PRESS

The Unsaddling Enclosure, Aintree, 1967, and a drawing made during the Greek Colonels' Coup, Athens, 1967.

The Israeli tank drove straight at us, flattening a Mercedes and a Buick on the way. My driver swerved into a field, his gun swinging on the door handle of the taxi. I was a war correspondent covering the Six-Day War.

Harry Evans didn't quite know what to do with me. He had bought me up for the SUNDAY TIMES because I had become famous for a certain type of drawing but he didn't want me to do it. How could he get rid of me? He thought reportage would soften my approach, and it did. He sent me to Cornwall, the London Docks; for an audience with God (De Gaulle) at the Elysée Palace in Paris; up north with Harold Wilson ("What's he bothered to come for," he said); to the Thomas à Becket to sketch boxer Henry Cooper training; to draw the deprived and poor in Paddington; to Washington for a portrait of Robert Macnamara; to Cannes for the film festival; to Plymouth, USA, for boxer Sonny Liston; Muhammed Ali in Boston, "Ahm prettier than that!"; crawling along two-foot-high tunnels miles underground in Mosley Hill Colliery, water dripping down my neck; to Aintree Race Course drawing sporty types; then, when the Greek Colonels carried out their coup, I was sent to Greece. I also marched against the Mafia with Danilo Dolci in Sicily.

Refugees cross the Jordan by of the Allenby Bridge
Gerald Scarfe

Gerald Scarfe Sicily

By a strange coincidence I found myself wearing the same uniform as Danilo Dolci. Dolci is a courageous priest who marched against the Mafia in Sicily in the 1960s. His crusade denouncing the stranglehold the Mafia held on the people of Sicily took him right through the main towns where the movement had been born. His uniform was a white polo neck, flaunting his presence and making him a sitting duck for any sniper.

I walked with him to one town where he lectured the locals in the town square on the evils of the Mafia. Engrossed in my sketching, I didn't notice a mob of youths gathering behind me, until one came alongside and said something unpleasant in Italian. They obviously thought that I was a sympathiser.

I ignored them and continued sketching uneasily. The ringleader taunted me again.

I was surrounded by them and felt trapped. I didn't quite know how to defuse a worsening situation. So I explained I was working for a newspaper, and turned my sketch-pad on to the ringleader and began drawing him.

Better buy some filthy postcards in Port Said, might make a good story.

Sent by the SUNDAY TIMES to see if the Suez Canal works under the Egyptians.

Sail down the Canal on an oil tanker. Arrested at Kantarra for sketching the Canal. Draw Arabs by the Mena House, eat pigeon by the Nile. Gallop Arab horses at dusk in the desert beside the Pyramids. Journey down the Nile to Luxor and the Valley of the Kings. Very hot. Better get rid of these dirty postcards before I return through Customs. Tear them into a million tiny pieces and surreptitiously drop them over the parapet of a bridge into the Nile. Sharp updraught of wind blows them back again and I am showered by a thousand pieces of feelthy confetti. Passers-by puzzled.

The effect was magical. Flattered and embarrassed, he melted into a grinning booby. Luckily the drawing was a good likeness and his friends began to barrack him about the size of his nose. The crowd began to laugh and when I showed him the drawing he nodded sheepishly. Collapse of stout party.

On the following page, the Casino Palace Hotel, Port Said, and Arabs at the town of Kantara on the Suez Canal, 1967.

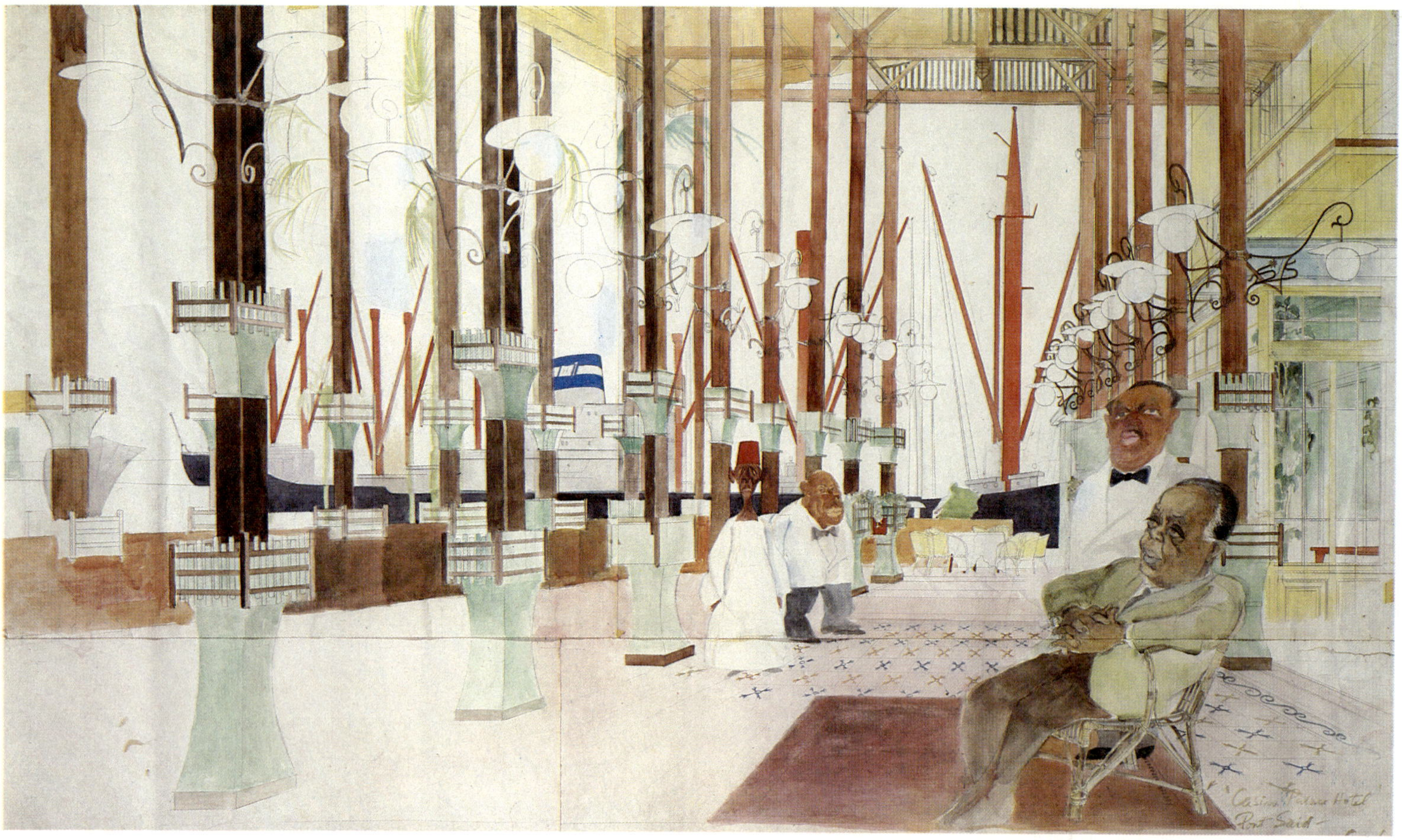
Casino Palace Hotel
Port Said

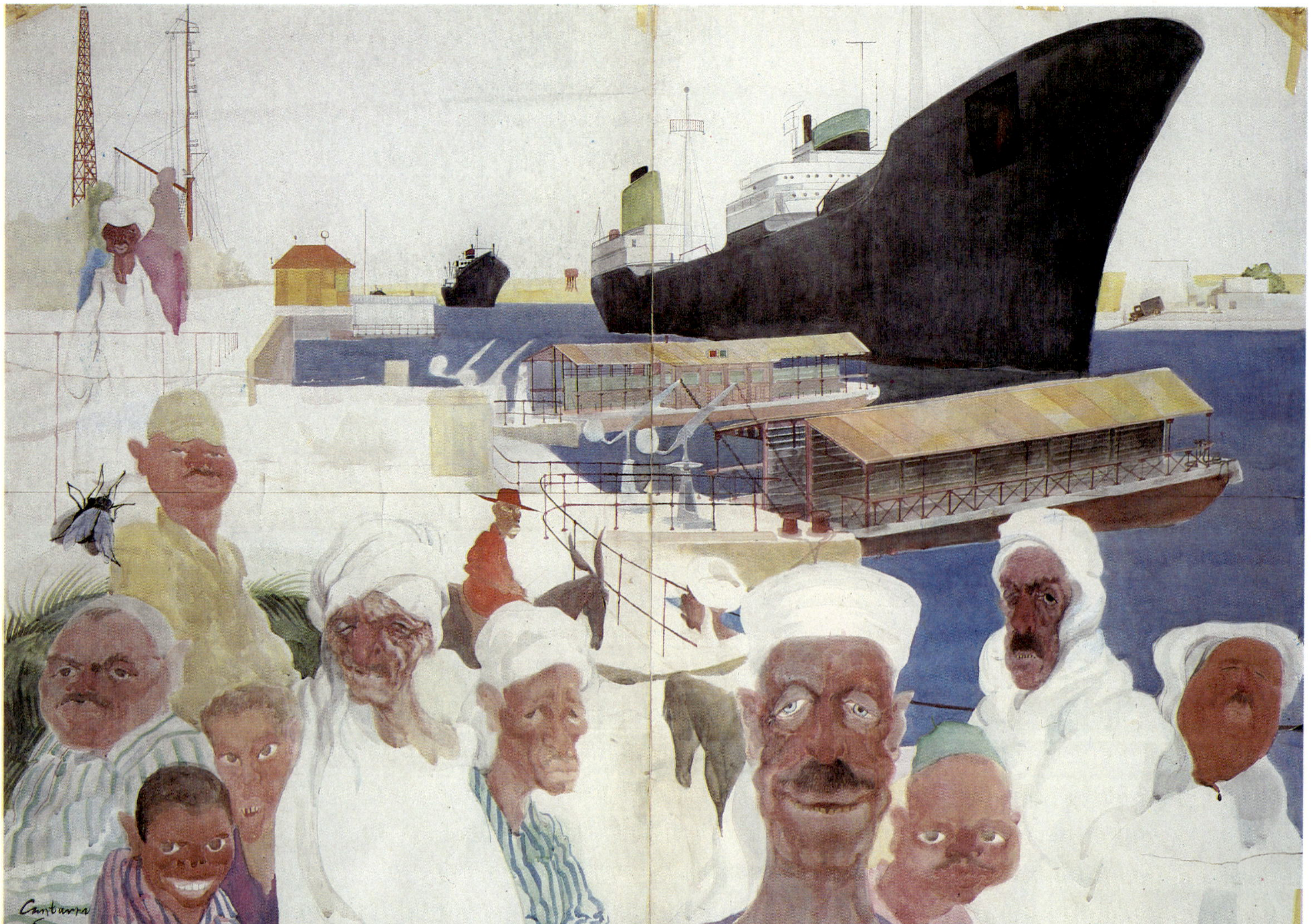
Cantarra
Suez
Gerald Scarfe

You're like me, Gerald," said John Lennon. "A cynic." I was sketching him for a Beatles TIME cover at his house in Weybridge.

Ringo's house had a psychedelic light show and a bar. He wanted me to do a drawing of him on the wall. I did while he posed.

Paul explained in St John's Wood how the secret of life was like a rose. I've forgotten how it goes now. It was in the days of the Maharishi.

I stayed with them at Twickenham Studios for a couple of days while they filmed 'Help'. Then I returned home with my pile of sketches, spread them around the walls and translated them into larger-than-life sculptural caricatures which were photographed for the cover.

TIME were delighted. They wanted to fly me over straight away and, when I arrived in New York, Henry Grunewald the Editor enthused and gave me many more commissions.

The first of these was John Kenneth Galbraith, the economist.

I flew to Boston to draw him. Armed with my sketches I moved into the Algonquin Hotel in New York, bought flour and wire and all the newspapers I could carry. Back in the hotel I shut myself in my room for days and had food sent up. I bent the wire into a linear caricature of Galbraith and covered it with strips of newspaper soaked in flour and water. Slowly over the days I built up a likeness of Galbraith. The maid regarded me with suspicion. God knows what she thought, but I obviously wasn't one of the Algonquin's intellectuals.

When I had painted the head it suddenly didn't look like him anymore. My work has a habit of doing this. I'm convinced it's a real humdinger, I go for a pee and when I come back it's a different person entirely. However it was too late. TIME was champing at the bit – the cover had to be printed. I had to deliver it immediately. I washed, dressed and, gathering up the three-foot-high head, swept out into the corridor and made my way to the elevator. The elevator doors opened. Six frightened pairs of eyes stared at me and my creation. In silence I got into the lift amongst them. I pressed ground floor. The doors closed and we descended. Not a sound. The model smelt of stale flour and damp newspaper. "Excuse me," said the lady on my left. "Isn't that John Kenneth Galbraith?" I was delighted: she'd recognised it! The doors opened, I stepped into the Algonquin lobby. Now I didn't mind the stares!

My next assignment was Rowan and Martin. I spent a wonderful week with them in Hollywood, sailing on the Pacific and watching stars at play.

Back to New York; this time my construction was so big that I built it in the conference room at Time Life Building. I wrecked the room, had it full of wood, plaster, wire, paint and all assorted junk. I occasionally noticed the sliding doors opening a few inches and eyes peering at me. When I looked up they disappeared. The next time it happened I leapt up and slid back the doors. There, rather sheepishly, stood an editor I knew and several visitors to the building. "Oh, hi, Gerry," he said. "Just showing the folks where you work."

I realised that I had become TIME's tame anarchist on the 26th floor.

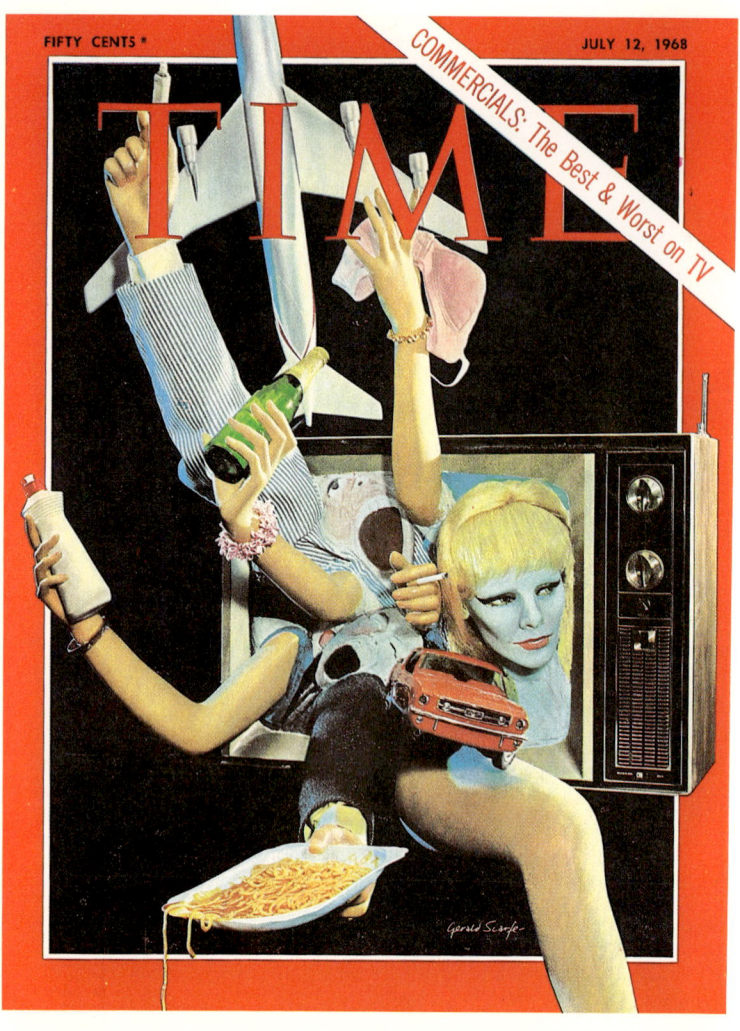

FIFTY CENTS *   JULY 12, 1968

COMMERCIALS: The Best & Worst on TV

TIME

FIFTY CENTS *   OCTOBER 11, 1968

TIME

ROWAN AND MARTIN

SOCK IT!

Gerald Scarfe

Richard Nixon was running for President; not many thought he'd make it. TIME magazine asked me to do a cover of him. He refused outright to see me. Omnipotent TIME was furious, no one told them what to do, let alone who would complete their covers. "We'll send you on his campaign plane as a reporter, he can't stop that." So, feeling rather embarrassed, I travelled with Nixon through North Dakota, Montana and Nevada. Everywhere we stopped I would be in the front row drawing the 'expletive deleted'. He was embarrassed, too. Eventually he thought, if you can't beat them better join them, and he would throw me a sweaty smile, "Hi, Gerry! Are your pencils sharp today? Ha, Ha!" I went back to New York, booked into the Hilton and completed a large papier-mâché head and shoulders of Nixon. I took it along to the Time Life Building and proudly presented it to the Editor in charge of covers. Embarrassed silence. Shaking head. Um! Er, it's a little extreme for us, Gerry. Could you try again? I later found out that in the meantime Nixon had come to look a real candidate for the Presidency and what's more the Covers Editor had joined his staff. What's sauce for the Beatles and Showbiz is not sauce for powerful politicians.

Nixon drawn from life, Cheyenne, USA, 1968 and on the following page the offending papier-mâché figure.
I appeared on this TIME cover: that's me bottom right, had a wonderful time painting the girl. Perks of the job.

TIME

THE BEATLES / Their New Incarnation

Gerald Scarfe.

ALAN CLIFTON

(REG. U.S. PAT. OFF.)

I travelled with Robert Kennedy for FORTUNE magazine in his private jet. He was charming and friendly. He came and sat with me and asked what I was doing and we discussed Harold Wilson and how most people in the USA would not know who he was. Big fish in our English pond look extremely small from other parts of the world. He was sorry, he said, for the girls who faithfully waited for him on the wet and windswept tarmac at every airport we visited. He would often invite them on his jet during the stop. I was in Los Angeles when he was shot (the drawing was made just before) and followed him to the Good Samaritan Hospital where he died. I then flew to New York for his lying-in-state in St Patrick's Cathedral and from there to Arlington Cemetery. I could not believe he was dead.

I had just stepped off the plane from New York when TIME rang. 'Please come back and report on the Republican convention in Florida.' The next day I flew to Miami and booked in at the Fontainebleau hotel (pronounced locally as Fountain Blow) then to the convention hall where blue-rinsed vulture-necked ladies and turtle-faced, wrinkled men took part in a grotesque, over-sized children's party, with banners, bands, rattles, whistles and balloons. John Wayne gave a heart-stirring speech about flying the flag. The whole thing was a bad movie.

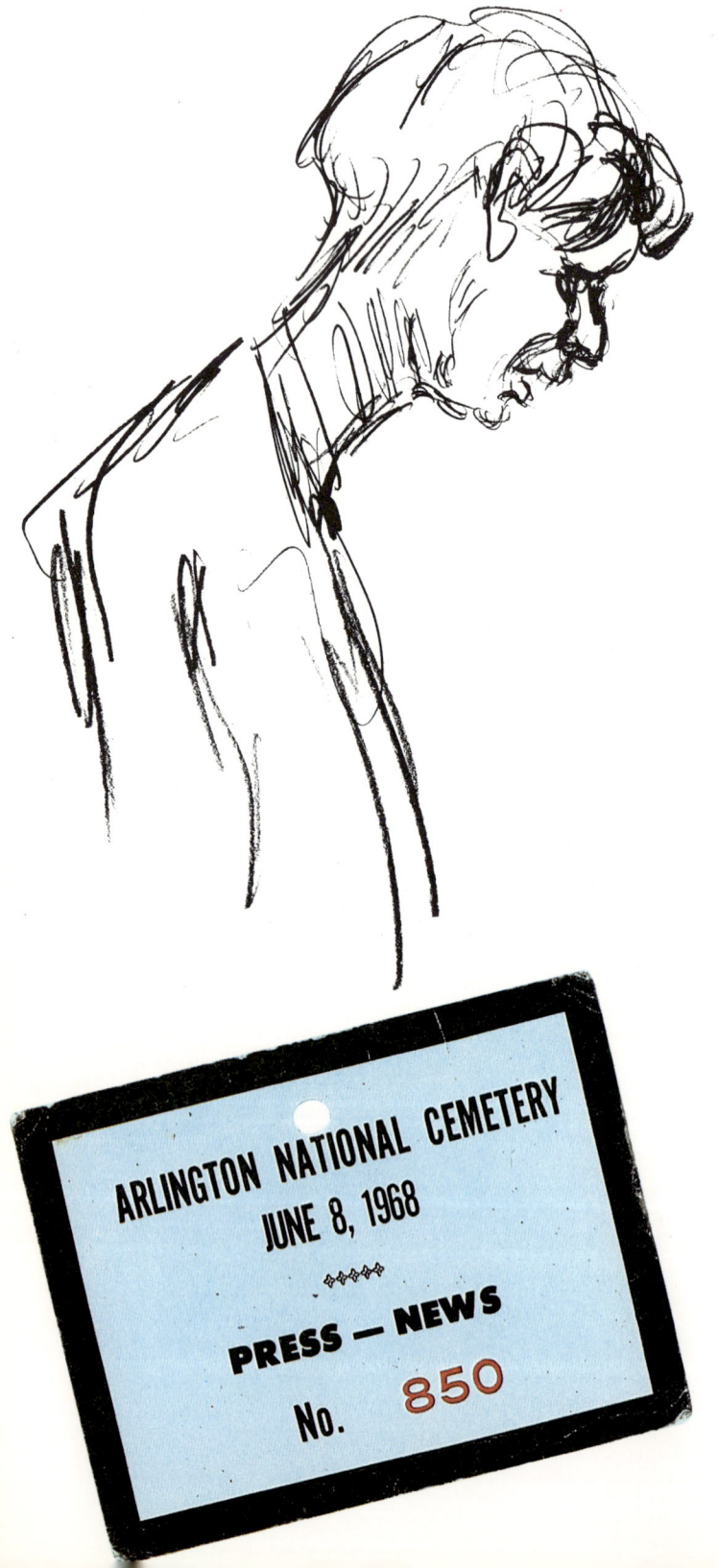

ARLINGTON NATIONAL CEMETERY

JUNE 8, 1968

PRESS — NEWS

No. 850

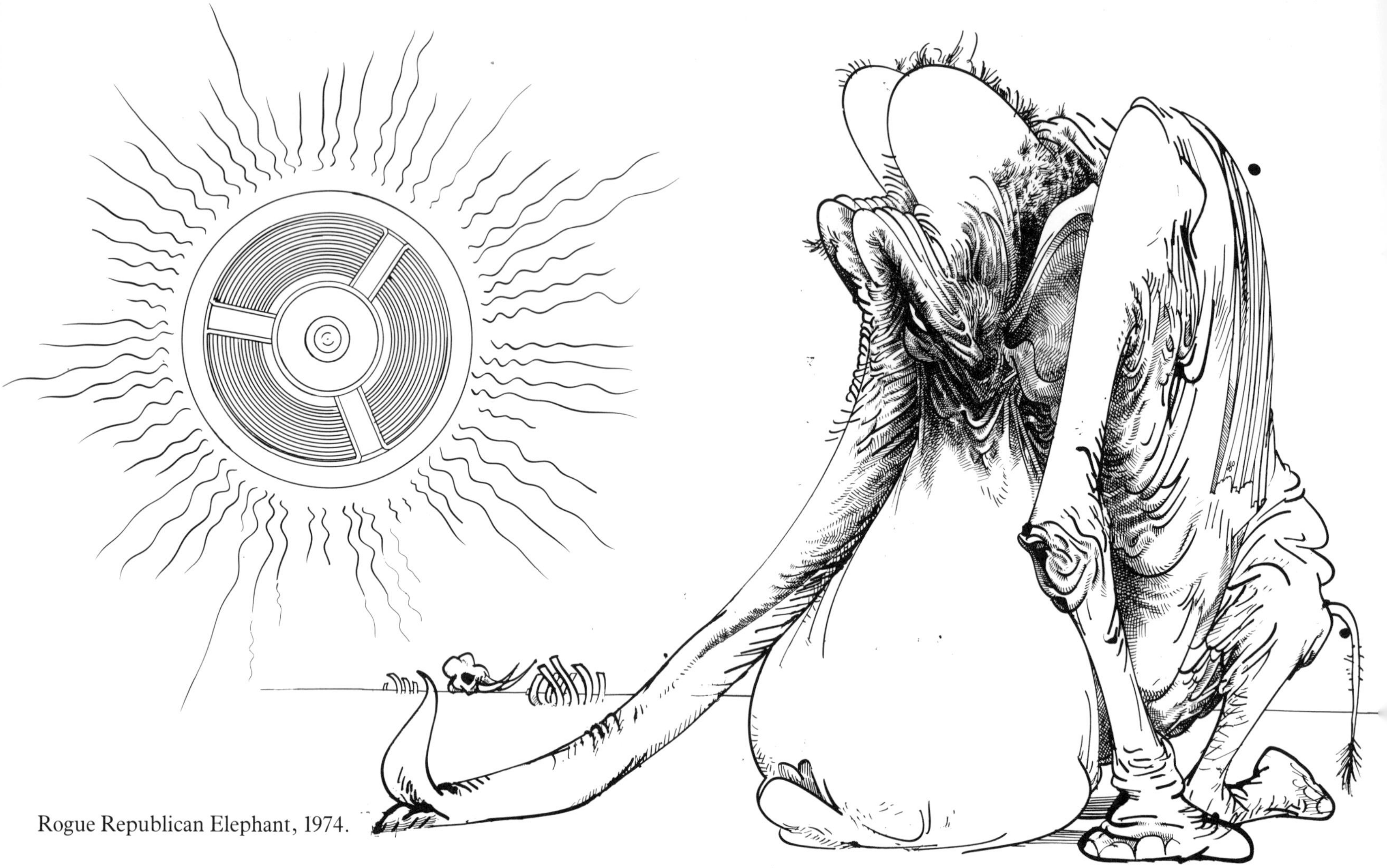

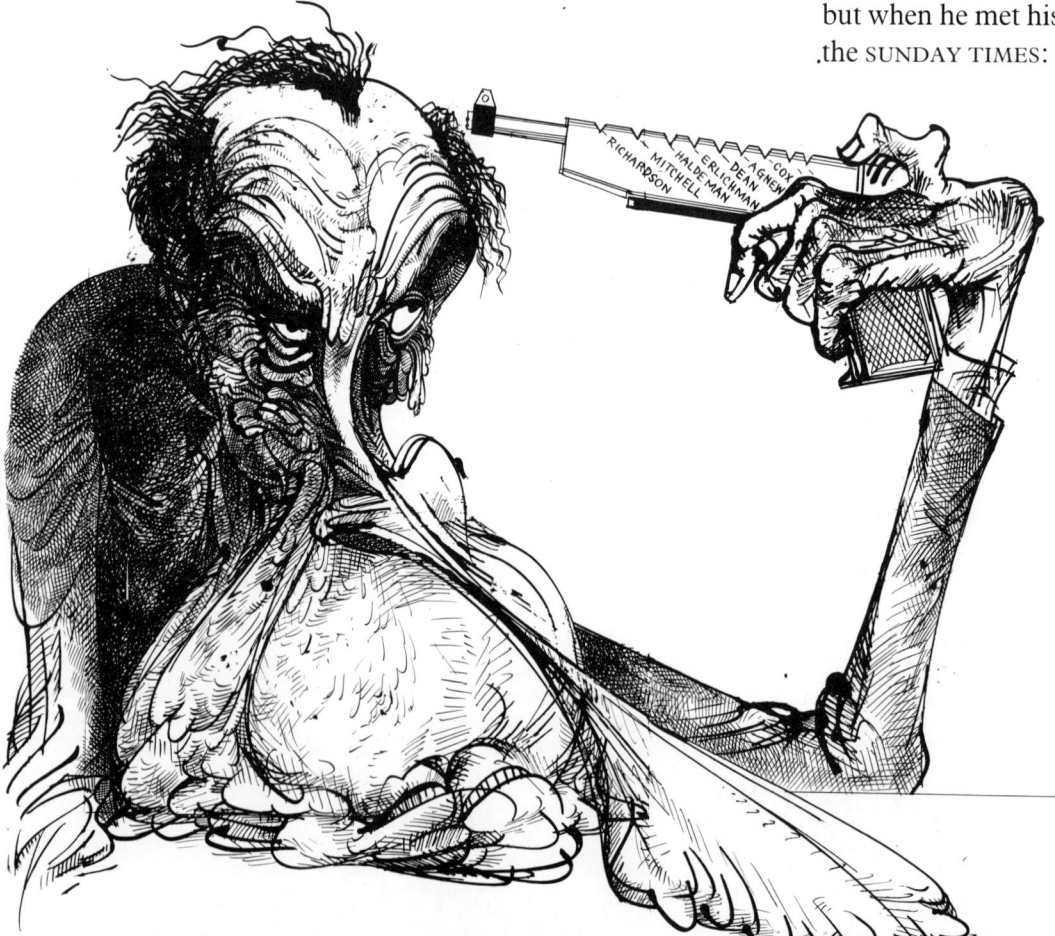

Rogue Republican Elephant, 1974.

I have to admit that I was obsessed by Nixon. I did not like him, but when he met his end in Watergate I published this lament in the SUNDAY TIMES:

'Though Nixon makes me sick,
I'll miss his every trick.
His used-car style
And sweaty smile
Made him a perfect (expletive deleted)'

Nixon wronged

I AM disgusted that you saw fit to publish Gerald Scarfe's anti-President Nixon cartoon (Leader page, last week).

The world may sleep sounder because of the alertness of President Nixon, but the media—which the President so correctly put in its place during his Press conference—is obsessed so very much with Watergate that it sees fit to attack him even when he takes action to protect the whole of the free world. And that includes the free Press.

You must indeed be asleep if you really think the Russians can be trusted, and it was only natural that they, too, would speak out against President Nixon's action. What he did was to show them that, in spite of all his troubles at home, he is all too alive and aware of the real evils which exist in the world.—John D Smith, Gosport.

PERHAPS HE'LL GET THE RIGHT MAN THIS TIME

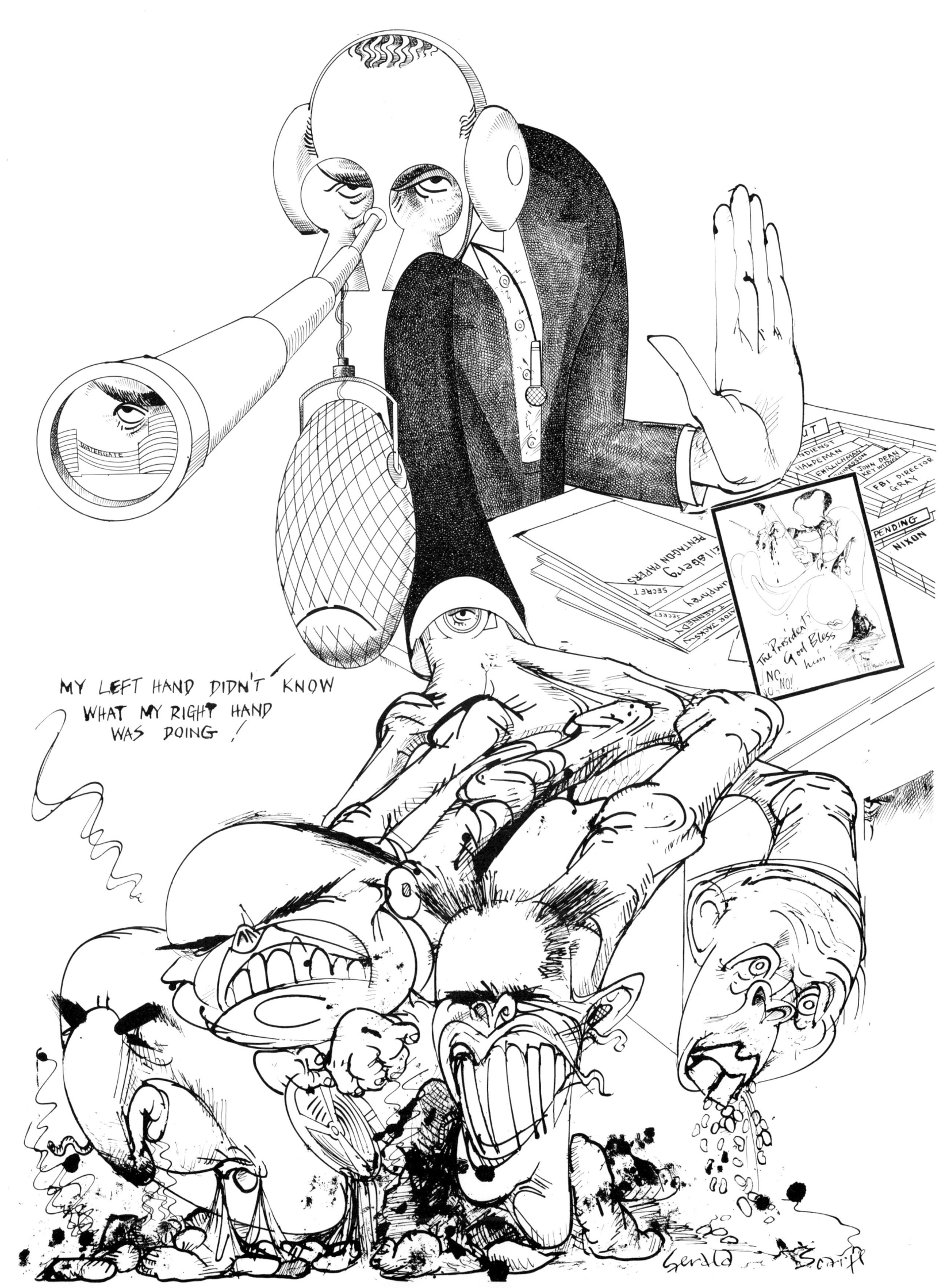

Six presidents I have drawn:
the charismatic Kennedy,
the old grafter Johnson,
the sweaty Nixon,
the stupid Ford,
the hopeless Carter and –
oh my God – Reagan...
How can it go on like this?

The Great Debate 1976

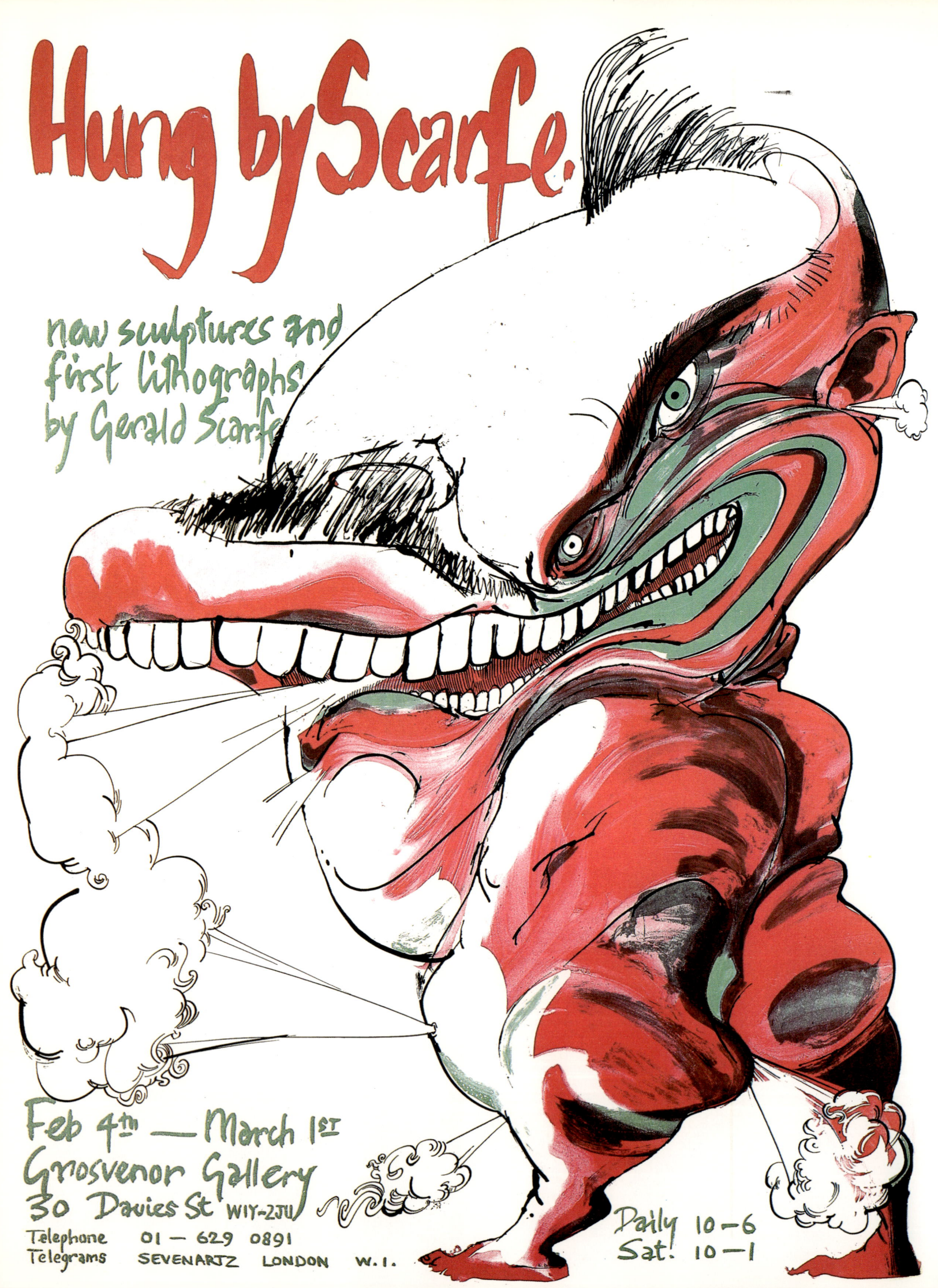

Sculpture was a new challenge because, unlike my drawings which are organised and presented to confine the viewer to one point of view, sculpture can be seen from all angles.

One must retain a likeness and still convince the viewer from all points of the compass. This challenge fascinated and inspired me.

Before now, when I drew my figures on paper, I sometimes had to twist their arms, legs and noses over their heads to make them fit onto the sheet.

In my 1969 Exhibition, 'Hung by Scarfe' at the Grosvenor Gallery, I was no longer restrained by the edges of the paper and my contorted cramped fingers began to grow, bulge and spill from their paper boxes and unfurl their crooked limbs and spew and sprawl across the gallery floor. I felt released, and the critic David Sylvester said to me at the time, "Now – let yourself go!" Nixon's jowls were no longer restricted by the edges of the paper, they were free, uncontrolled, they flowed across the room and tripped up the gallery director Mr Estorick. "What the hell's that?" he growled, irritably.

It was a great release for me too. I seemed to be at the beginning of something new again. It was also wonderful to see

Left: Ted Kennedy. Below left: 'Christian Unity': Rev. Ian Paisley and Archbishop of Canterbury. Right: Aristotle Onassis and Jackie Kennedy.
Overleaf: 'We're learning to accept the blacks bit by bit', Dr. Christiaan Barnard. Prince Charles's Investiture. The Marquis De Gaulle. Landscape USA. 'Revolution, Lovely Revolution', Vanessa Redgrave.

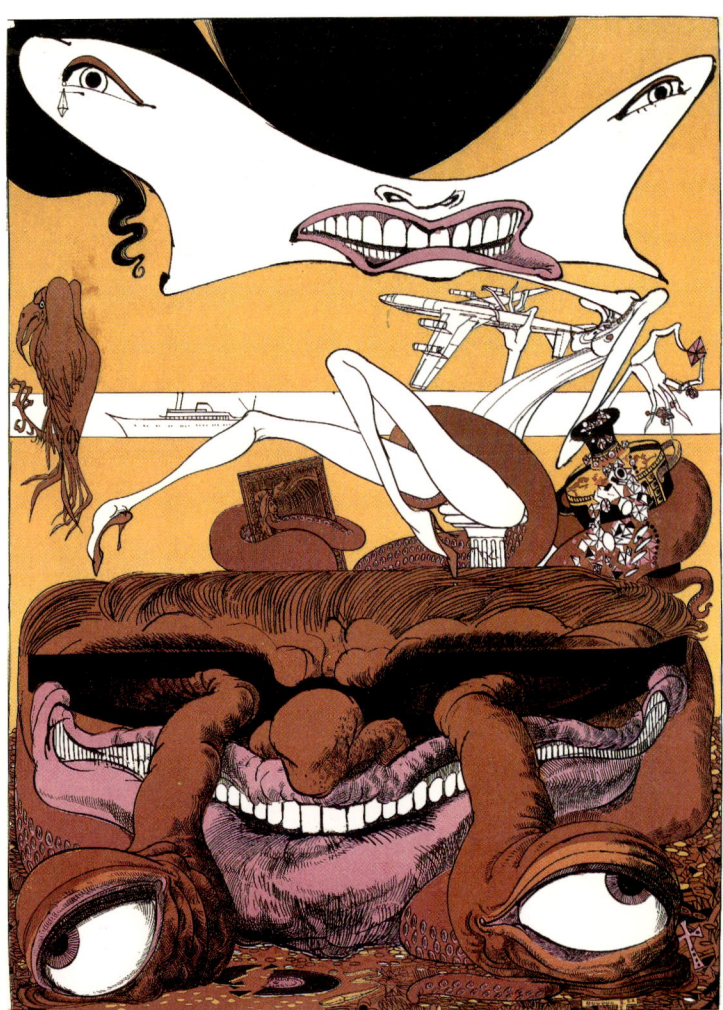

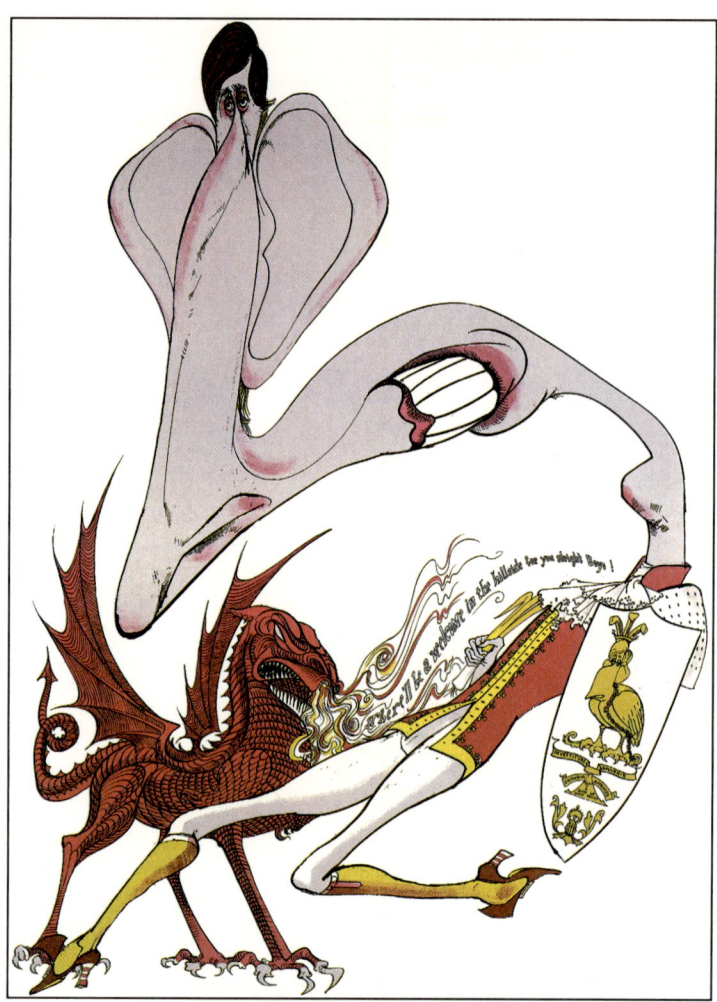

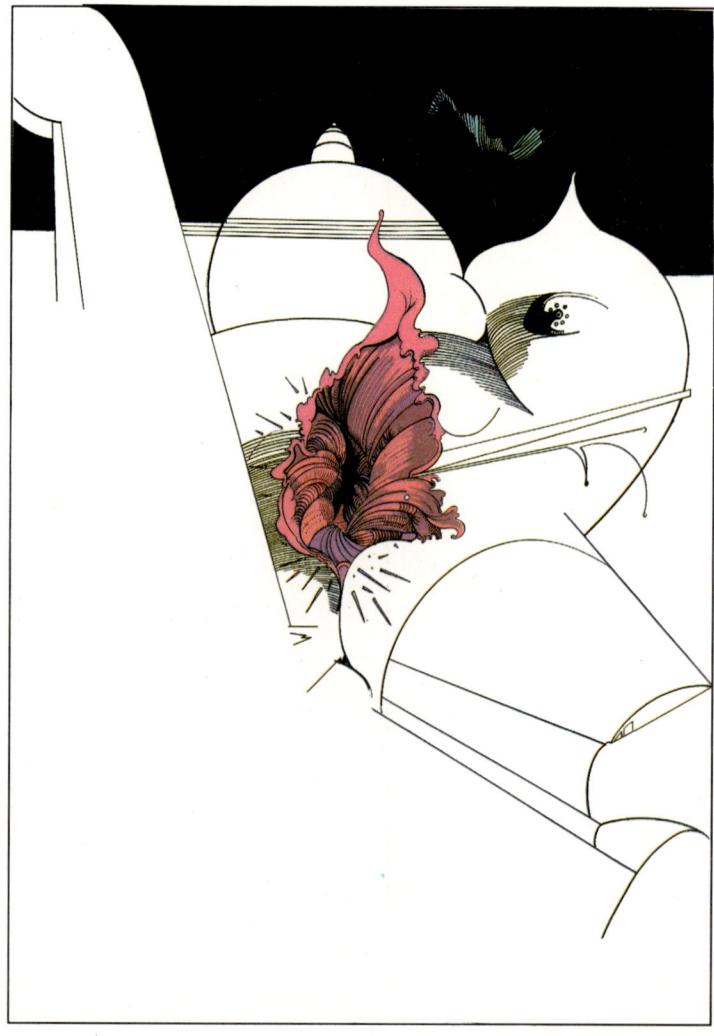

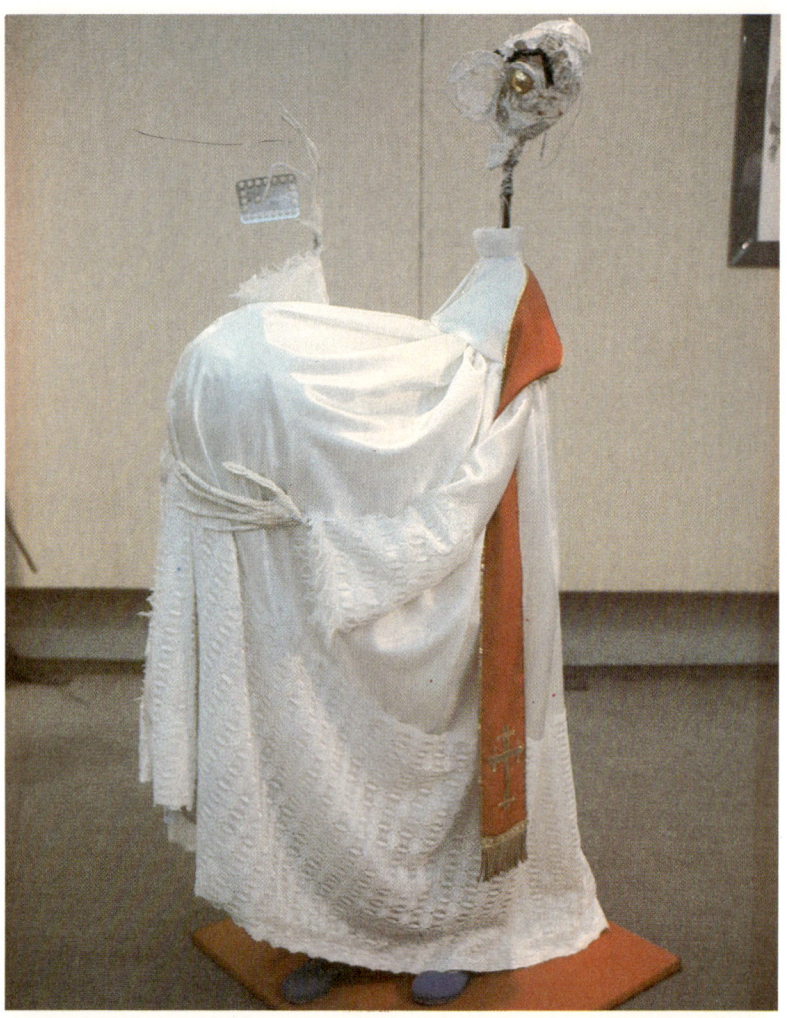

the public amongst my creations. They mingled with them and became part of the show. I saw them laughing out loud and realised I was really in the business of entertainment.

Now that my figures could release their limbs it also meant that I could achieve simpler shapes. I began to aim for simplicity, leaving behind the nooks and crannies that I had explored so often in my PRIVATE EYE drawings.

'At the Grosvenor Gallery, Gerald Scarfe has clothed his scabrously pointed cartoons with plaster, chicken wire and yards of material and also produced a series of screenprints.

Gerald Scarfe's cartoons are too familiar to need much elaboration. They are, I suppose, the embodiment of Swiftian venom in pen and ink, with the same obsessive relish for every human orifice as a potential sink of corruption. Behind each puckered or bulbous lip lies a writhing mass of lies waiting to spew forth, each hand stretched in benediction is really a grasping claw. His targets in the present exhibition, the first public display of a most secretive artist, are now new and the figures he has created are such vulnerable Aunty Sallys as Onassis, Ian Paisley and Enoch Powell. But his big treatment of them would draw a last rictus of pleasure from Gillray's gaping jaw.

All the figures are larger than life, except for Field Marshal Montgomery and the Pope who have both shrunk to less than human stature and rattle around in their clothes alarmingly. The Pope, precariously held together by chicken wire, clutches the Pill as if it were the rock which occasioned the text 'Tu es Petrus'. Montgomery, the most successful figure in the show, hovers ghoulishly over a chessboard, on the point of moving a tin soldier to swift extinction, with his vulpine face eagerly watching the camera. For the men we love to hate Scarfe pulls out all the stops. The Rev. Ian Paisley leans from the cross as if it were a soap-box, and Enoch Powell, as a Janus-headed blackbird, bends like a contortionist to a battery of microphones. Onassis becomes an enormous octopus with gobstopper eyes and a filmy nightdress in one tentacle, while Prince Charles, elaborately hosed and gartered for his inauguration, is hardly visible beneath the kind of ears elephants fly with in nursery picture books. They will all give enormous offence in some quarters and hours of pleasure in others.'
Paul Grinke *The Spectator* February 14 1969

Top: 'Thou Shalt Not Pill' – The Pope. Bottom: 'The Bodysnatcher' Dr. Christiaan Barnard. Opposite page: Rev. Ian Paisley.

Stomachs split open. Entrails spilled out. Flowers grew from horrific monsters. Johnson defecated bombs over Vietnam. In a nuclear blast a figure was stripped to the bone and disintegrated before our eyes. My self-portrait decomposed in five seconds flat, but the thing that upset the BBC was Harold Wilson. Wilson saying, "Over the years many people have changed their position," but what disturbed the BBC more was that he was saying it out of his bottom.

We had a serious meeting about this with the Heads of Department at BBC Centre. Richard Cawston wanted it taken out. I refused. I was pleased with the Lip Sync. Stalemate. Compromise. Harold would appear with a small censored notice on his bottom. Honour all round. It looked funnier than ever.

It was all for a BBC documentary in 1968 about my work: the world seen through my eyes. I called it 'I Think I See Violence All Around Me'.

Funny business, making films. It is a corporate enterprise. Unlike the writer, artist or composer, who need only a pen or pencil to express themselves, the director has to deal with a whole string of people before he can see a result. I found myself in some unexpected situations in an effort to explain my work. Sitting expectantly, alone in a trendy King's Road restaurant. Lights, camera. No action. I am to be filmed amongst the Swinging Sixties people I satirize. We wait. Nobody comes. Where are they?

"We have closed the restaurant," says Alvaro. "What! It's the customers we want!" says the director. "You couldn't organise a nail into a block of wood," says the cameraman. "Come outside and say that!" says the director. They disappear into the street.

Half an hour later they come back the best of friends. They've had a couple of pints in the Chelsea Potter.

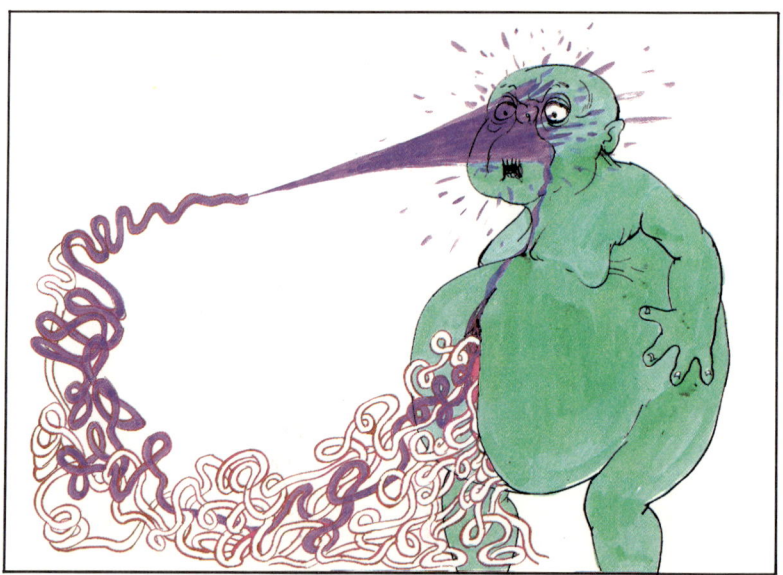

Opposite: Because of my apparent obsession with flesh, blood and entrails, I am filmed in an abbatoir. Reality is more unbearable to draw than imagination, 1968.

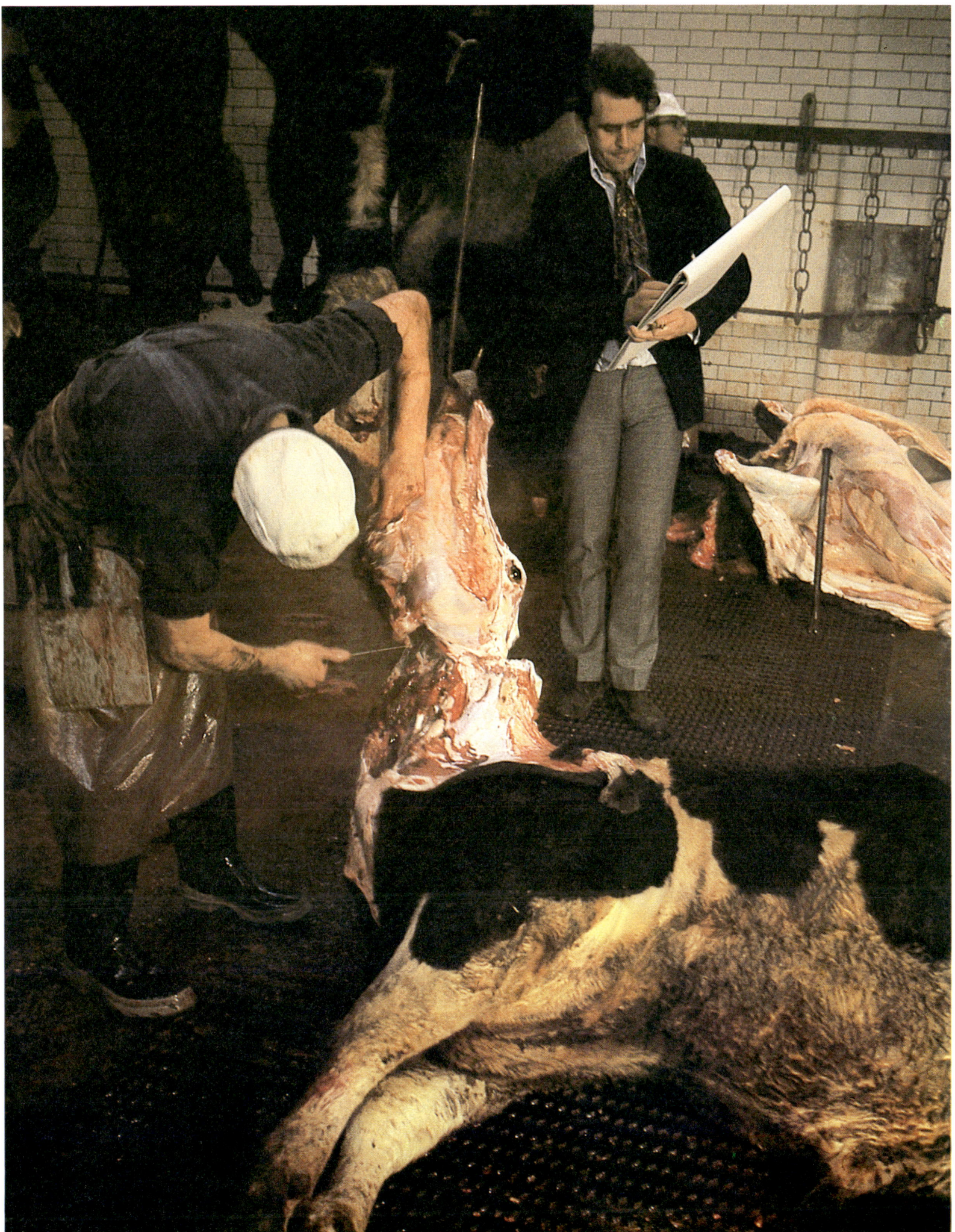

In 1968 I had my first exhibition in America at the Waddell gallery, and then because of its success I was given another in 1970. I don't sell my work but luckily the gallery owner, Dick Waddell, was rich enough to give me a show without selling anything. However, Nelson Rockefeller wanted to buy his sculpture, and Dick persuaded me to part with it. Apparently it sat at the top of the stairs in the Gracy Mansion, the Governor's residence in New York. Gallery openings can be depressing affairs for the artist. The same fashionable New York crowd came to every affair, jam-packed so hard that the drawings and sculptures not only weren't looked at, but were in danger of being damaged. "Mr Scarfe, I got to tell you you're a genius," they trotted out as I'm sure they did to every artist while upsetting white wine down his pictures.

CARICATURES IN LIFE-SIZE SCULPTURE BY
ENGLAND'S FOREMOST POLITICAL CARTOONIST

GERALD SCARFE

U.S. ELECTION '68

OCTOBER 15—NOVEMBER 9

WADDELL 15 EAST 57 NEW YORK

Gerald Scarfe
60-70

A ten-year commentary in
drawing lithography and
sculpture by Englands foremost
political caricaturist
FEBRUARY 24   MARCH 27 1970

WADDELL GALLERY
15 East 57 New York

I took my sculptures on the Johnny Carson television show. I explained that drawings bottled themselves up inside me and I didn't feel right until I got them out onto the paper – "a bit like being constipated," I said. "Uh huh," said Johnny Carson, "that's a no-no."

Below left: Ronald Reagan breaking through the silver screen.
Below: Nixon, McCarthy, Wallace, Johnson, Humphrey, Reagan and Rockefeller with gold teeth, 1968.

Bottom: The hippy-basher, Mayor Daley of Chicago, 1968.

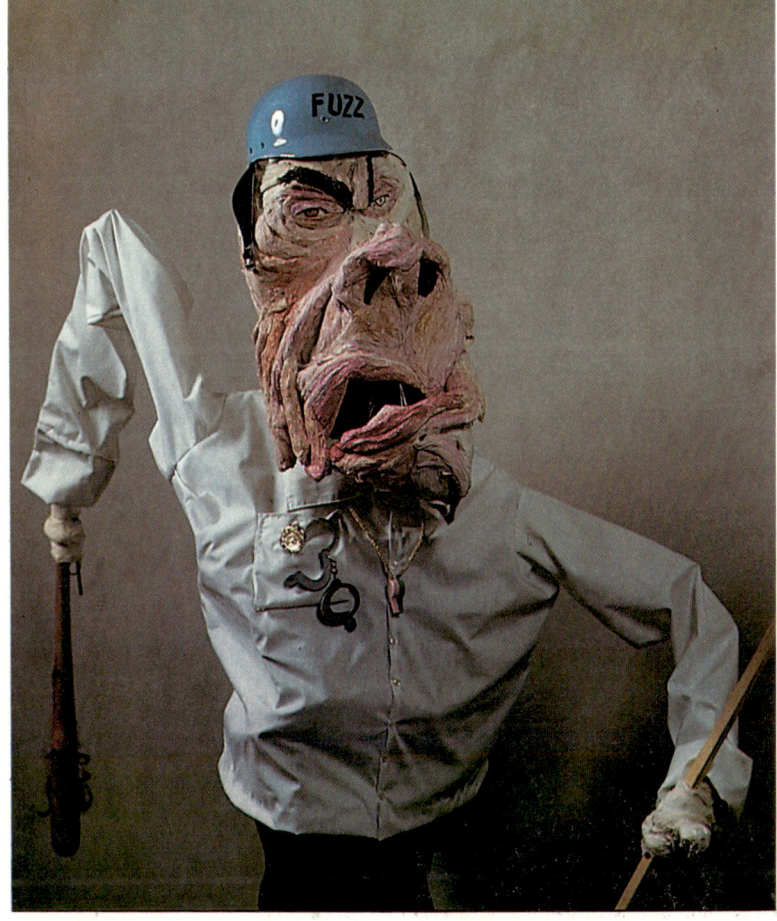

We discover just before opening the show in Chicago that the model of Jackie Onassis has been damaged irretrievably.

I have an idea. I ask the gallery director to nip out and buy a fairly expensive mirror. He arrives back with it and I ask him to smash it.

"Smash it?"

"Yes, smash it. I see her as a cracked mirror."

As he dutifully brings down the hammer, the flying glass cuts his hand badly. On the other side of the gallery stands my model of Field Marshal Montgomery playing a game of chess with toy soldiers.

I have another idea!

I seize the bleeding man, run him over to Monty's chessboard and sprinkle the blood from his bleeding hand over Monty's toy soldiers.

Nothing like authenticity.

Robert LaPalme was a great fan of my work, and every sculpture I completed he wanted to put on show in Montreal. So every time a sculpture had finished its round of the galleries I sent it to Robert in Canada.

After some years I decided to recall what amounted to most of my sculptured work to England, only to find to my devastation on its arrival that most of it was either badly damaged or destroyed. Robert was apologetic. They had been badly handled. I flew to Montreal in a fury for a meeting with Mayor Drapeau and we eventually arrived at a settlement. Alas, most of the work from this period does not exist anymore.

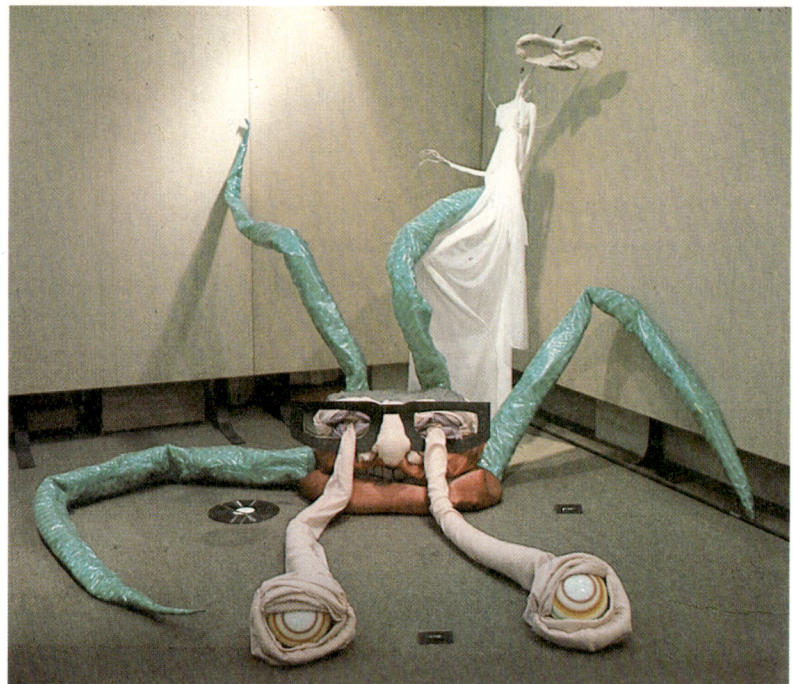

The Royal Family. Top: Jackie and Aristotle Onassis. Bottom: 'Monty'. Opposite top right: My studio in 1968. Bottom: John Lindsay.

David Frost had a nest of mice in his head and I had to do something about it.

He had sat in the corner of my studio for some months wearing a blazer and flannels and I had my suspicions all wasn't well with him when I heard scratching and scuttling coming from inside his papier-mâché skull. I told my assistant Ed to take the whole lifesize model across the road in Cheyne Walk to get rid of the mice.

At twilight he left the house with the model and a broom. Laying the figure of Frost on the pavement alongside the small park opposite, he started to wallop it with the broom. The mice ran out and a car skidded to a halt in the middle of the road. "Oi!" shouted the driver. "Leave that old geezer alone!"

They said that John Lindsay, Mayor of New York, was destined for high office. He told the citizens there were too many cars in New York. He told them they should take to cycling.

I made a sculpture of him riding a real cycle for my exhibition in New York. Politicians love to have their fame captured in stone or marble but it seemed right to me to make these ambitious creatures in papier-mâché and cloth, for like my newspaper cartoons they were transitory materials.

You see, right, what has happened to the papier-mâché after mice, beetles and time have had their way.

As for the real John Lindsay, I have not heard of him since but his bicycle is very useful, I still ride it.

built a thirty-foot-high sculpture of Gulliver in my garden in Chelsea for an exhibition of my work in Osaka, Japan. I made him entirely of welded scrap metal. The whole house and garden was full of scrap metal and oxyacetylene welding equipment. It was a disgrace.

The funny thing was that my neighbour who had complained about the previous owner of my house playing the piano didn't say a word.

It had been commissioned by the Central Office of Information for Expo 70. When I had finished eight or nine soberly-suited men from the C.O.I. filed apprehensively into the alien territory of my studio. They had come to look at Gulliver. He had been made in two halves, torso and legs. Unfortunately only the torso was on view.

Silence and shuffling from the C.O.I. gents. "I think he's absolutely wonderful," said the leader. "But isn't he a little short for Gulliver?"

In order to clothe some of the other figures in my exhibition I bought the entire wardrobe of a defunct theatrical company and, as it was bitterly cold working outside on Gulliver, my brother Gordon, who was helping me, took to wearing some of the costumes.

One day he opened the door to the gasman wearing three frock coats, one on top of the other, and a Thomas Wolsey skull cap.

The gasman didn't say a word – probably thought it was the thing down in Chelsea.

Sumo wrestler, Tokyo, Japan, 1970.

In 1971 the SUNDAY TIMES sent me to cover the cholera outbreak in India. I flew to Calcutta and checked into my hotel. A quick shower and straight to the bar like a good journalist, to meet a photographer friend.

We ordered two whiskies – "No water!" Water carries cholera. The barman put ice in one glass. "Er, no ice," we shouted together. He emptied out the ice and put the glass in front of my friend and a new glass in front of me and poured the whisky. Just before we drank my "friend" swapped the glasses. "No, you don't!" I said. He smiled sheepishly.

The following morning the photographer and I left the hotel early and picked our way through the sleeping ranks of those who spend the night on the pavement. In Calcutta the pavement is "owned" by some small-time entrepreneur who "rents" it by the foot to the poor homeless. They sleep on pieces of cardboard or on the bare stone itself.

We drove to Bodartala Hospital, a long low breezeblock building with corrugated iron roof. It had been raining and great brown puddles lay on the dirt road. The doors of the hospital were open and I could see figures lying inside.

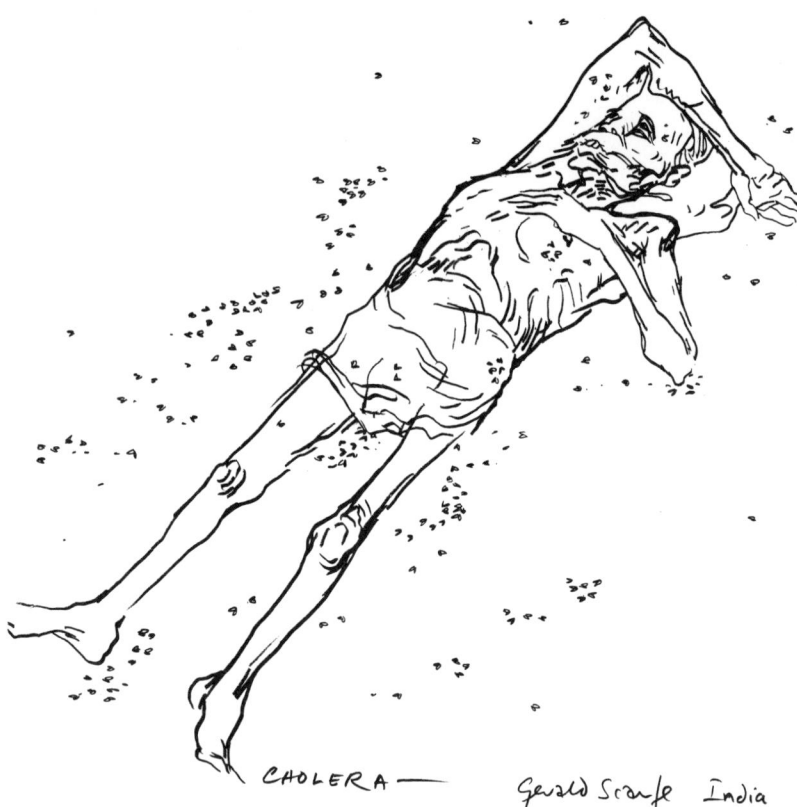

CHOLERA — Gerald Scarfe India

We went in and saw what seemed to be the aftermath of a battle. Every available space in the sparse room was covered by recumbent forms. What beds there were had at least two or three people on them and two or three people under them. Between the beds every inch of the floor was covered with people in various stages of death. The whole place was black with flies.

I had the same feeling of panic that I had experienced in a Saigon morgue, made worse by the fact that these poor people were alive. I felt I could not invade their grief and misery and dispassionately attempt to draw them.

As I hesitated in the doorway, my photographer colleague pushed past me firing off shots with his Nikon. "Insensitive swine," I thought, as I watched him picking his way through the dying. I went outside again feeling a complete failure. I had travelled thousands of miles and risked cholera to report this assignment. It was my job to let people at home know what was going on. "I should do it," I thought, and went back into the hospital.

I feverishly drew the poor lady on the left who was too far gone to care what was happening and, as I drew, I became engrossed in putting down as faithfully and quickly as possible the image of the dying woman and my embarrassment left me. I moved on and started another drawing. Often drawings are made in a state of high tension and nervous energy. The figures became objects with dimensions that I must try and imitate on paper. My sketchbook became a screen behind which I could distance myself from the pain just as the photographer used his camera.

Unwisely I drove my hired Cortina into the Catholic Bogside area of Derry in Northern Ireland. I had to circumnavigate several barricades of burnt-out cars. Once inside the deserted area I stopped and moved into the passenger seat in order to rest my drawing board on my knee and began sketching one of the barricades.

After about half an hour I was startled when a young man rapped on the window.

"What are you doing?" he said.

"I'm making a drawing."

"Who sent you?"

"I'm from the SUNDAY TIMES in London," I said.

"Ah," he said. "Well, we might need your car."

"What do you mean?"

"Well, we might need it. It's rented, isn't it? You won't have to pay."

"Yes, but it's not insured." (This was true – Avis would not insure me. It was too much of a risk.)

He seemed satisfied with this and went away.

I decided to work on and got to the point of the drawing you see above, when a Zephyr screeched to a halt across the front of my car. Three men leapt out. One, unshaven with long, lank hair, got into the driver's seat. I realized later that he had sat on an open razor blade I had been using to sharpen my pencils. That could have caused trouble.

Two more got into rear seats and stuck automatic pistols in my ribs. "Don't move," they said. "This is official." "What's going to happen?" I said with a slow-motion state of calm. "We're going to drive you somewhere," one said. The driver put the car into gear and moved slowly forward. No one talked. Eventually we stopped in a square of modern flats. I still had the drawing on my lap.

"I'm making this drawing for the SUNDAY TIMES," I said weakly.

"The SUNDAY TIMES has done us a bit of no good," said one.

"Murray Sayle wrote that we were passing gelignite in the Bogside Inn." Another one looked at my sketch. "You're a brave drawer," he said. "Get out!" said the other. "What's going to happen?" I said. "Get out!" he said again.

As I got out, prickles running down the back of my spine, I thought they would shoot me. One got out of the rear seat with his gun. "Have you got all your pencils?" he said. "Sorry about all this. That's the way back to the centre of town," he pointed. I walked slowly away from my hired Cortina, still expecting a bullet.

As I reached my hotel I wondered if the razor blade ever found its target.

Later they blew up the post office in the next road and attempted to blow up my hotel.

I left the next day.

I ran out of the gentlemen's lavatory in Covent Garden with a bucket of water and threw it over the pavement hoping it looked as though it had been raining. Five 18th-century gentlemen looked on.

"Do I shout 'Action!," I asked Norman Swallow.

"If you like," he said. "Turn over," said Mike, the cameraman.

"Action!" I shouted.

The five 18th-century gentlemen started leapfrogging amongst the colonnades of St Paul's Church, laughing and shouting. It was wonderful, I was a director. I felt happy, such power. A lorry full of 20th-century vegetables backed across my creation.

"Cut!"

The BBC had asked me to write and direct a film on "Hogarth".

I had five actors dressed up romping around the Kent countryside. Silly business, I put them in a field with some sheep.

"Action!"

"Just a minute," they said. "What shall we say?"

"Oh, anything you like – Action!"

"But what shall we do?" they said.

"Just go over there and run about," I said, getting irritable. "Action!"

I had my comeuppance when I got the rushes back to my cutting room in Ealing. They were almost unusable.

I changed my tack. What would Hogarth be if he were alive today? An artist? A writer? A photographer? A television reporter?

I set about exploring these possibilities in what I hoped were Hogarthian contexts. Pubs, bars, gambling establishments. Playboy club.

My cameraman and I managed to bluff our way into Boodle's Club in St James's by mentioning the name Hogarth (very acceptable) and film a medical dinner. Very jolly, very Hogarthian.

"May we offer you a brandy?" asked one member.

"No thank you," I said, "I've just bought one myself."

"Good God, bought one yourself?" he said. "Must say the standards of this club have gone down."

Very Hogarthian.

Below left: Two limited edition books I produced myself.

Opposite: Directing a bunny and a turkey, 1971.

What's it like to have a genius in the family?" Said my editor, Harold Evans, to my mother at the opening of my new show. "It's all very well," answered my mother, "but I wish he'd draw something nice."

I was asked to exhibit at the National Portrait Gallery in London in a show with David Hockney and David Bailey. I set about making new sculptures for the show but this time, remembering that John, Paul, George and Ringo had been eaten by beetles, I used more durable materials. A fibreglass Edward Heath who oozed across the floor as a spilled egg, dropping from a cracked polystyrene shell.

A collapsed old armchair in the basement became an expensive pun, 'Chair Man Mao'.

Nixon is an example of my pushing caricature to an extreme. I wanted to encapsulate him in the simplest shape I could achieve. He is made of wood and his jowls are separated from his face and hang independently.

Enoch Powell is no more. He was one of my favourite sculptures. A series of four figures made of cloth, wire, leather and metal were linked to one another. It showed how my work evolved. Above you see the unfinished sculpture, the seated figure looking moderately caricatured.

It was a very good visual explanation of how I start with a fairly representational figure and develop it until it becomes a much simpler, almost abstract, symbol. Four linked figures becoming more and more caricatured as they progressed, ending up with steel jaws gripping a golliwog.

Simplifying my work was one of my constant aims although I frequently became waylaid. I made a set of lithographs at Curwen Studio for this exhibition. I think the Queen is a good example of the simplicity I mean.

The BBC featured Enoch when I was interviewed for an arts programme and I left him there overnight. The next day he was discovered badly beaten up and partially destroyed, and that was the end of Enoch.

I've always wondered whether the vandals were anti-Scarfe or anti-Powell.

All I have left now are the steel jaws.

'There is also – and this is perhaps the most telling part of the show – a roomful of biting satires by Gerald Scarfe. There are cartoons in which caricature is carried to lengths rarely equalled or even attempted, and sculptures in which bile blossoms into luxuriant baroque varieties or is boiled down to austere paradigms of dislike – for instance, a remarkable rendering of Nixon's face in wood, in which the features are dissected and re-assembled so that his pendulous jowl actually hangs from a hook.'
Nigel Gosling *The Observer* March 21 1971

Pausing only to buy a screwdriver at Woolworths, I made my way to Newport Art Gallery. I strode into the Gallery and started unscrewing pictures from the wall.

The director of the Gallery was appalled. He ran around flapping his arms. He told me to stop or he would call the police. I told him to go ahead. After I had taken down about ten pictures the police arrived and the director pointed me out in excited fury. I thought he would explode. "Now then, sir," said the Inspector. "What's this all about then?"

I explained that my exhibition from the National Portrait Gallery was to be shown at Newport but a Councillor and the Committee had objected to three of my drawings, calling them "Lavatory Wall Artistry", and wanted to take them out of the exhibition. On hearing this, I had told the Arts Council, who ran the exhibition, that it was understandable if they didn't want to show them but they must remove the whole of my work or none of it. I had taken great trouble to pick a balanced, representative selection; the drawings they wanted to remove were sexual in content but as an artist I felt that there was no part of human activity that I should not show in my work, and indeed I was known for the use of human sexual activity as a vehicle in my drawing. Therefore it would be an incomplete collection if they were not included.

What had spurred me to take this action was that the Committee had gone ahead with the exhibition without the three controversial drawings against my will.

"Well, Mr Scarfe," said the Inspector, "you are completely within your rights to remove your property."

I did.

The exhibition closed and the Gallery director exploded.

WOMEN'S LIBERATION FRONT OR VENUS RISES

SCARFE 'STORM SHOW' OPENS

AN ART exhibition which was the centre of a row over three drawings by cartoonist Gerald Scarfe opened in Newport, Mon., yesterday, while talks went on to decide whether it should be abandoned.

The three drawings which sparked off the trouble were not on view.

They were banned after the chair...

Mr. Cefni Barnett, said the show was going on pe... the outcome of talks be... Newport Corporation a... Welsh Arts Council, w... organising the exh... with the Arts Cou... Great Britain.

Newport's town cl... **John Long**, said ye... "Various points ar... discussion with t... Council and a dec... the exhibition will... soon."

The ban on the... by Mr. Venn, age...

Banned all his

GERALD SCARF... been banned fr... Chelsea home...

Scarfe show shut-down likely

By A. J. SICLUNA

SNAP, THE Welsh Arts Council exhibi- tion, is likely to be removed from Newport Art Gallery today. Yesterday the WAC's assistant... moved exhibits and un... supply to the exhib... tion.

Scarfe art ban

An art exhibition which was the centre of a row over three drawings by cartoonist Gerald Scarfe, opened yesterday, while talks went... should decide whether it... three drawings which were... the trouble at the art gal... at Monmouth...

This followed a me... ing with Newpo... amenity and... services committee which, he, claims, was treated... "intolerance and ...ourtesy."

"I have been w... Welsh Arts Council f... ...ars and never hav... ...ated so much like... an errand boy... ...nes today,...

Newport ba... on three Scarfe nud...

By A. J. SICLUNA

THREE DRAWINGS by art... Scarfe, one of which depic... Harold Wilson surrounded by... of Zurich, have been withdr... exhibition which opens next... port Art Gallery.

The decision was mad... this week by Newpor... council amenity and leisur... services committee when... they examined material for... the exhibition Snap, which... is organised by the Welsh... Arts Council.

Coun. Clive W. Venn, the... chairman of the committee,... said today: "Two of the... drawings are lavatory wall... art and the third attacks... the integrity of a Prime... Minister. Scarfe is a bril-... liant artist, but I could not... allow these exhibits to go... forward. I think Scarfe... tends to mix up his sense... of values."

The three drawings, no... behind locked doors, dr... a certain amount of co... ment from London visi... of Snap.

For Swansea...

One is entitled to...

prieve
r Scarfe
rtoon

controversial art exhibi-
at Newport, Monmouth-
, where three Gerald
fe cartoons were banned, is
tay open—and one of the
oons may be shown.

he town's amenities com-
ttee held an emergency meet-
on Monday night to discuss
e repercussions of their ban-
ng of three Scarfe cartoons,
belled "lavatory-wall artistry"
y the committee's chairman,
ouncillor Clive Venn.

The town clerk, Mr John
Long, said yesterday that the
committee would be prepared to
hang one of the three cartoons,
depicting Aubrey Beardsley,
e it was catalogued.

st Scarfe takes
bits from Snap!

NDED that three of his drawings have
hibition at Newport, travelled from his
and took down his remaining exhibits.

The police were called | property if I felt like it," he
Newport Art Gallery, | said.
t left after officials | His action, he said, was in
had been told he was | support of his view that no-
entitled to move his own | one should decide what an
property. | artist should or should not
Now, more than 20 of Mr. | display. The exhibits in
Scarfe's drawings are in the | Snap, he said, comprised a
care of the Welsh Arts Coun- | balanced selection. Thus, if
cil, the organisers of the ex- | the council objected to some
hibition Snap. | exhibits, the whole sections
Mr. Scarfe said, "I had said | should be removed.
I did not want my exhibits | Mr. Peter Jones,
shown at Newport after the | director of the
ban and I decided that the | Council, said t
only way to make my point | Newport auth
clear was to go down and | of his work
ake the drawings off the | tion.
alls." | The row
| started las
Level-headed | Coun. Clive
| of the Nev
Newport Borough Council. | leisure se
said were planning to | said three
ge whether the three | taken out
nned drawings should be | Two, he
cluded. | wall art"
"I felt disinclined to let the | an atta
uncil review my drawings, | Minister
do not know what their | On
lifications are and it | Arts Co
nt leave me open to | the exl
her insults," he said. | held, b
hen Mr. Scarfe arrived | nounce
le gallery he was told he
not take down the "level-
ngs but after discussions he was
d to proceed.
ad to go out to buy
crewdrivers
wings and
They
at I wa
to take

● Gerald Scarfe

Ban on three cartoons

JUST LAVATORY WALL ARTISTRY—COUNCILLOR

THREE DRAWINGS by car-
toonist Gerald Scarfe have
been withdrawn from an
exhibition next week at
Newport, Monmouthshire.

The order came from Coun.
Clive Venn (45), Conservative chairman of the New-
port Amenities and Leisure
Services Committee.

"I am no prude," he said yesterday — "I will

them to be lavatory wall
artistry."

The exhibition is organised
by the Welsh Arts Council.

Mr. Venn is backed by his
committee — and also Mr.
Cefni Barne director of

nett, "but when you have
people of all ages, views and
sensitivities coming in, one
has to exercise a little care."

The subjects of the banned
works are the Female
Liberation Front; Mr.
Harold Wilson and the
Zurich; and

Scarfe works banned

● THREE drawings by the
cartoonist Gerald Scarfe have
been withdrawn from an exhibition in Newport, Monmouthshire, organised by the Welsh
Arts Council. Councillor Clive
Venn, chairman of the Amenities and Leisure Services
Committee, said the drawings
Women's Liberation

3 Scarfe drawings banned from art gallery

DAILY TELEGRAPH REPORT

THREE drawings by Gerald
withdrawn from an Arts
tion at Newport art gallery,
yesterday after an objectio
councillor who described t

Sex art row exhibition for Swansea

EVENING POST REPORTER

SWANSEA TODAY decided to accept an art exhibition that this afternoon was being withdrawn from
Newport art gallery after a row over it
content.

But the city may not get
the controversial

*I*saw murder, rape, incest and decapitation but I had a slap-up supper afterwards. The theatre world is the perfect antidote to my anxieties. Nothing is real. All is pretend, all make believe, don't take it seriously. It's a reflection or a dream which ends at 10.20 when the curtain comes down. If only the lights could go up and I could find that Famine, Cruelty, Poverty and Nuclear War were all figments of the imagination. "It's only the theatre, dear boy," I would say.

I went to the theatre to draw a dress rehearsal one day, got lost in the maze of corridors backstage and suddenly found myself on stage in the middle of a sword fight. Alan Brien wrote in the SUNDAY TIMES: "A mad Byronic figure erupted onto the stage and fell into the orchestra pit, it was Gerald Scarfe."

Nicol Williamson asked me to show him the sketch I'd made of him. "Oh," he said, "you've been drinking again, Rembrandt. The trouble with you, Gerald, is that you're moribund."

The only time I've ever acted myself was when Bill Wyman, the Rolling Stone, wanted me in his film, 'Digital Dreams'. One morning, Lights! Camera! Action! I found myself in a dramatic scene with James Coburn dressed as a druid in our kitchen. Never again.

These drawings were made for the SUNDAY TIMES. I like the theatre. Well, it gets me out in the evenings. It's nice to have an evening out. My wife's an actress, you know.

James Coburn and unknown in 'Digital Dreams', 1984.

ANTONY SHER 'RED NOSES'

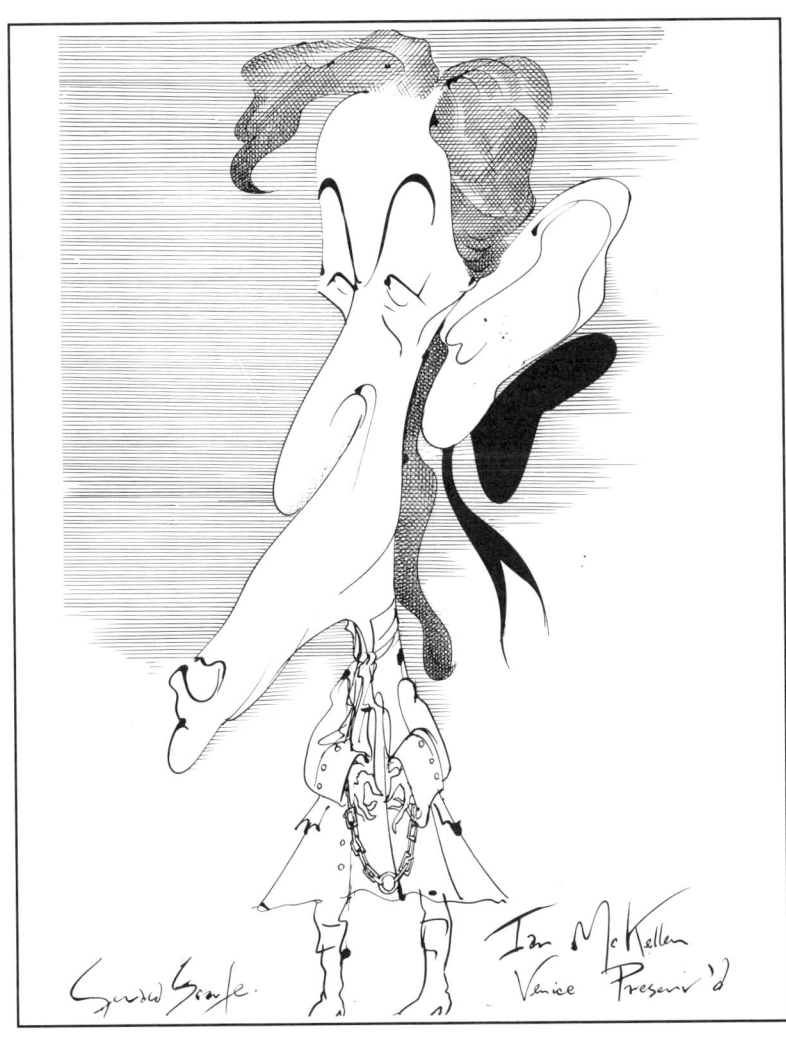

ALBERT FINNEY AND COMPANY
SERJEANT MUSGRAVES DANCE - OLD VIC

Ian McKellen
Venice Preserv'd

Peter O'Toole
PYGMALION

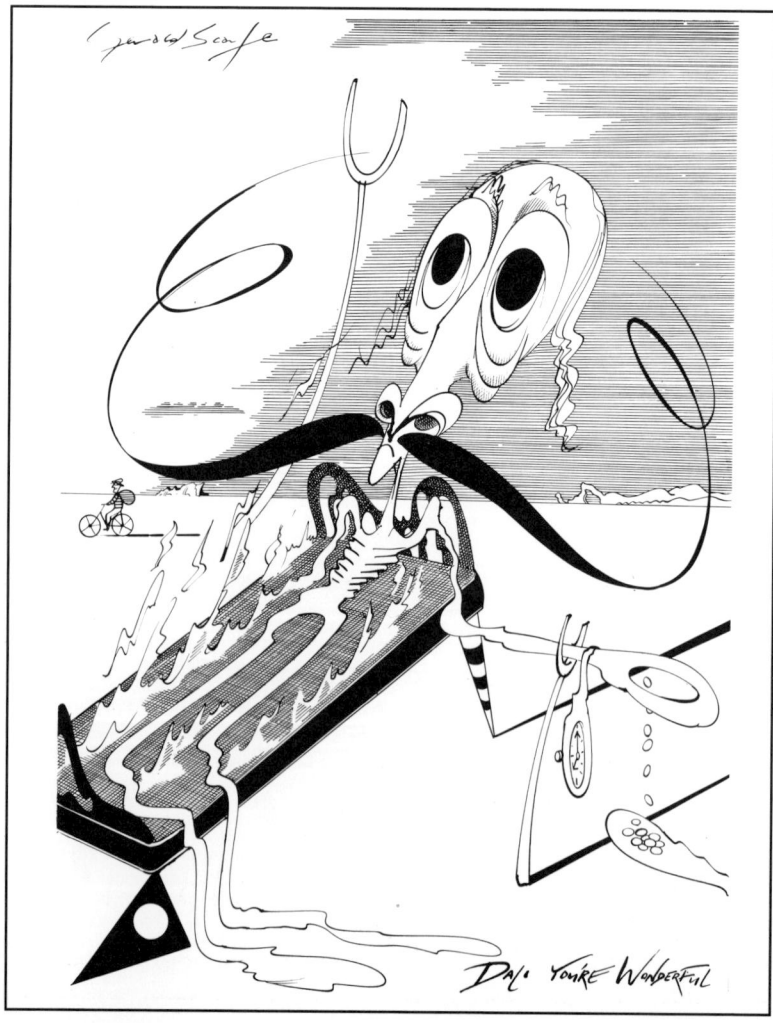

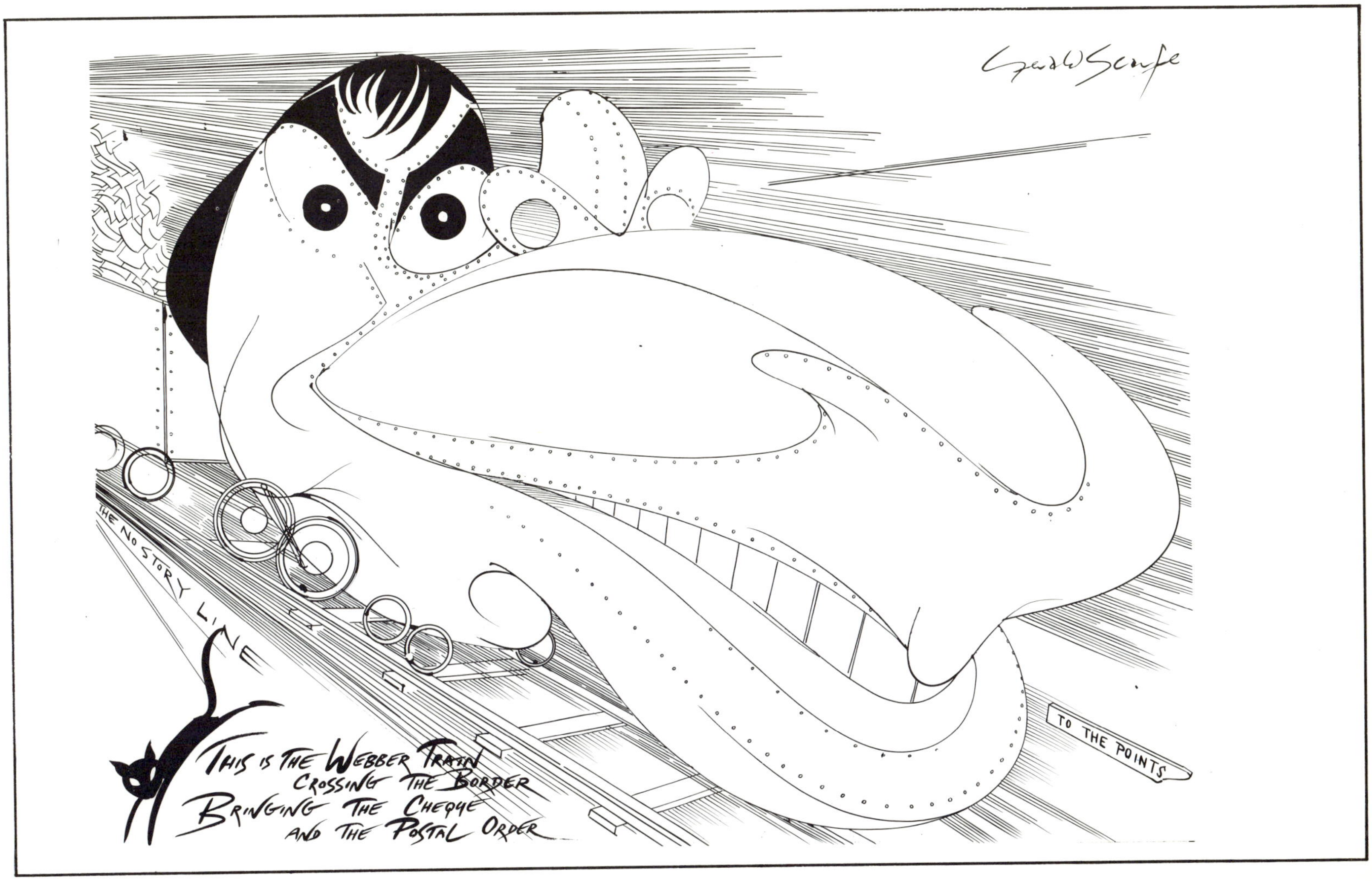

"Oooo! Don't draw me, will you!" they usually say to me. "Goodness knows how you must see me." Well, the truth is I don't think I see them any differently to anybody else. I do not see people with elongated noses and floppy ears loping around. They look normal to me. Well, normalish.

When I start to caricature someone I exaggerate their features or I may imagine them as something else entirely, a lug worm, or a vacuum cleaner. What I'm trying to do is simply bring out their essential characteristics. I find a particular delight in taking the caricature as far as I can. It satisfies me to stretch the human frame about and recreate it and yet keep a likeness. There comes a point in that stretching process where, like a piece of stretched chewing gum, it breaks and the likeness is lost.

The advantage of working on a daily or weekly newspaper is that the readers can be slowly led over a period of time to accept the extremes of caricature. If I make a fairly representational caricature of Ronald Reagan in January and exaggerate it slowly through the year, by December, in theory, the reader would be conditioned to accept a circle with two triangles on top as Ronald Reagan.

Imagine yourself sitting at your desk and the door opens and an artist comes in and thrusts a piece of paper three feet by two with a 'joke' drawn on it, under your nose.

"Go on laugh damn you."

What do you do?

That's what it must be like when the cartoonist confronts his editor. God, what's this one about? Who's that? – Ronald Reagan? or Gorbachev? What are they doing? Why do they look like sponge cakes? Who's the man upside down in the background?

I have learnt over the years to go in firing from the hip. "This is Reagan and this is Thatcher and they are symbolising Western Unity." Relief on Editor's face. Pass.

Then it's over to you, the public, to sort it out.

I am fighting for attention amongst screaming headlines, dramatic photographs, and advertisements designed for impact. I have either to shout louder than they to survive, or make a drawing which is simple, direct and immediate. An example of this simplicity is 'A to B, Children's Problem'.

The whole process of drawing can be wonderful, ideas flowing, an urgency and necessity to get them down before they evaporate.

I love ideas and, when they rush on to the paper, there is nothing better.

But beware those days when nothing, nothing, nothing will happen.

No wonder we believe in the muse. I end up trying to trick myself into working, rushing it, sidling up to it, caressing it. But nothing happens. The pen won't work. The ink is too thick. My hand is like a steel claw or a piece of mountainous dough.

The work stuttering and spluttering on to the paper.

It's hell!

Where did it go?

It was here a minute ago.

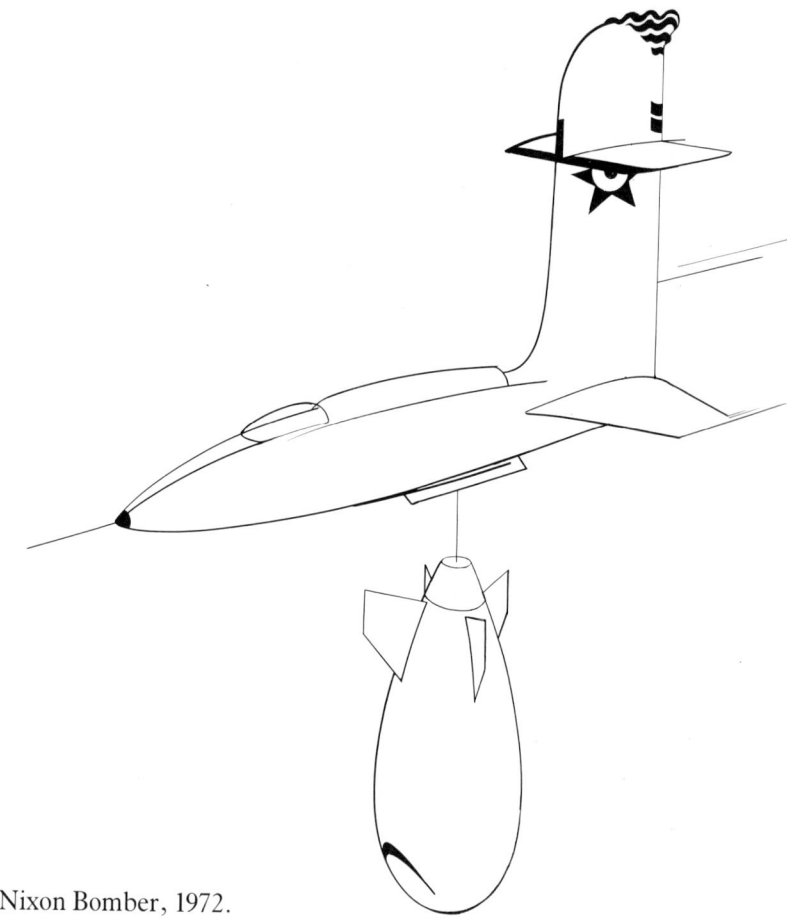

Nixon Bomber, 1972.

CHILDREN'S PROBLEM
JOIN A TO B
(Baffles World Leaders)

Above: Biafra, 1970.

Opposite: Idi Amin, 1976.

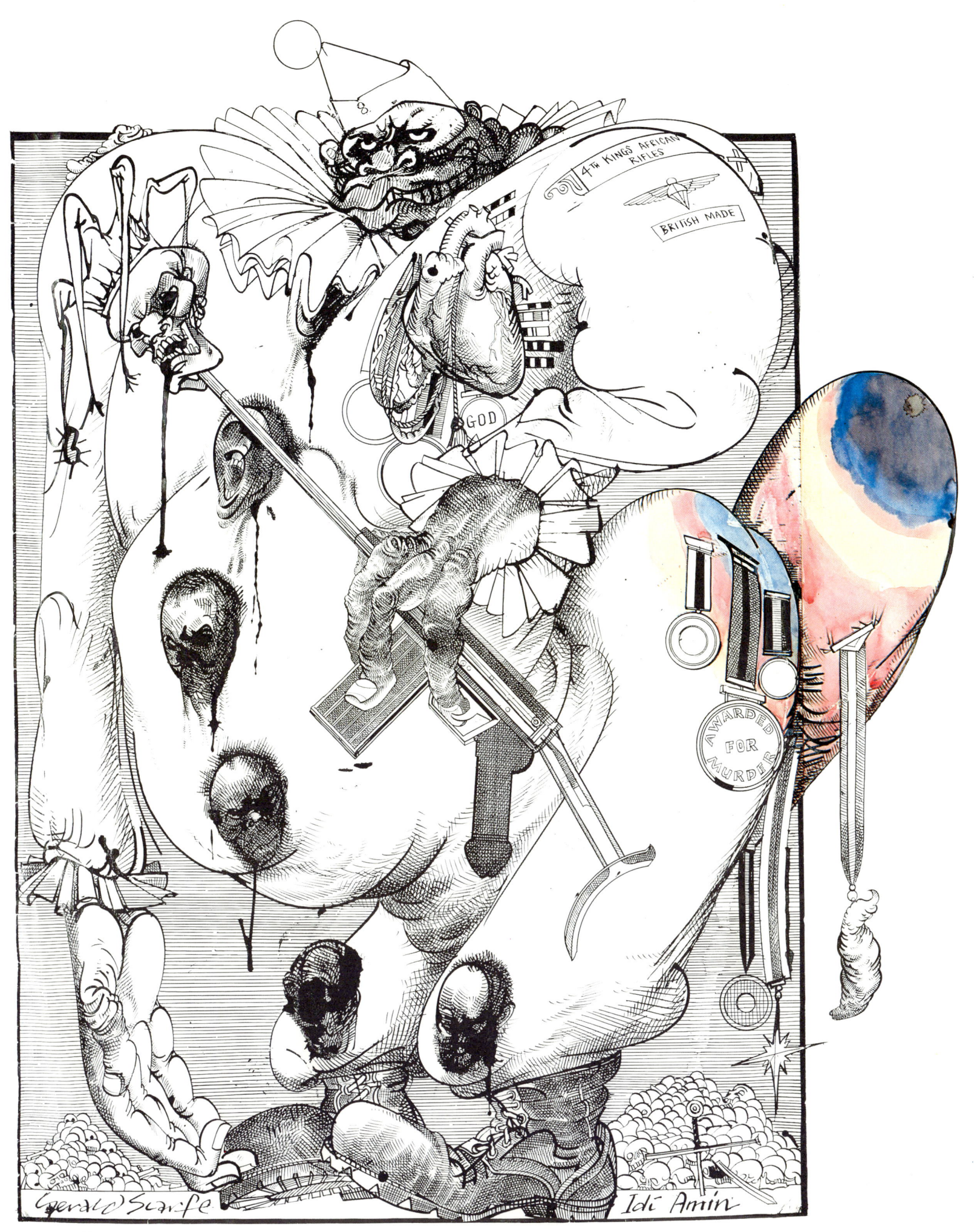

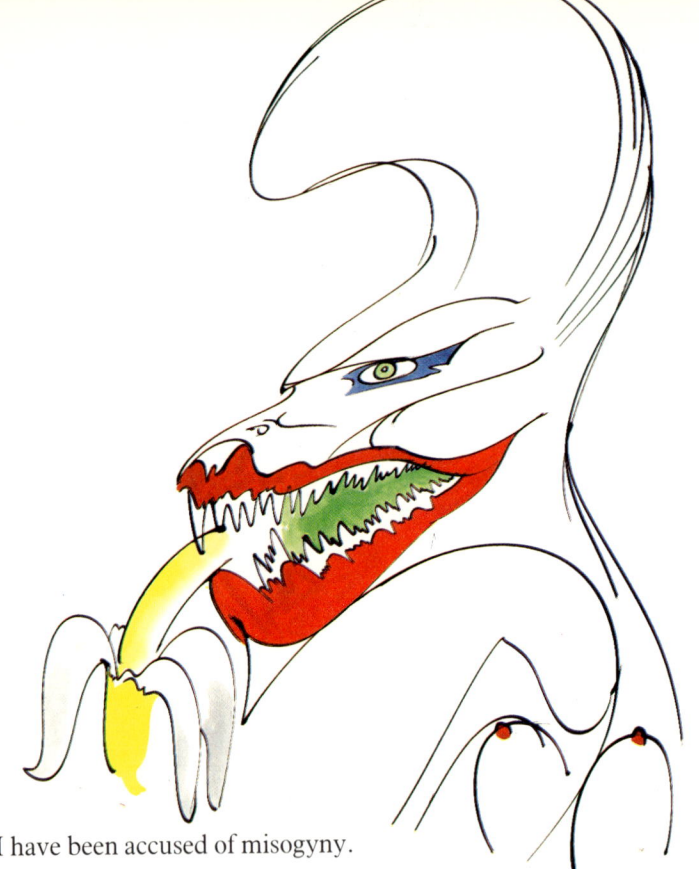

I have been accused of misogyny.

Harry Evans was furious with me. I had deliberately tried to slip a penis into the SUNDAY TIMES, he stormed. I had no idea what he was talking about. He said, "You know very well, Reggie Maudling's chin looks like a penis." I looked at it. He was right, it did look like one. "I'm sorry," I said, "I didn't intend it." He didn't believe me. I told him penises are in the eye of the beholder – but he wasn't amused. We changed it for the second edition. I sent him a little drawing of Maudling with underpants on his chin.

He was always worried, too, when I drew rockets. It's not easy being a cartoonist.

In general people I draw do not react to my drawings. Most of them are figures in public office and perhaps it would be beneath their dignity to react. Indeed, I think some of them enjoy it. It's better to be portrayed as a dung beetle than not to be mentioned at all. Vicky always said that his victims got to look more like his drawings, even consciously exaggerating their hair or whatever to comply with their caricature. I can't think of an instance where one of my subjects has spoken to me sharply about their drawing.

The fans of these public figures, though, are a different kettle of fish. I made a drawing of Mick Jagger and received a letter from one hundred and fourteen schoolgirls from one school. "Dear Mr. Scarfe," it said, "for what you have done to our Mick we are going to get you and cut your balls off. Yours sincerely, Angela Morris, Betty Duckley, etc., etc.," one hundred and fourteen signatures.

Sweet things.

My drawings are of course very personal acts made in the privacy of my own home, but when they leave my hands they escape into hundreds of thousands of copies and may be seen by millions of people. I don't think about that when I make the drawing – it's just between my imagination and that piece of paper – but if a drawing is particularly ferocious or overtly sexual and someone looks at it in my presence I have to admit to sometimes feeling shy; I feel so personally about it it's almost like undressing in public. My drawings are often a cry against that which I detest, and in showing my dislike I have to draw the dislikeable. To horrify people with a drawing of the waste of war I must make a horrific drawing of war, and when I come to draw people, their bodies become vehicles for their emotions – greed, lust, cruelty. It is not that I have a dislike of human flesh: it is that I have a dislike of human frailties and the flesh becomes a medium for

SPOT THE DIFFERENCE

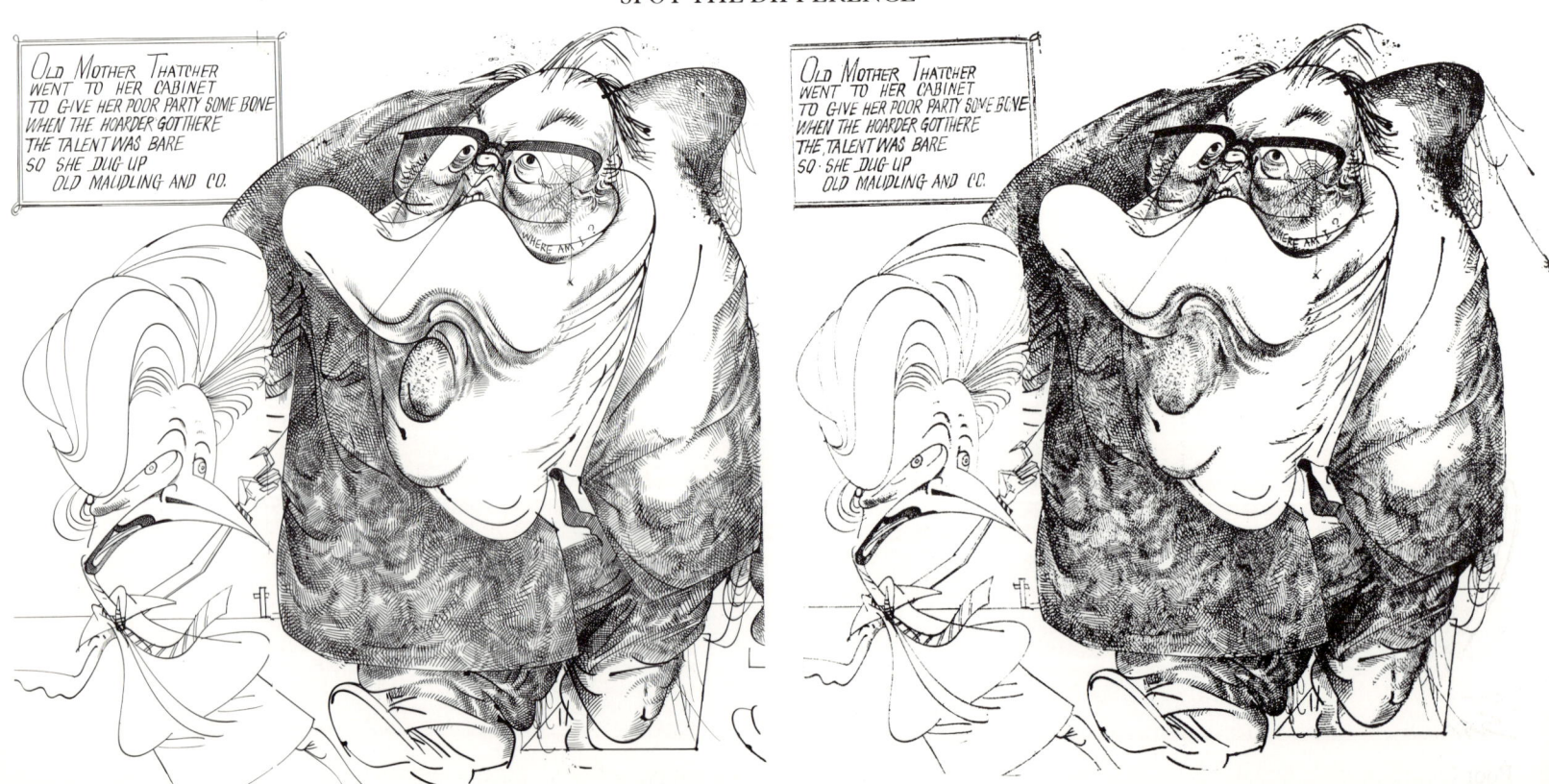

depicting them. However, as there is a percentage of prudery in my make-up I am embarrassed if for instance the drawing is overtly sexual and the onlooker is shocked, although that is what I set out to do.

Denis Healey bore down on me at the Labour Party Conference in Blackpool. "Look!" he said, jabbing a finger in his mouth. "My teeth are not! – not!," he emphasized, "as big as you draw them."

They were.

Blackpool or Brighton at conference time is the natural habitat of the politician. Here I can draw them unobserved, braying at breakfast, basking on the prom, lolling at their watering holes, snorting at the best troughs in town, slumbering in the afternoon boredom of unmemorable speeches (waiting always for the main chance).

I'm not too keen on politicians. What arrogance and stupidity makes a mere mortal think he is the one chosen to lead others?

On the week of Rupert Murdoch's take-over I made this drawing of Ronald Reagan symbolising America stepping out of Vietnam and into San Salvador. It was reported to me later that Murdoch had said, "Poor old Ronnie! We must get rid of this pinko artist."

Denis Healey.

Poor Old Ronnie, 1982.

Enoch Powell 'A Nasty Shock', 1973.

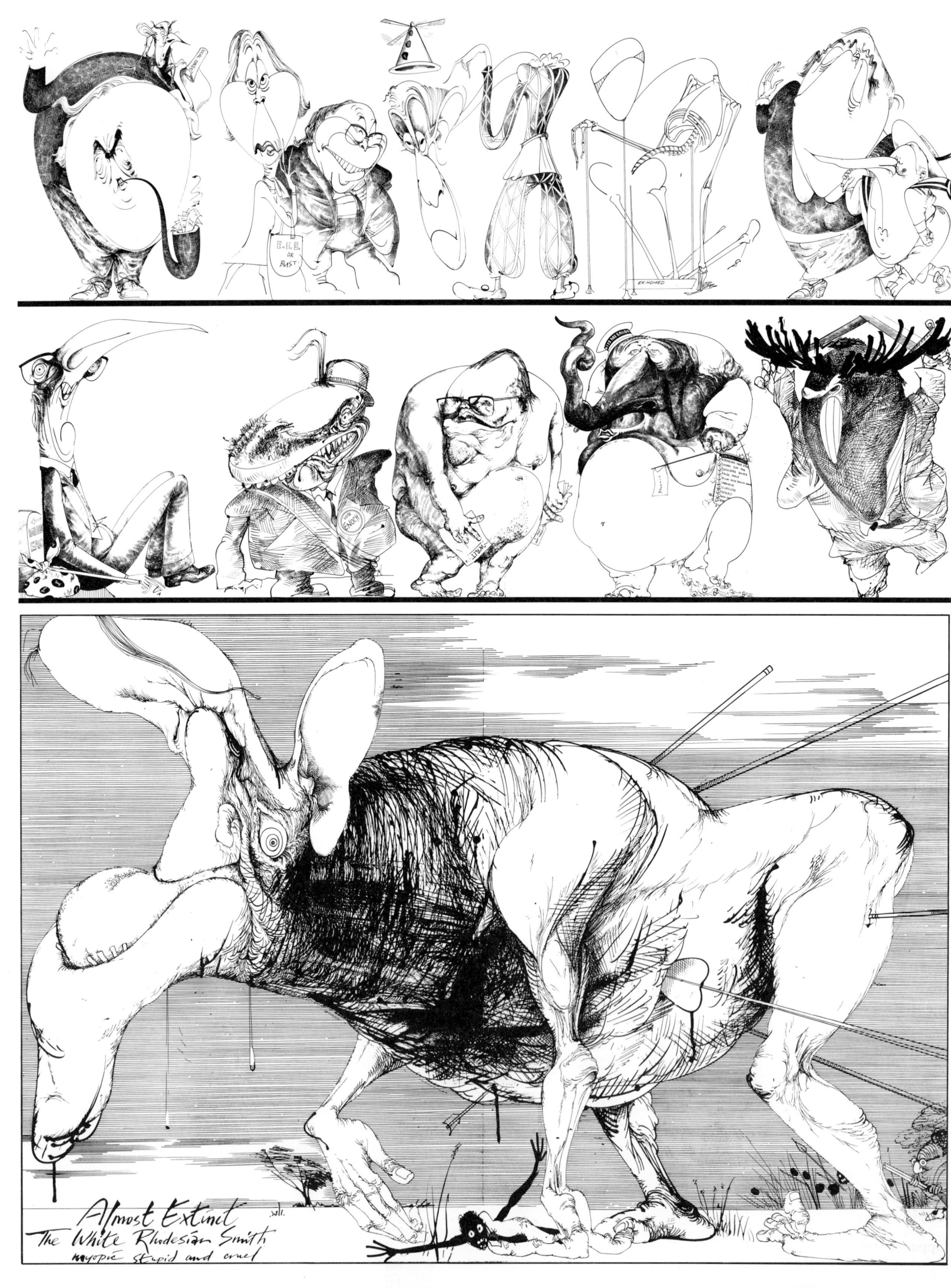

Almost Extinct
The White Rhodesian Smith
myopic stupid and cruel

Putting on my smock and beret I stroll down to the studio at the end of the garden. It's a beautiful sunlit midsummer day. The door stands open and the smell of honeysuckle and oil paint blend in the hot air. I tell my model, Marie-Claire, to get dressed as I won't be needing her anymore today. Time for a quick aperitif before I dash off my latest masterpiece.

Well, sometimes it is like that, apart that is from the smock, the beret, the honeysuckle and Marie-Claire. I do go to the studio and pick up my pen and the drawing miraculously appears in front of me – just as I imagine it, as if predestined.

Other times I have a vision and I rush to the drawing board and slam it down while it hovers on the back of my mind's eye. It doesn't work and I try again and again and again until, after ten efforts, it becomes just lines, hieroglyphics without meaning, like saying the word bicycle over and over again until it becomes senseless. I can no longer feel the image I had. It disappears and fades from my mind like a face one can't quite recall, it gets fainter and fainter until I am left with only the image that my continual drawings have left.

Nothing to do then but go away from the drawing board and rethink it and then try again. Eventually it arrives in some form or other but sometimes it's quite different to my original concept.

I love magic tricks, mirrors. I love setting up a reality and knocking down that reality to show the reality behind that reality, and then knocking down that reality to show the reality behind and then… I'm lost.

Drawing politicians over and over again is a tedious business and I'm always looking for a new way to depict them to relieve the boredom. Who are these fools anyway? Trying to run our lives.

I'm very fond of transmogrification, of turning Gorbachev into a hammer and sickle, Reagan into an ageing Mickey Mouse and Margaret Thatcher into an old boot.

There are many different ways of approaching a caricature. Sometimes it shows the essence of the person, the way they stand, walk, or it can depict them as a political symbol, or show them as some aspect of the policy of their government.

Therefore a character may appear a tyrant in one drawing, a weakling in another.

I do not sketch out my drawing in pencil first but bash straight in with pen and ink hoping to get every line in the right place first time. Unlike an oil painting, where each succeeding layer hides the last, there is very little room for error. The simplicity of shape, the volume of the figure, the likeness, if it is a caricature, *all* have to be achieved in the initial drawing. It's tricky.

Being an artist is a weird job. Nobody needs you. They think they ought to, but don't really know why.
Superfluous.

Opposite top left to right: Harold Wilson, Shirley Williams, Roy Jenkins, Jeremy Thorpe, Alec Home, Willie Whitelaw and Ted Heath.
Bottom Row: Lord Carrington, Enoch Powell, Reginald Maudling, Ted Heath and Denis Healey.

Opposite bottom: Ian Smith, 1976.

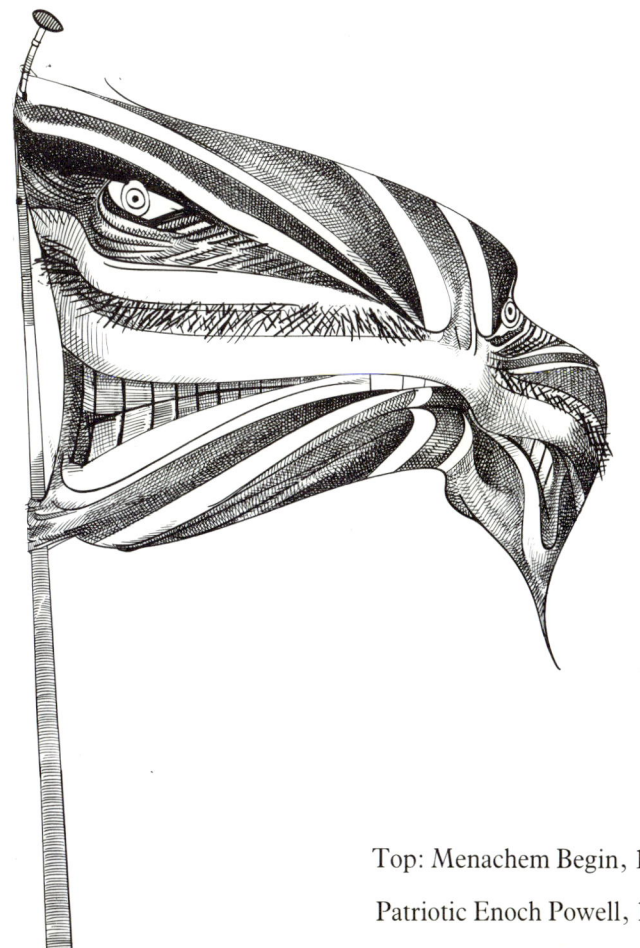

Top: Menachem Begin, 1979.

Patriotic Enoch Powell, 1974.

For my political work I watch television news and current affairs programmes, read articles and generally keep myself aware, so that I become a type of filtering plant for all these ideas in the hope that they will flow down my arm and onto the paper.

Cartoonists and journalists live off bad news. Being a cartoonist is a heart-rending business. I am continually crying out against a sea of troubles, and by opposing not ending them. You see in the cartoon above that most of the troubles of the 1970s are still with us. There always is war, famine, oppression and poverty.

Incidentally, people ask me, do I think my drawings change anything? Answer: "Not a jot." So, why do I bother? I don't know. I feel I must cry out – perhaps it can raise the public conscience, prick the public nerve. But the poor public nerve is numb with bombardments from all quarters. We sit with great heaped plates of food in front of us, watch television pictures of the dying and the starving and feel a momentary pang of guilt which moves on when the pictures change.

Opposite top left: Human Embryos 1985

Top: Nothing changes.

Opposite: Chernobyl 1986

Left: Optimistic Cartoon.

The Altar of Causes 1975

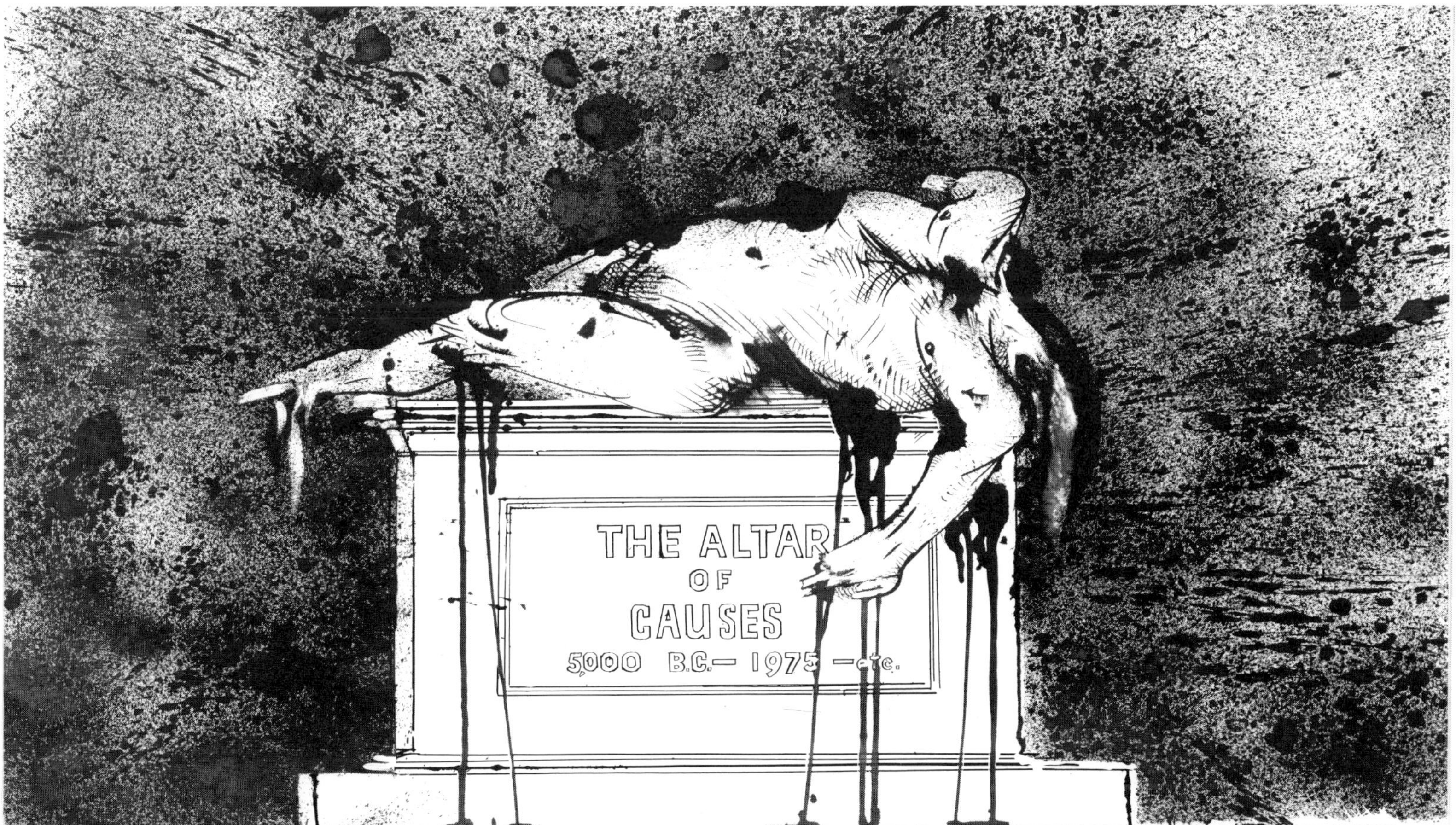

My drawings were so enormous that they became a joke in the process department. Some of them were up to five feet long. If a nose got longer I cellotaped a bit of paper on to accommodate it. They had special cameras to handle them. The only problem was that my line got very thin if reduced. Sometimes they had to be photographed out of focus to make the line thicker.

I was sketching Prince Philip as he moved amongst invited guests at the Royal Geographical Society, and as I glanced up from my sketchbook an equerry blocked my view. 'You have incurred the Royal displeasure,' he hissed.

Whatever the subject, I make my drawings without any sense of embarrassment. I draw my subjects without reservations, they become objects, graphic puzzles that have to be captured on the paper. I don't mean that I have no feelings for them, on the contrary, at the time of drawing my feelings are usually running high, but the effort to capture it all on paper doesn't leave room for any worry as to what people will think.

However –

After they are finished there are times when I would rather not meet any subjects. We were invited to dine at Kensington Palace with Princess Margaret.

It was an interesting evening but I felt a bit embarrassed as I had once drawn her as a warthog.

With a certain amount of application one can achieve a fairly high standard in drawing. They say genius is five per cent talent and ninety-five per cent hard work.

The crunch comes when you have achieved that high standard of drawing and don't know what to do with it. That is why so many artists abandon the academic representational drawings of their student days for apparently bewildering departures into the abstract. Having achieved basic drawing instruction they are searching for their particular contribution, something that will make them unique.

The rules of art are there to be broken, in fact I'm not sure there are any rules, only personal rules.

I find I respect an artist who can draw because one can feel it as a solid basis to his work.

That is why I appreciate the work of Picasso or Matisse. Whenever I need inspiration I turn to Michelangelo, da Vinci, Rembrandt, Goya, Daumier. But I think art is ultimately just a wonderful way of expressing yourself. If you're happy with it, it's successful. Many Sunday painters get more joy from their work than Matisse or Lautrec ever did.

Above: Lord Home. 'The Arms Salesman', 1970.
Top right: 'Pollution', 1970.
Opposite: Nuclear Power, 1986.

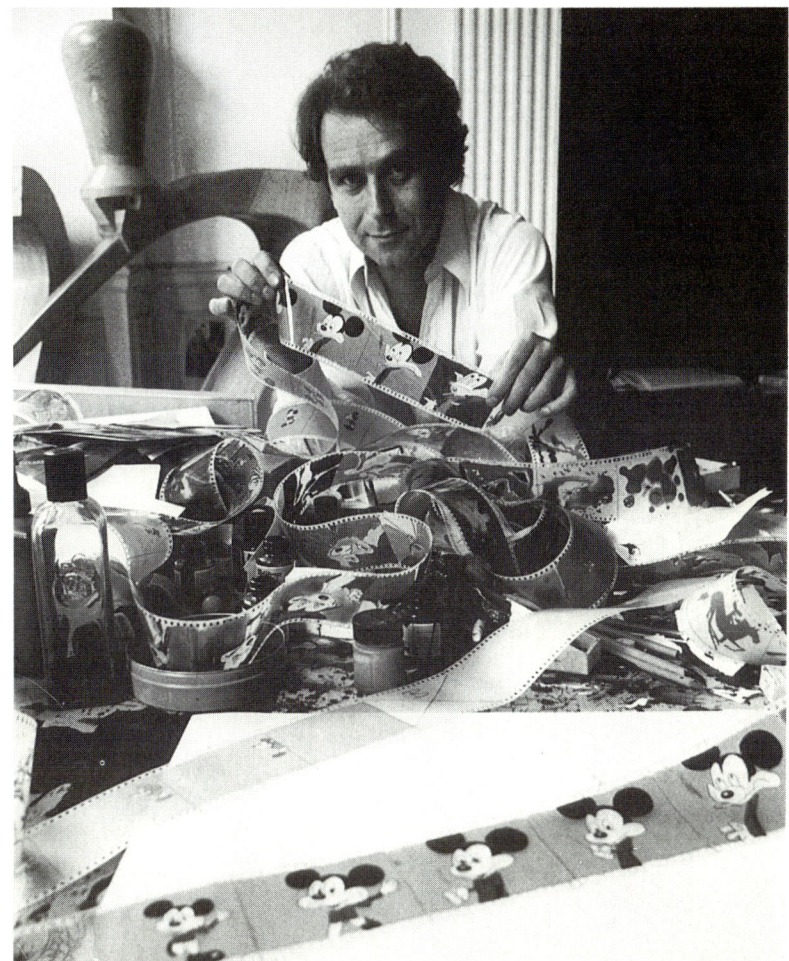

T he Movable Feast Lady is here," says the tannoy. I have just finished turning Donald Duck into a hot dog so I am feeling peckish. The Movable Feast Lady sells avocado and prawn sandwiches, chocolate brownies and coffee and, after having completed over two hundred drawings today, I am ready for some. I am in an air-conditioned office in down-town Burbank, making my first animated film and doing the thousands of drawings myself.

The BBC has asked me to go to Los Angeles to experiment with an animation system.

My drawings become a stream of consciousness. A character given birth on celluloid takes on a life of its own. He amazes me with what he does. I cannot draw fast enough to see what happens next. Some days and nights I draw three or four hundred drawings, hour after hour, before my wife, Jane, and I drive home to Beverly Hills in the early hours of the morning.

During the day Jane and two other ladies paint all the drawings with brightly coloured inks.

I draw everything American I can think of – John Wayne, Indians, Coca Cola, Mickey Mouse on drugs, Frank Sinatra, Black Power, Freeways, Playboy girls, billboards, astronauts and the Empire State Building, etc. Broken only by the 'Movable Feast' lady and the occasional dip in my brother-in-law's swimming pool.

I am supposed to be there ten days but stay for six weeks: hence the title "A Long Drawn-out Trip".

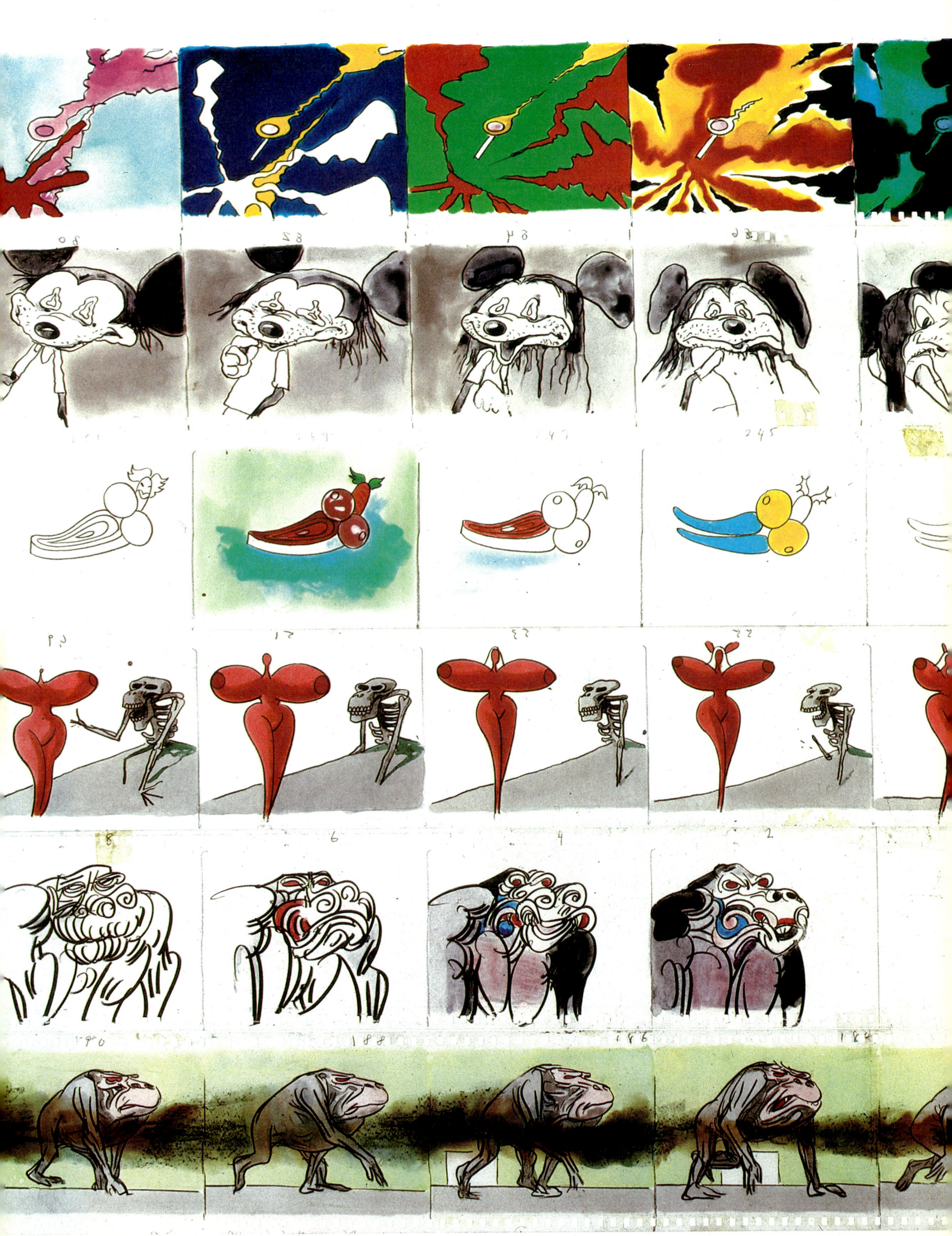

Rhinoceroses can fly, boiled eggs can sing and the Maharaja of Jaipur can transform himself into a potted shrimp. Animation is magic.

To make a static drawing move and come to life is an artist's dream. Yet it has been so unexplored as an art form. Disney, marvellous though he is, had such a strong and far-reaching effect on the industry.

I couldn't help wondering what Picasso or Matisse would have done with this art form. There is no reason why it should all be cute little ducks and big bad wolves. I suppose to a certain extent the middle European school of animators have tried to use their craft to make some comment but there is only so much you can take of butterflies symbolising freedom. The Pink Floyd had enthused over my 'Long Drawn-out Trip' and had asked me in 1971 to make some animated films for their concerts. But it wasn't until 1974 that I agreed. It seemed like a lot of work and I feared it might stop the flow of my other work. It did. Directing animation is a full-time job.

I set up a studio of about forty animators in the Fulham Road. I tried to train them to think my way but some were too caught up in the Disney system to change. So many animators are trained in the 'squash and bounce' school, a phrase derived from the exaggerated way in which the animated characters walk, rising up and sinking down on every footstep. But I was lucky and found a handful who worked hard, two in particular, Mike Stuart and Jill Brooks, produced some of the best animated work I have ever seen for 'The Wall'.

Walls scream and flowers turn to barbed wire. The dove of peace explodes and from its entrails a terrible eagle is born. This menacing creature tears great clods from the countryside with its gigantic talons, destroying whole cities. Swooping low it gives birth to the War Lord, a gargantuan figure who turns to metal and sends forth bombers from its armpits. The bombers turn to crosses as the frightened ones run to their shelters. The ghosts of soldiers fall and rise again continuously and on a hill of bodies a Union Jack turns to a bloody cross. Blood runs down the cross and through the corpses and pointlessly trickles down the drain. Cathedrals are crushed and reform as glittering gods and gigantic hammers march smashing all in their paths.

Although I wrote the script and did the original designs on which the film was based, unlike 'Long Drawn-out Trip', where I did every drawing, on 'Wish you were Here' and 'The Wall' the animators did most of the final drawings. There were hundreds of thousands.

At first I thought, how wonderful, I just think up all the ideas and make the original drawings then my animators do all the donkey work. Then, although I was writing the script, designing the characters and directing every stage of the film, I felt that frustration that all directors or executives must feel, of not being able to do it all yourself – in fact of not being able to do any of it yourself. It becomes an administrative job organising, checking, thinking of ways around disasters, cutting corners and worrying about why the new chinagraph pencils haven't arrived and why there is no paper in the lavatory.

To give the illusion of smooth movement there are twelve drawings per second. So many drawings and each one could take a day or more to do. It is a long, long business.

Shout 'Action' at 11 o'clock on Wednesday and 'Cut' three months later. Animation goes its own laborious way, however you try to hurry it. After I've written the script and designed the characters I make a storyboard of their actions. I next make individual drawings of the characters in various attitudes. These drawings are then passed to the key animators with a description of the actions they should take. They make the main drawings – if the character were getting up from a chair they make one of him sitting, one half way up and one of him standing. These drawings are filmed to see if they look convincing. If so they are passed to an assistant animator who fills in the gaps. Then they are filmed again. If passable (unlikely), the drawings are cleaned up and given to tracers who laboriously trace the drawings on to cellophane. They may then be filmed again. Next painters paint the colours in on the reverse side of the cellophane, one colour at a time. The drawings are all spread out on racks to dry.

Meanwhile other artists are drawing the backgrounds. Finally it is all cleaned and checked, and then, when dope sheets telling the cameraman what to do in detail are completed, it is filmed.

At a showing of the rushes you could find that the cameraman has left out one drawing and it all has to be filmed again. Sometimes they refilm many times. Back-breaking, heart-breaking – but, if it works, it is magic. If it doesn't it's just expensive.

The flowers grow up, make love, fight and the female devours the male (I know, I know!).

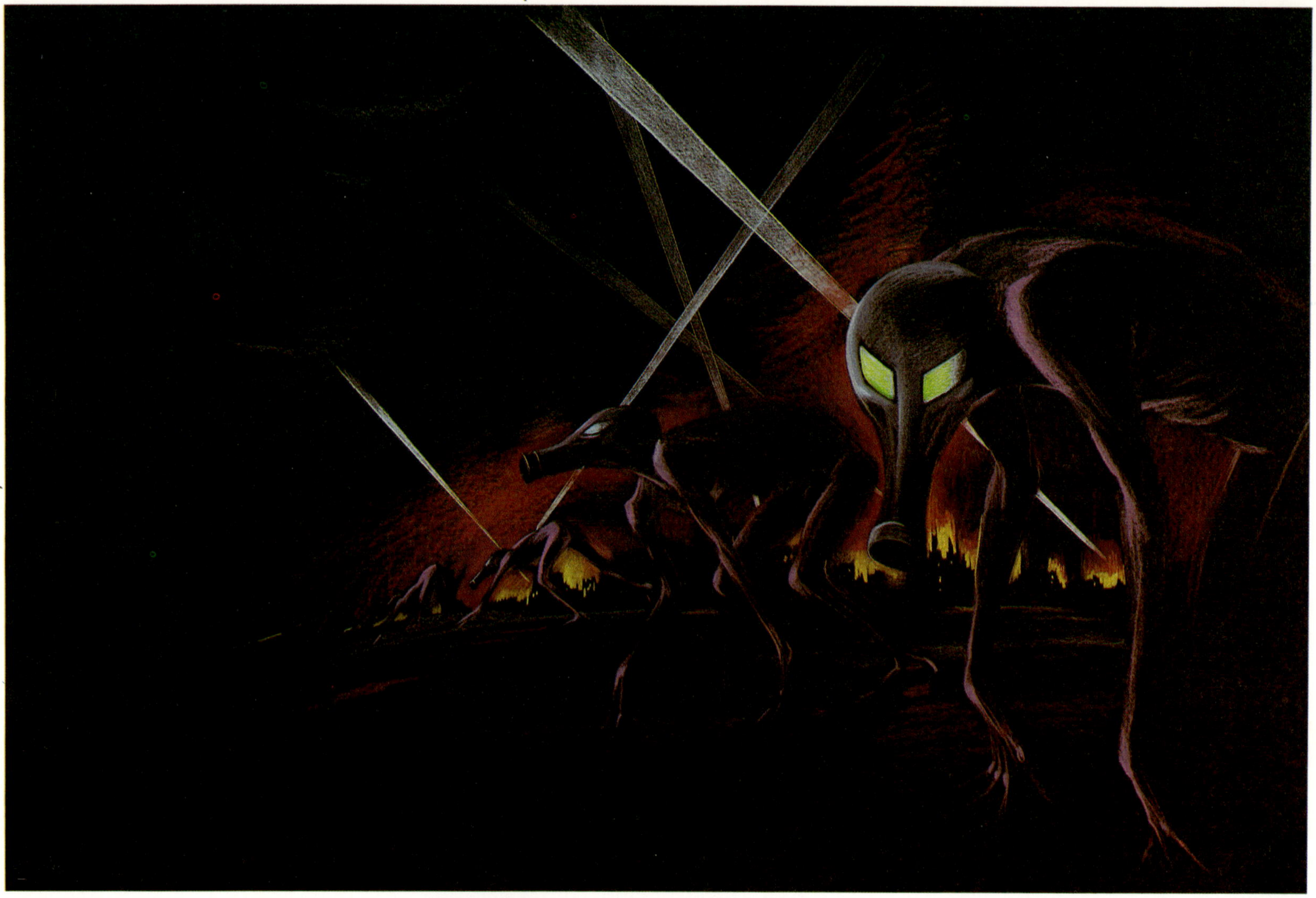

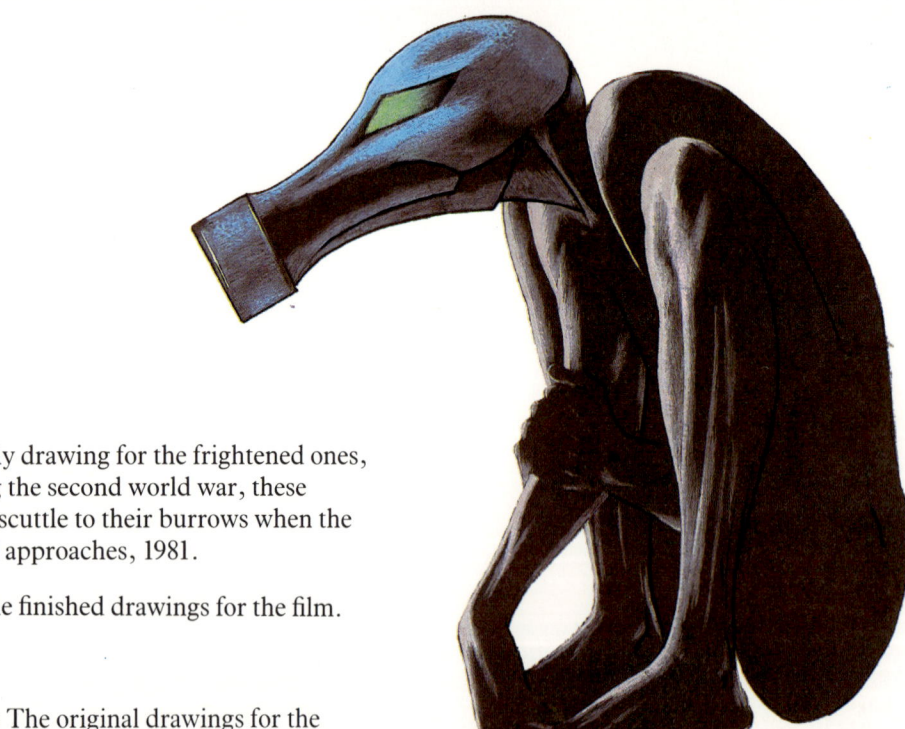

Above: My drawing for the frightened ones, set during the second world war, these creatures scuttle to their burrows when the War Lord approaches, 1981.

Right: The finished drawings for the film.

Opposite: The original drawings for the crashed eagle of war. 1981

Overleaf: The original drawings for 'The Hammers' and 'The War Lord' and how they appeared in the film, 1981.

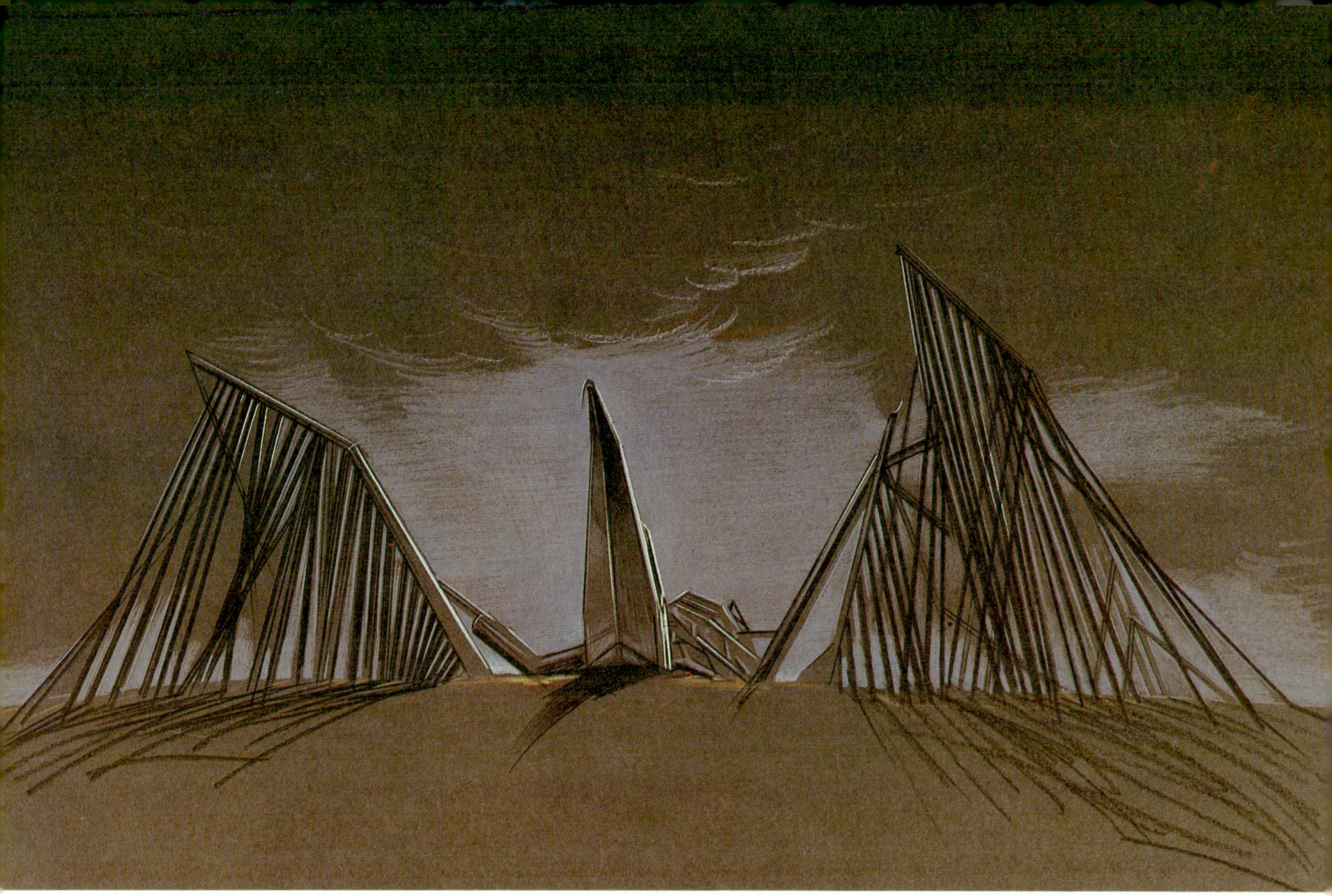

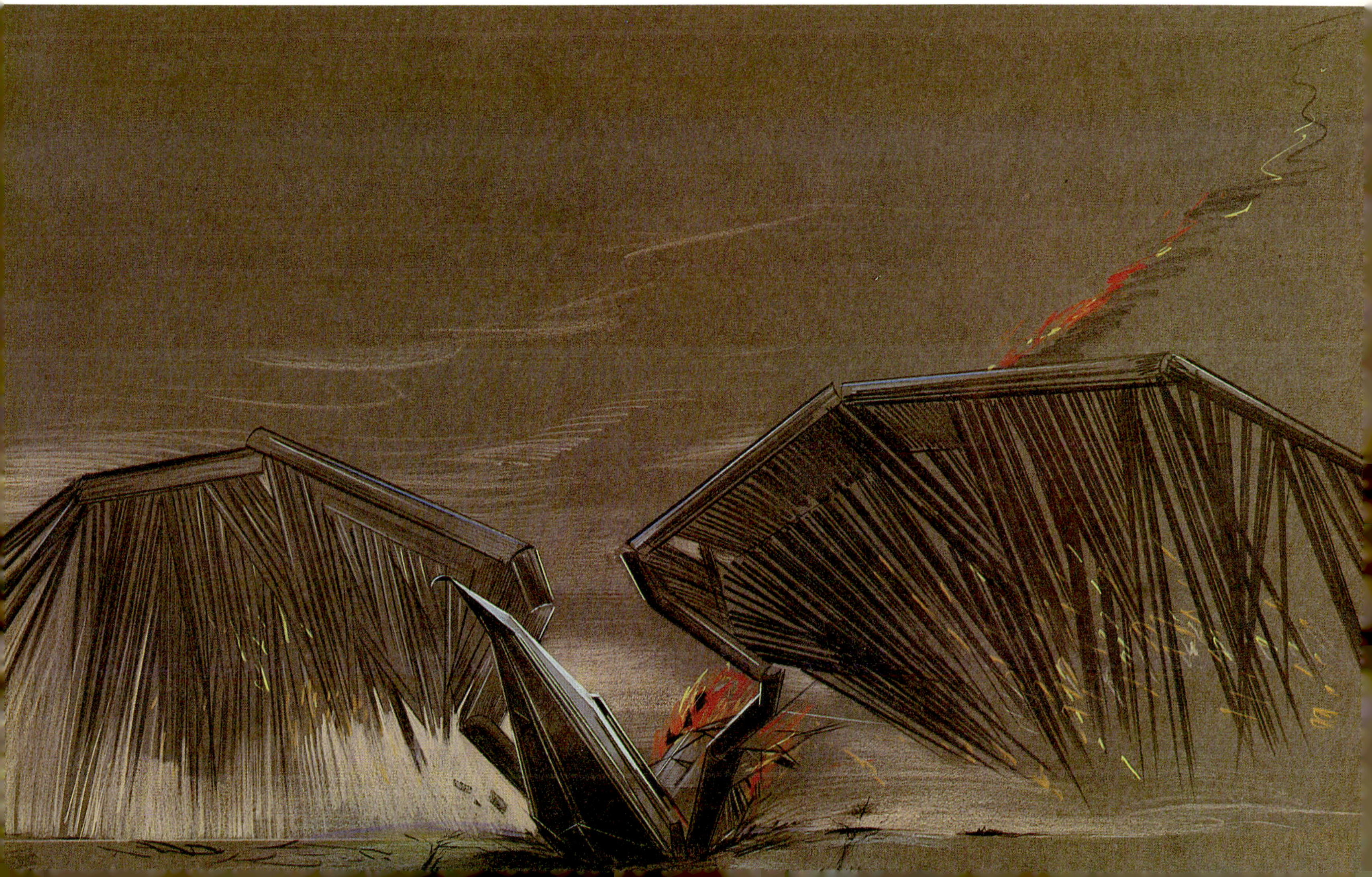

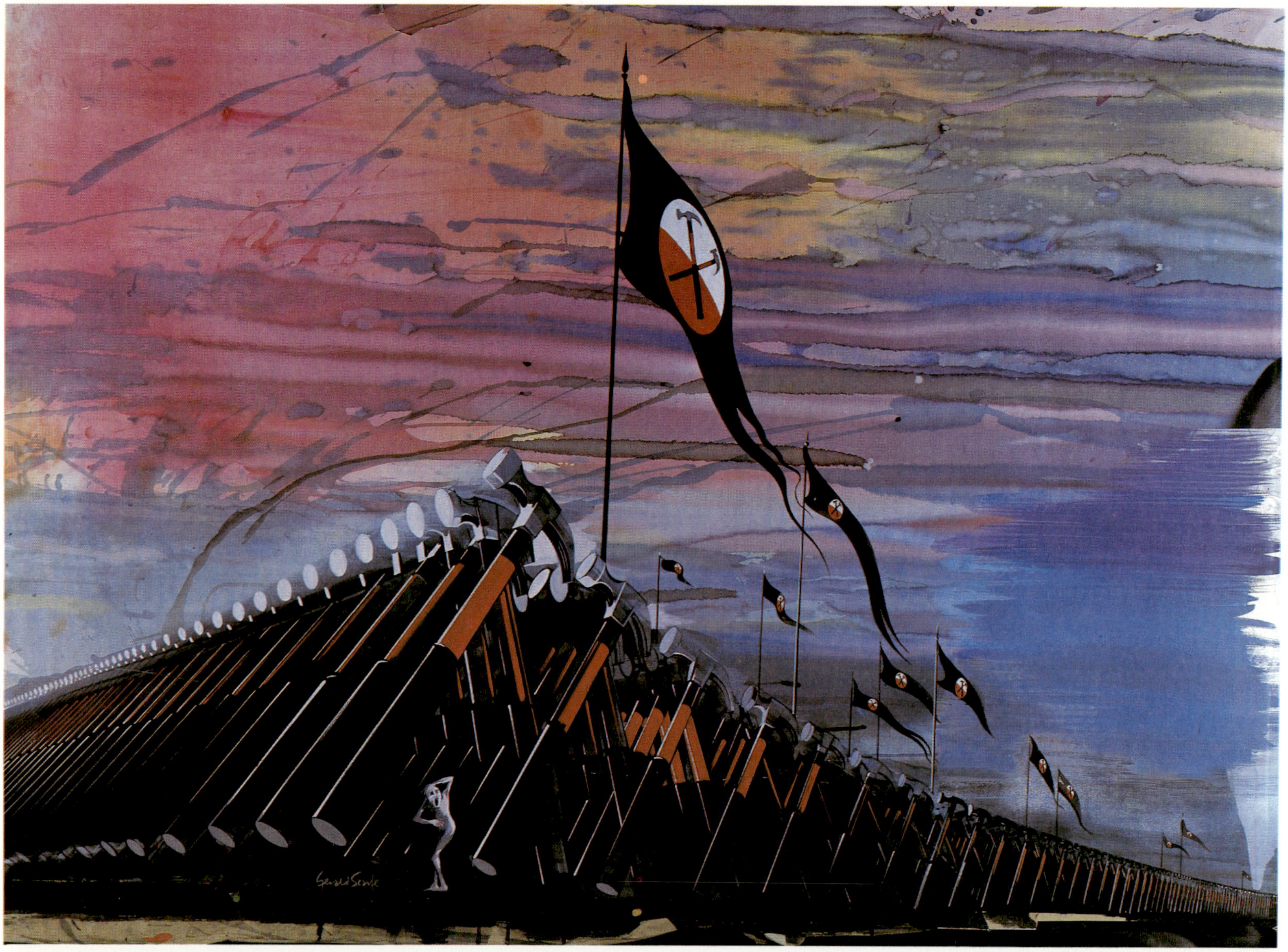

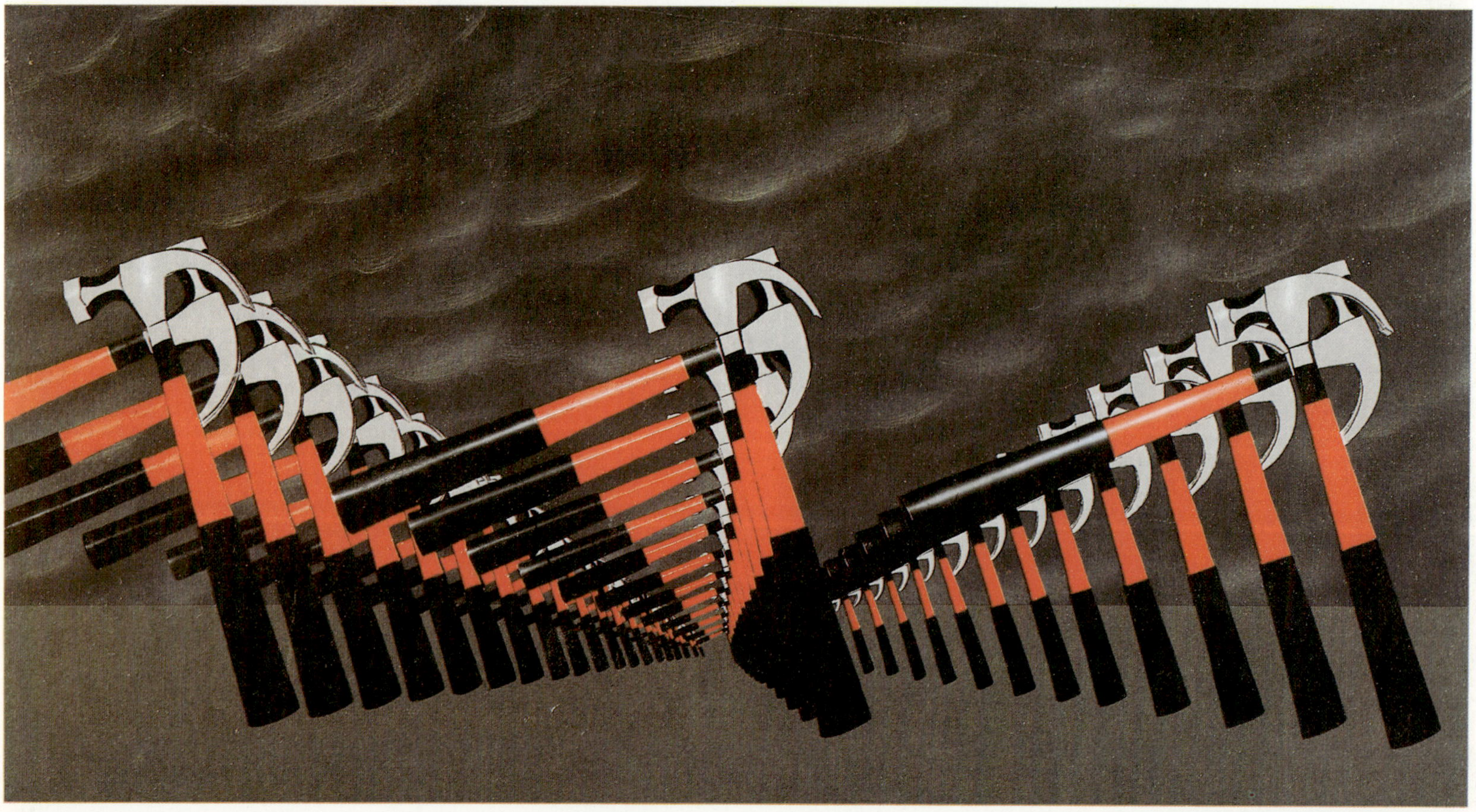

Animators are special beings with a slow tick-over rate. They go their own speed, bent over their desks for eight hours a day, listening to Radio Four or Capital Radio, through earphones in a world of their own.

Animation is very like the party game Chinese Whispers, where everyone sits in a circle and the first person whispers a sentence to the second and the second repeats it to the third, and so on. By the time it comes full circle the sentence bears no resemblance to the original.

I found it's much the same way in animation, by the time I received the finished film it bore very little resemblance to my original ideas. However, as with all art forms, accidents that happen during the creative process and lead one in a different direction can sometimes have results that are better than you could hope for.

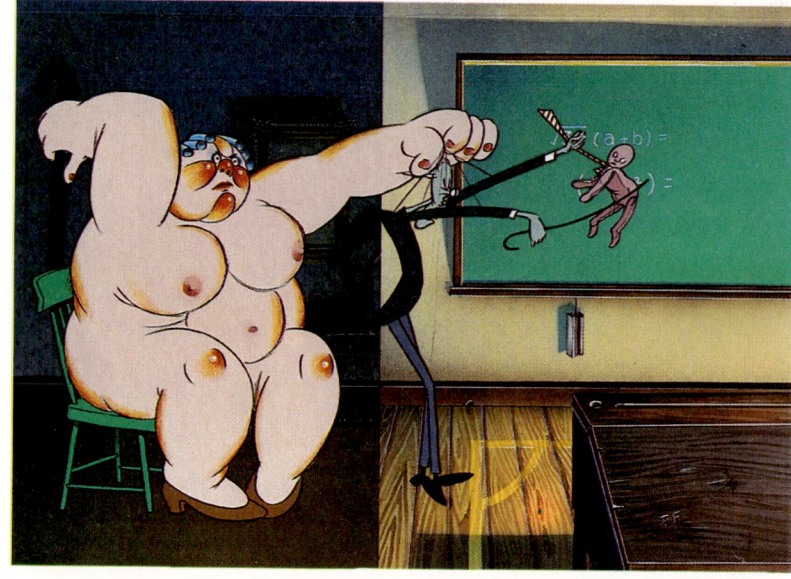

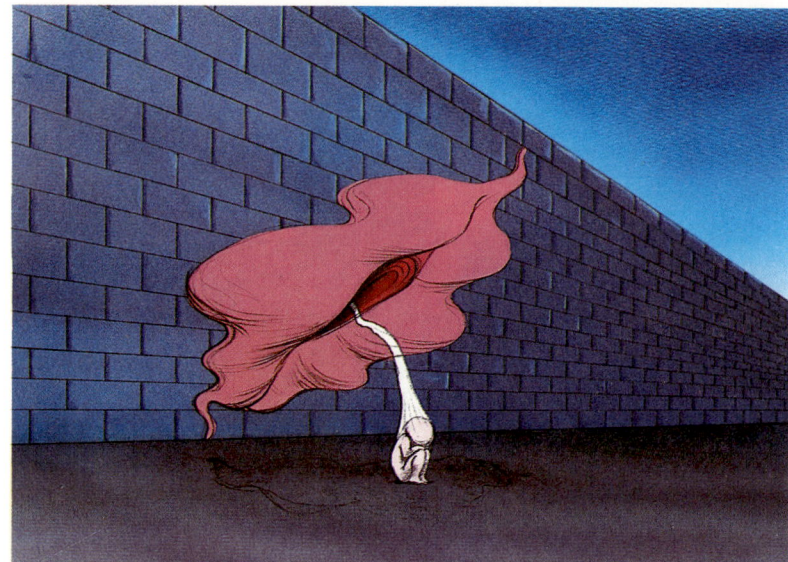

Stills from 'The Wall', drawn by animators from my designs.

The helicopter takes off from beside the Hudson River, wheels right and flies dangerously under the bridge. "I do that once in a while," says the pilot, "to liven things up." We bump our way over the silver and grey evening map of New York to Nassau Coliseum. The band and I jump out – duck under the rotor blades and into the black limos.

The big blue silhouette of the Arena stands out against the yellow and orange sky and we drive up the ramp and into the mouth of the monster building. The huge steel shutter slides down behind us. We are backstage at the Coliseum, a vast dry dusty cavern of concrete pillars, giant travelling boxes, a mass of electronic equipment, cables, wires, ropes, a giant circular cinema screen, guitars, keyboards and empty beercans.

Roadies with I.D. badges step back as their bread and butter whispers by. Steel barriers and heavy heavies guard the band's area. We get out in an area of pretend civilisation, a large astroturfed square, sided by four trailer caravans, café chairs and café parasols over the café tables – very tasteful – very nice. To amuse the band there are pinball machines. Each caravan is loaded with drink and food. Here the band rests.

Outside, thousands press against the turnstiles, patiently filing to the seats. Excitement mounts. Stalls sell T-shirts, programmes, souvenirs, badges, sweatshirts, posters, postcards, buttons, hamburgers, frankfurters, soft drinks, beer, sandwiches – anything. The area fills and the noise increases.

The show starts. There is nothing like the roar of a crowd, ten thousand strong, giving its appreciation in these vast arenas. It's the most exhilarating sound. It's no wonder that Rock stars go slightly mad with self-importance.

As the band plays, a huge alienating wall is built across the front of the stage spanning the whole arena, cutting the audience from the band. My giant puppets stalk the stage like great ghosts and three of my animated films are projected onto the huge wall simultaneously and synchronised with the live band. It all works like a dream. It's a success.

It always amazes me to see the end result of what started as a few scribbles on a piece of paper. Roger and I had sat for hours planning and designing the show in detail, and here it was, a giant Roman Circus.

After the show the band came back onto their safe green astroturf looking tense but relieved. The sidewalk café tables are peopled now with grinning hangers-on.

Going home – the long black limo.

We drive back to New York, the bottles of drink clinking gently as we speed over the concrete slabs. The Rock star, a hunched figure in a racoon coat, sits in the middle of the black leather seat clutching a beer can.

Although we are doing sixty miles an hour a lunatic bearded figure stares in at the window. "Hey, Roger! Will you sign my album?" He leans further out of his driving seat causing his car to bounce and sway. It feels like disaster to me. Our driver knows what to do. He accelerates – so does the lunatic. We are joined now by another bounding lunatic on the other side of the limo. The three cars speed down the motorway neck and neck. Oh, I've had enough of Rock and Roll.

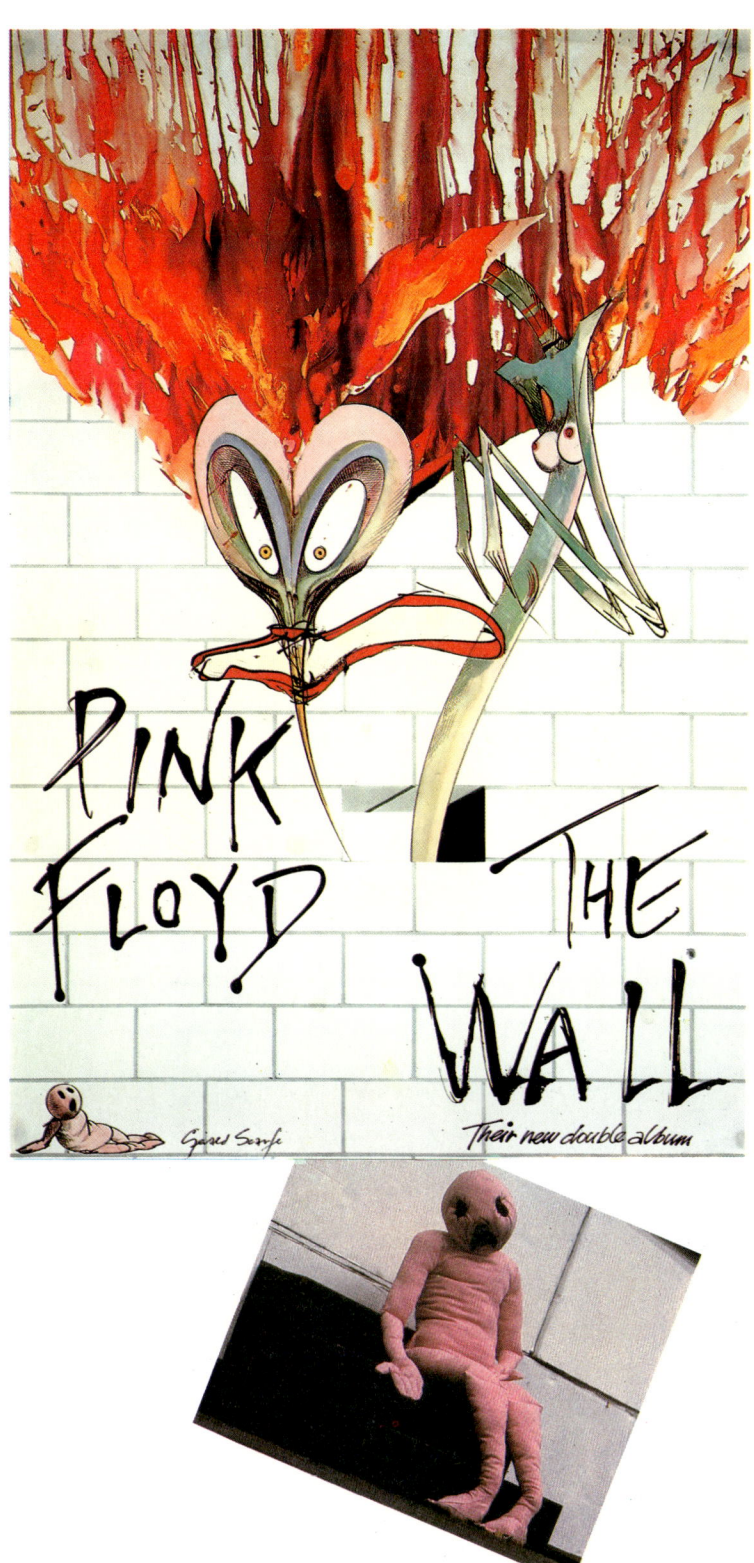

P.S. Small last night party somewhere in New York. Goes on too long. Must catch my plane. What time is it? My God, seven o'clock in the morning. Straight to the airport. Fly to London. Only took an hour. Surprising. Oh, I feel awful. I must go home and do my SUNDAY TIMES cartoon.

When I look at it on Sunday morning I have no memory of doing it or, worse, of what it's about. Yes, I've had enough of Rock and Roll.

Right: During an exhibition I held at Earls Court ten drawings were stolen. I have never recovered them. 'The Wall' was such a complex show it was only able to play limited concerts. It travelled to Dortmund, Los Angeles, New York and London.

Below: This gigantic inflatable of 'Mother' had fans built into its balloon-like body. They slowly filled the creature with air so that it grew and towered 30 feet above the audience.

Above: 'The Teacher' who worked on the same principle and had a wonderful effect in the concert as he loped across the stage. Here it was being filmed on location. Compare the telegraph pole for size.

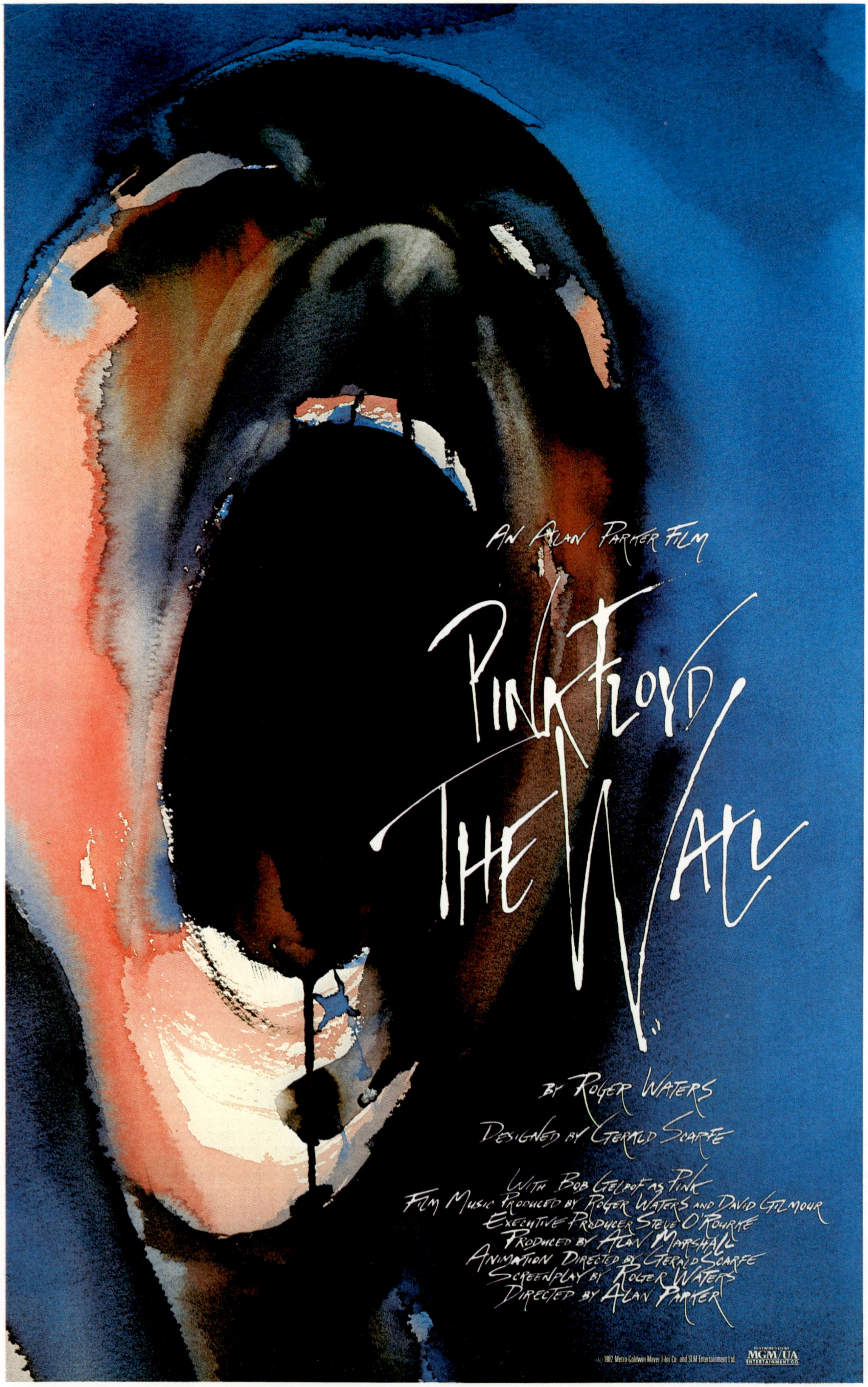
An Alan Parker Film
Pink Floyd
The Wall
by Roger Waters
Designed by Gerald Scarfe
With Bob Geldof as Pink
Film Music Produced by Roger Waters and David Gilmour
Executive Producer Steve O'Rourke
Produced by Alan Marshall
Animation Directed by Gerald Scarfe
Screenplay by Roger Waters
Directed by Alan Parker
© 1982 Metro-Goldwyn-Mayer Film Co. and SLM Entertainment Ltd.
Distributed by
MGM/UA
Entertainment Co.

There I was, beautiful sunny morning, driving down to Pinewood, bottle of Jack Daniels sliding about on the floor under the back seat. I was designer and director of animation on the MGM film PINK FLOYD THE WALL. I'd always wanted to make a real movie and work on that huge screen and reach all those people. My wish had come true, and I was miserable. After the show of 'The Wall', Roger Waters and I had shut ourselves away in Cheyne Walk for weeks, writing and drawing scenes until we had the semblance of a script and storyboard. From that script and storyboard to Hollywood was a long hard emotional haul. I had imagined a collaboration between three people with different art forms would be fruitful – it was not fruitful, it was hell. What else do you expect when you put three megalomaniacs in a room together? they said.

The film world seems to me to be peopled by near criminals who will practically kill to get their puerile tripe onto the screen. The rewards are so large and their greed is so great.

This is my sketch for Bob Geldof's transformation in the back of a limousine into a Führer-like monster. The inset shows the prototype for Bob's costume and how faithfully the props department tried to follow my sketch.

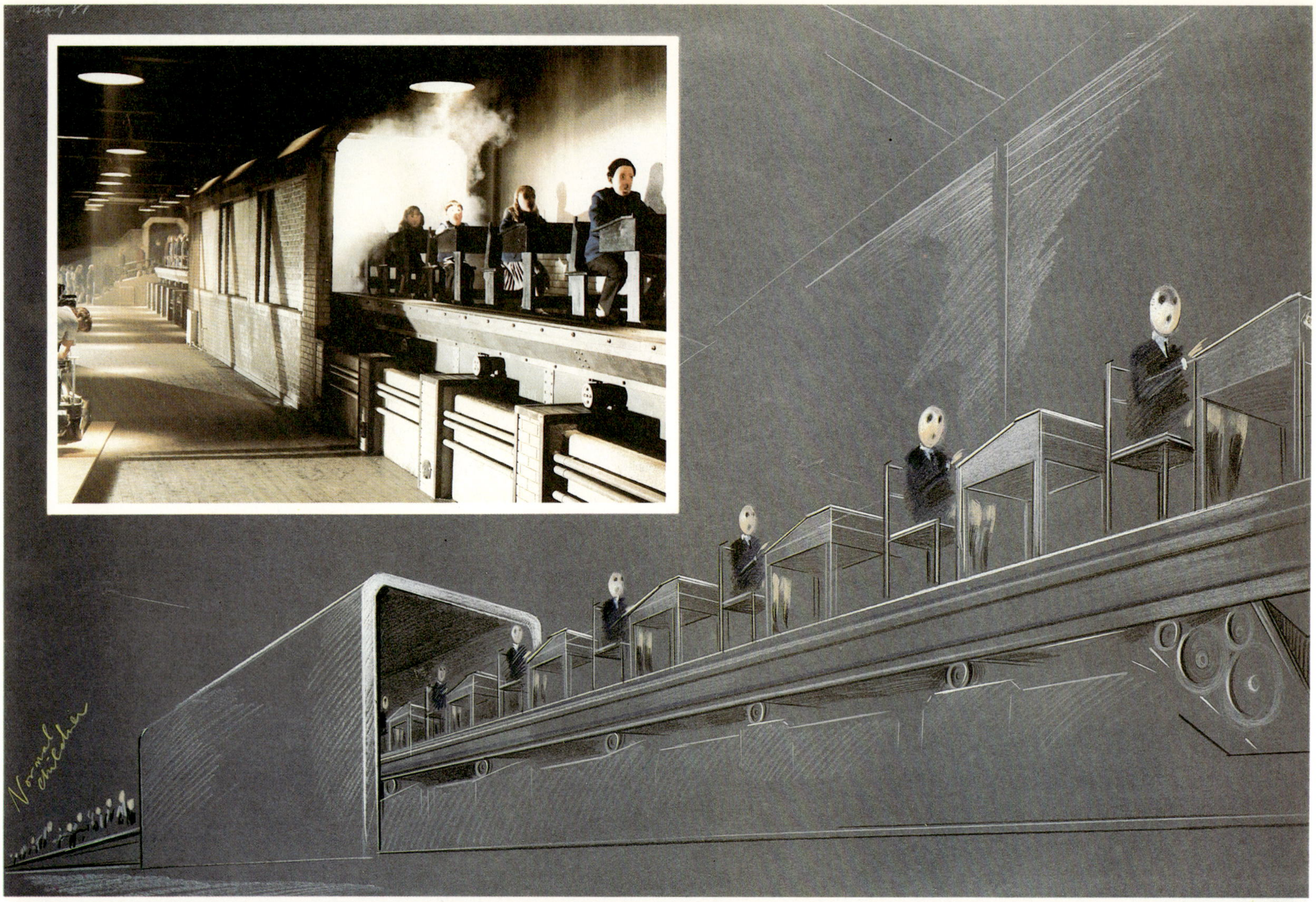
Normal children

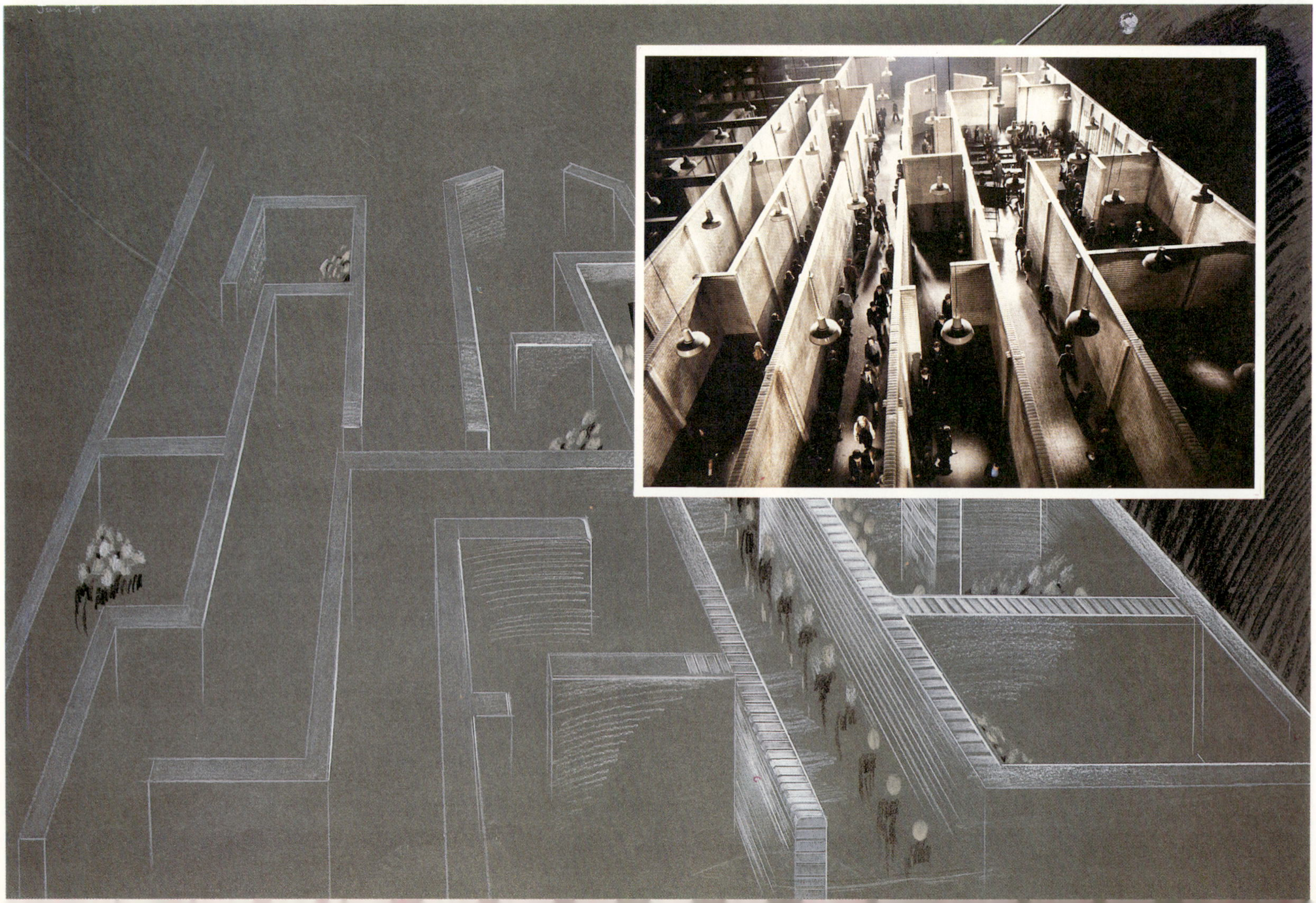

Sunshine glints on the silver bucket cooling my Champagne in my suite at the Carlton, overlooking the sunny Mediterranean. A gentle breeze blows through the open window causing the curtains to billow. Down for the Cannes Film Festival. This is more like it. This is the film world I recognise. I knew it was there somewhere.

London Première, crowds, lights and applause. Concorde to New York. Which wine should I choose? Champagne in my suite off Park Avenue. Interviews, interviews, interviews. Big black limo two blocks long to the New York Première. Can't bear to see the film again so we play pool somewhere in Manhattan.

Then to Hollywood. West Coast Première. Bob Geldof and I are promoting the film. More Champagne in my Beverly Wilshire suite. White limo three blocks long to the Première.

Sir Bob and I tell each other our life stories as we fly to Toronto. More interviews. My God it's boring. Can't wait to get home.

In my designs for the live action 'education' sequence in 'The Wall', I was once again able to express my feelings about this subject, but this time build sets and fill them with actors. Opposite, above: 'The Conveyor Belt' – children are processed and stereotyped. Opposite, below: 'The Maze'. This sketch became a set costing £100,000, see inset photograph. Above: 'The Mincer' – the final part of the system through which children are pushed into society.

Overleaf: Four designs for the live action sequences.

Two roadies ogle a groupie.

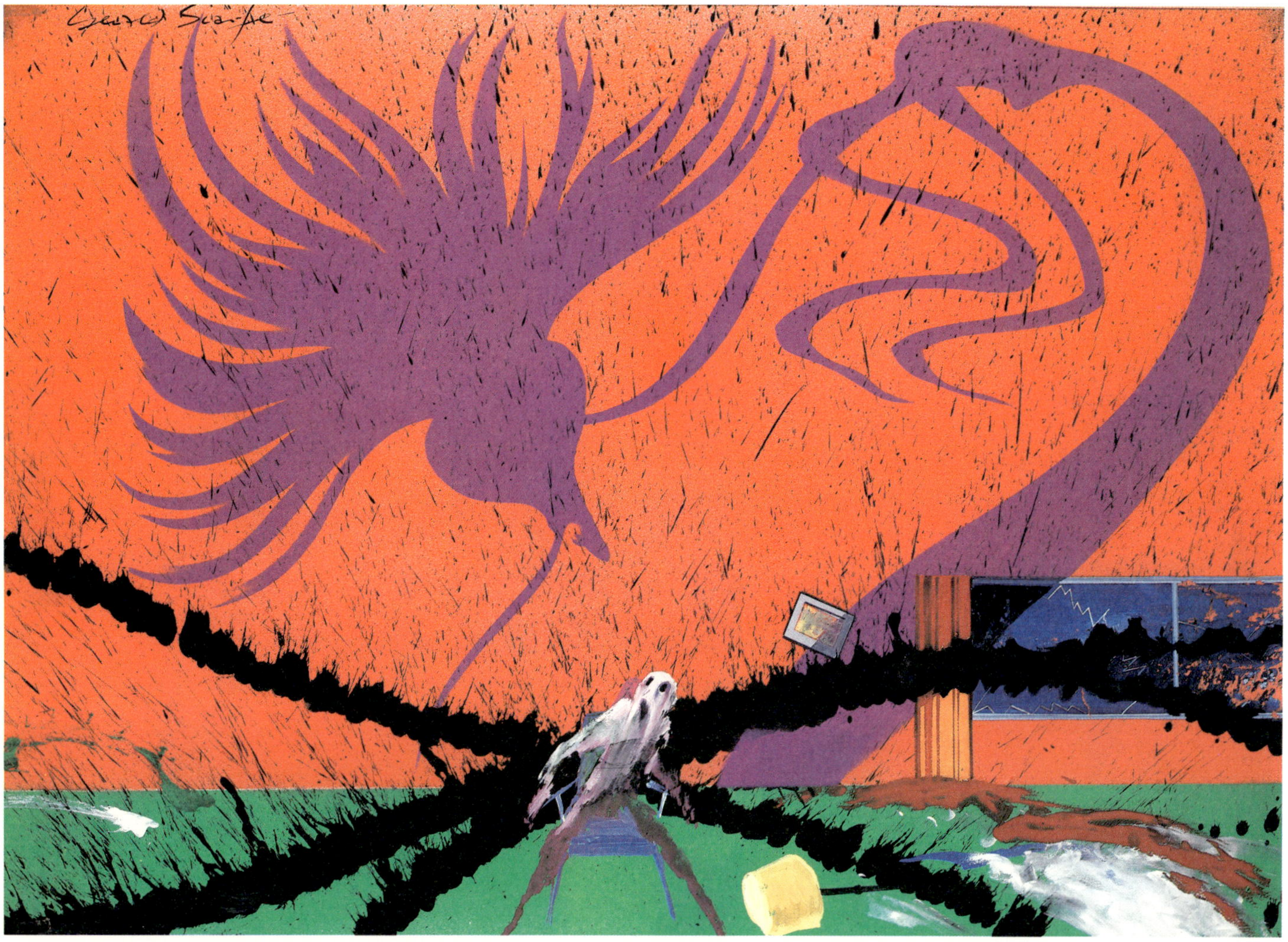

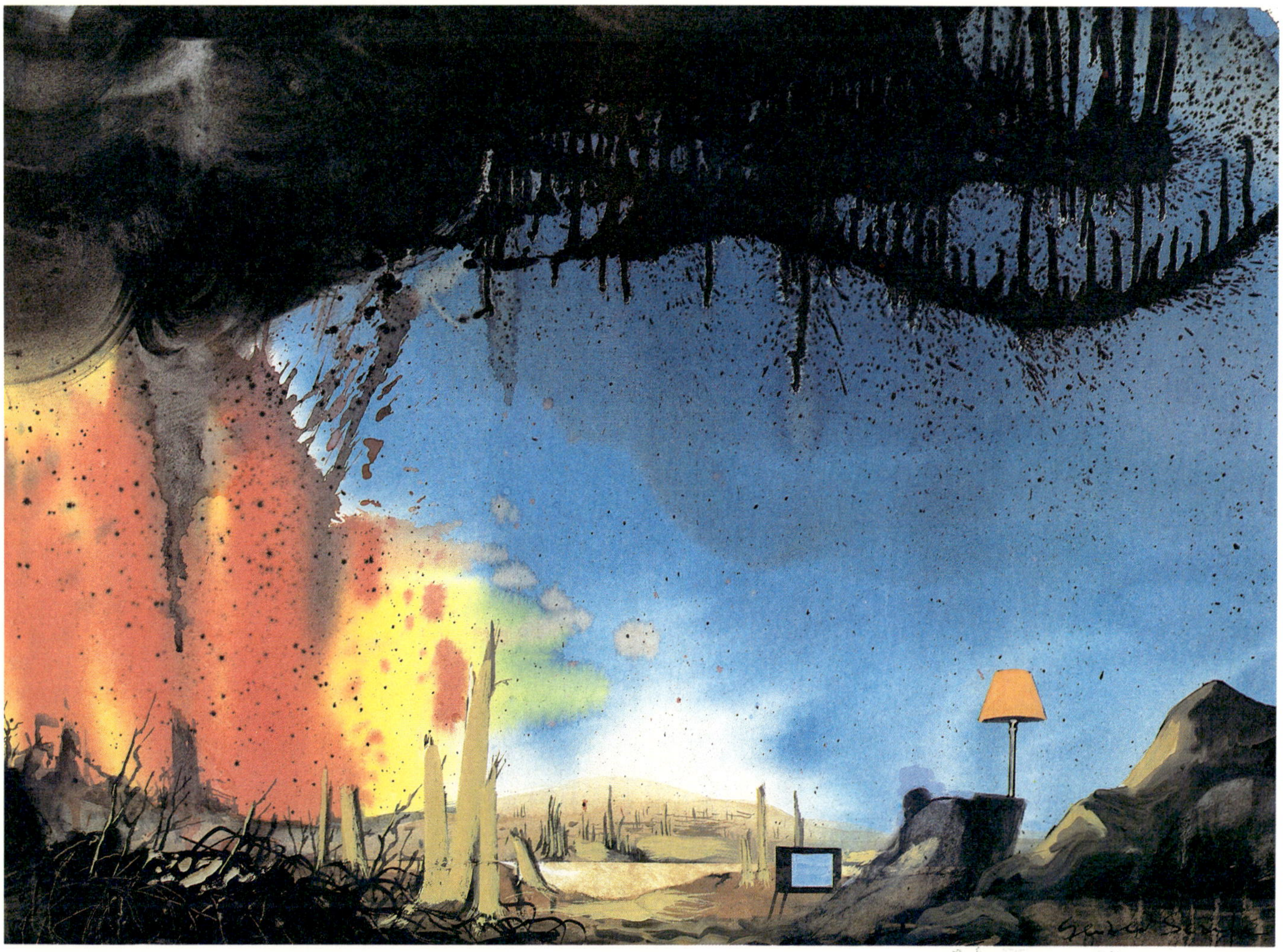

Playing cards designed for the Victoria and Albert museum, London.
Featuring: Francis Pym, Margaret Thatcher, William Whitelaw and Geoffrey Howe.

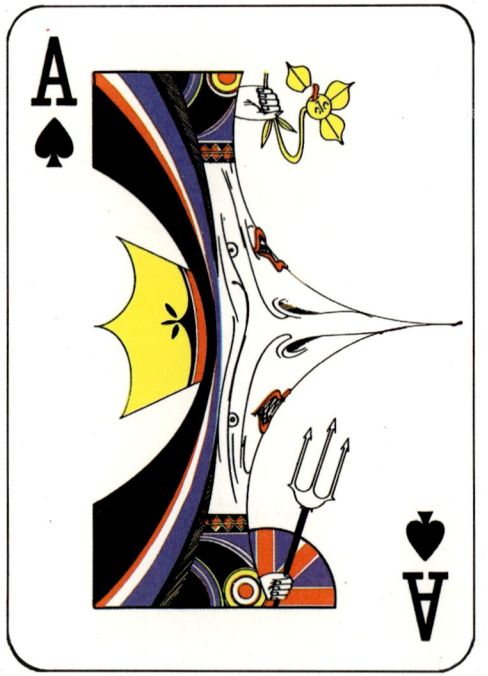

I haven't had a lot of encouragement from the art establishment. I feel as though I have had to make my way up through the back roads parallel to the main motorway.

I told David Hockney that I would love to have an exhibition.

"Why don't you contact Alan Bowness at the Tate," he said. So I rang the Tate and spoke to the director Alan Bowness. I asked him if there was a small gallery where I could hold an exhibit.

"Well," he told me, "I must tell you frankly, I don't like your work." This seemed to me a bit of a setback, but he said he would send his deputy David Brown to look at it.

David Brown duly arrived, consumed a great deal of brandy and left, and that was that. I never heard from them again.

However, my exhibition at the Festival Hall was seen by 140,000 and was so successful that they immediately re-ran it for three more weeks. Wherever it travelled it broke attendance records. So I don't feel too bad.

EXHIBITION
24 April-14 May

Monday-Saturday 10 am-10.30 pm   Sunday noon-10 pm   Admission free

GLC
Working for London

Opposite: Margaret Thatcher – statue for a very public place.   Above: Ronald Reagan as Mickey Mouse, 1983.

Michael Foot, the Labour Party, 1983.

My poster for Bradford, which showed Mrs. Thatcher in bed surrounded by screaming ghosts pointing accusing, skeletal fingers, was banned. Bradford's Conservative council was in office by a very small majority, and there was an election coming up. "Yes, I banned your poster," said the gallery director proudly. "Might be a bit embarrassing. Ha Ha! Have another sherry." I was quite happy, as they had substituted a gun-toting, ageing Mickey Mouse Reagan for the poster.

Rather like a parent visiting his grown-up children, I followed my exhibition around the country, from Cleveland in the North to the Isle of Wight in the South, being fêted by mayors and councillors.

designed this backdrop for a show for Peace called 'The Big One' at the Dominion, London.

I took the drawing to John Cavanagh, a scene-painter in Hammersmith. He was tremendously proud of the work he had done for Bridget Riley and insisted on showing me the original prints she had given him. They were framed beautifully and cushioned by soft tissue paper. He handled them with loving care and discussed how fine they were. Obviously a man who appreciated works of art. I handed him my drawing and left.

When I want back several days later he had torn it in half. "Easier for two of us to paint it," he said.

'In the Beginning, Part II'.

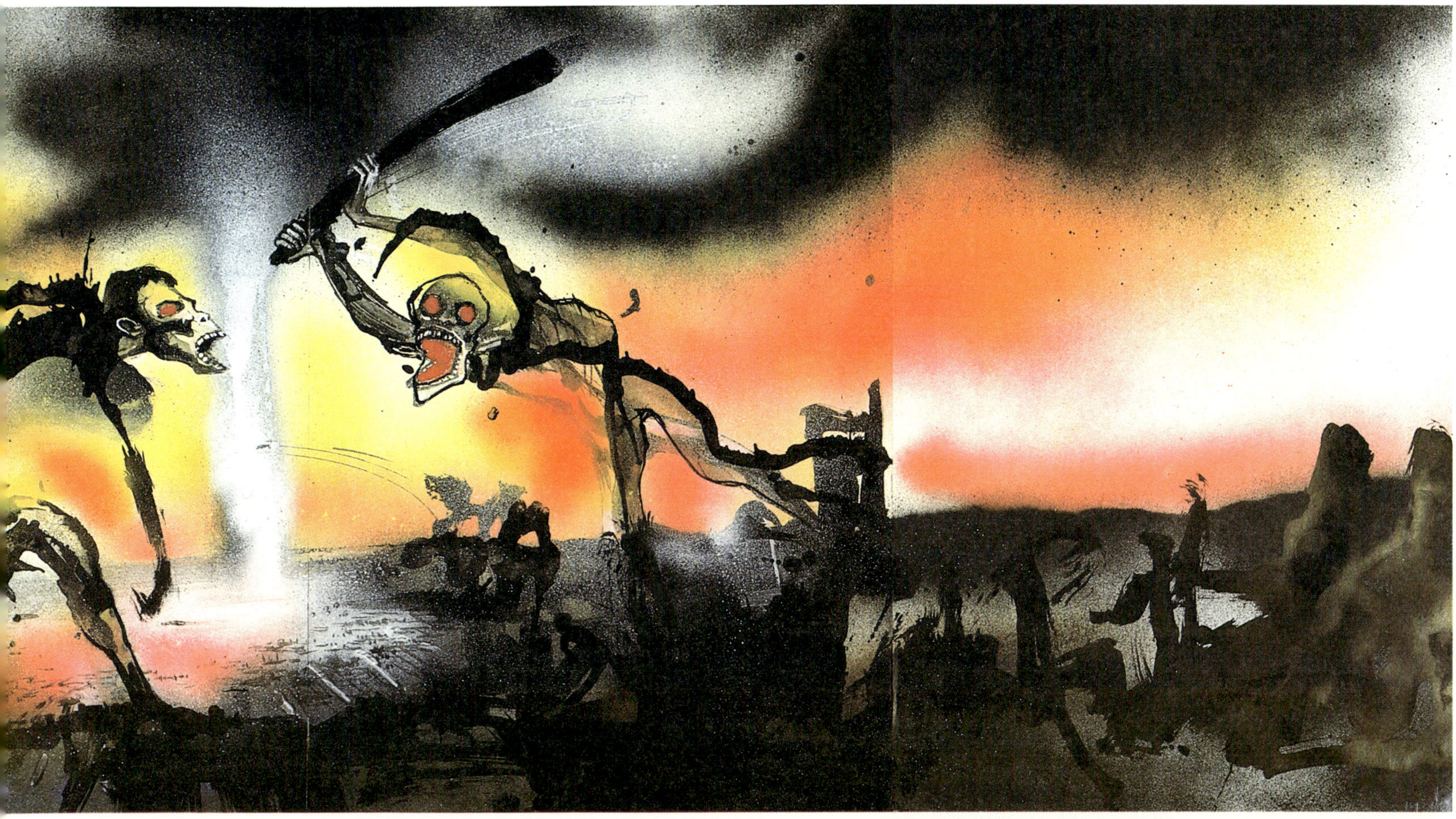

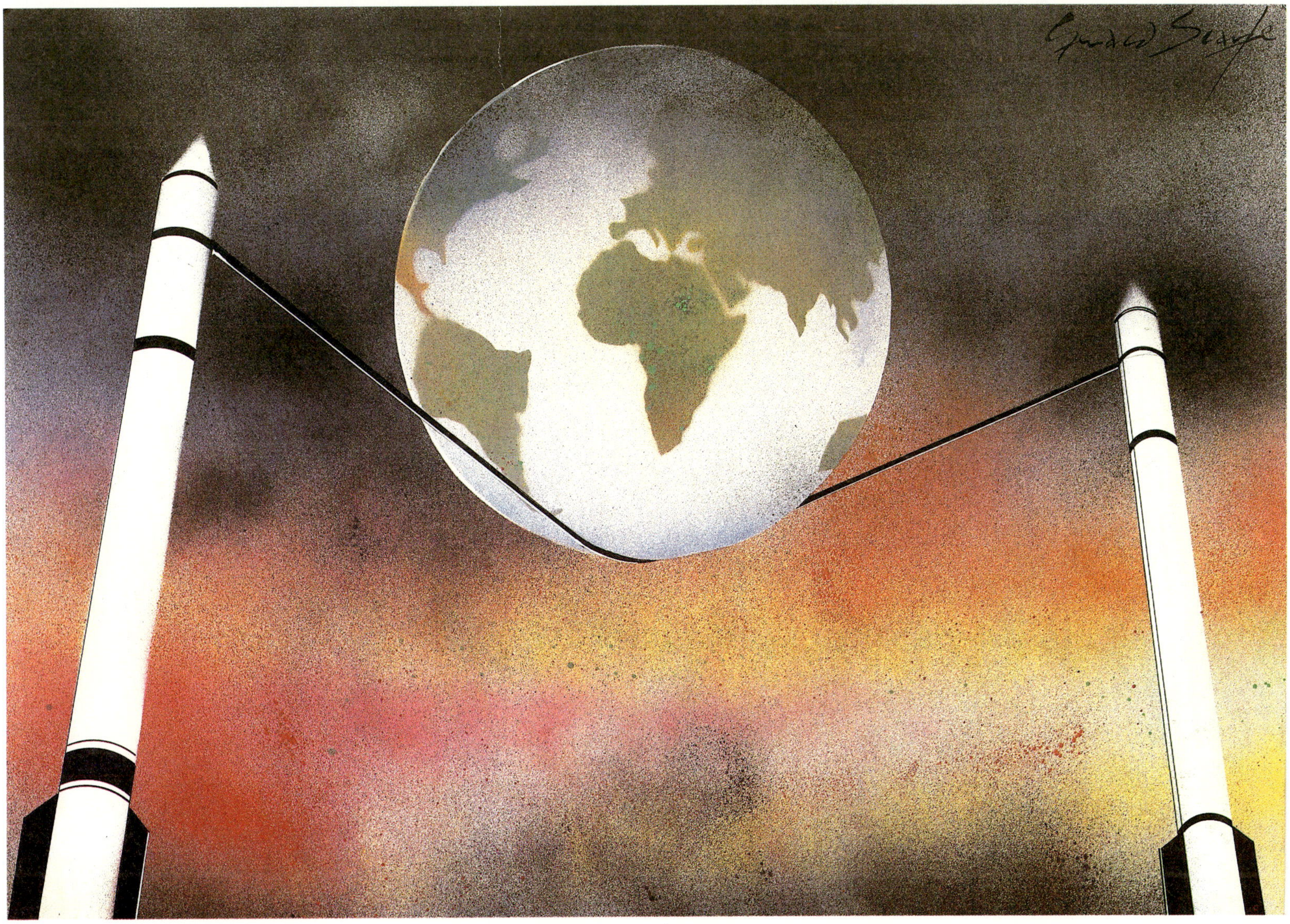

 ripes, it's the wife!" said Reg. Reg was an animated dog that I designed for 'The Pros and Cons of Hitchhiking'.

I quite liked Reg. He was a lazy wastrel and frightened of his wife. "Come down here at once and do something useful" she yelled at him while he was floating high on drugs. I made caricatures of all the band. They didn't go down too well. When I walked into the bandroom backstage in Stockholm there was an unfriendly silence. Eric glared at me. He didn't think it looked like him. Time I was going, I said. I felt like Reg.

The show toured Europe and America.

Alan Price and I and Braham Murray, the Director of the Royal Exchange Theatre in Manchester, wrote a musical based on Hogarth's 'Rake's Progress'. Alan wrote the music and lyrics, I did the designs and costumes, Braham directed.

I would travel up to Manchester several mornings a week in the Pullman to see how the building of the costumes and designs was progressing. I liked the Pullman because I could pass the time eating a very large English breakfast.

A proscenium-arch theatre demands designs that work within a box. No one has to see the back or the side of them. Designing for theatre in the round means the audience must be able to see what is going on from every angle. Scenery or furniture must be recognizable from the back or the side, and must not obscure the audience's view.

Everyone is very generous in the theatre world. They want to make a success of everything. The prop department made my flat designs three-dimensional realities. The costume department worked non-stop to interpret my sometimes very brief scribbles made on envelopes.

Because I could not use much scenery I covered the floor with my version of Hogarth's Rake.

I loved the whole exercise but in a way I was glad when it was over – those breakfasts were killing me.

Opposite: The unemployed go down the drain, and the newspaper editor, 1985.

PLATE 8

'The Lady Mayoress' design and costume, 1985.

Below: costume designs – Lord Helpass, depressed housewife and punk.

Top right: the floor of the Royal Exchange. Above: Chief Barker, punk,
Barbara Cartland, housewife and Serccio Formani, 1985.

The Coliseum commissioned a thirty-foot-high flat cut-out caricature of Lord Harewood for his surprise Farewell Concert – could I please make it in his favourite shooting outfit. Certainly, I said – but what did it look like?

The next day a motorbike messenger arrived with Lord Harewood's trousers in a plastic bag – they had been stolen from his wardrobe by Lady Harewood and should be returned as soon as possible before he noticed.

In 1973 my name was put forward as designer for the Glyndebourne production of 'The Rake's Progress' by Stravinsky, but John Cox, the Director, thought my work lacked humanity, so David Hockney got the job and I had to wait ten years before another chance came up.

So I was delighted when David Pountney of the English National Opera wrote and asked if I would like to design the sets and costumes for an opera, 'Orpheus in the Underworld'. I jumped at it.

We began meeting with the writer Snoo Wilson in Cheyne Walk and it soon emerged that this was to be a very jokey production. We decided to have a great number of cloths or backdrops very much in the Victorian tradition and I started work on my paintings. I felt that first and foremost it should be fun. Not too many of my messages about life, just entertainment.

First the sets. 'Orpheus' is set on Earth, in Heaven and in Hell. Great scope for invention. But more difficult than it seems. What does Heaven look like? Does it have golden clouds with people playing harps? No, David wanted it to be a lunatic asylum and I tried several sets in this direction but somehow they looked dull and predictable. Lunatic asylums had been used before. I wanted something more unusual, funnier.

Offenbach's written direction says, "The Gods are asleep," so I set about designing individual beds for the Gods. Mars had one that was made of fierce weaponry. But where did these beds go? They still looked insignificant. I jacked them up on long legs. I suspended them from the ceiling. But nothing pleased me.

Suddenly it came to me. Why not have all the Gods in one bed, which was at once like clouds and like eiderdown. I could put the whole chorus of forty people in one bed and that would fill the stage – just one huge bed in the middle – no need to worry about any environment, just give it a sky background.

Next problem: how to make the bed. It could be a huge inflatable one, but with quick scene changes how would they get it off the stage in time for the next scene? It had to be light and movable. The chorus could carry it off. How would they get it through the wings. It would have to be in segments. Why not make it a series of flat segments, painted pieces of portable scenery which would give the illusion of a bed, and put the bedhead on the backdrop. That was it!

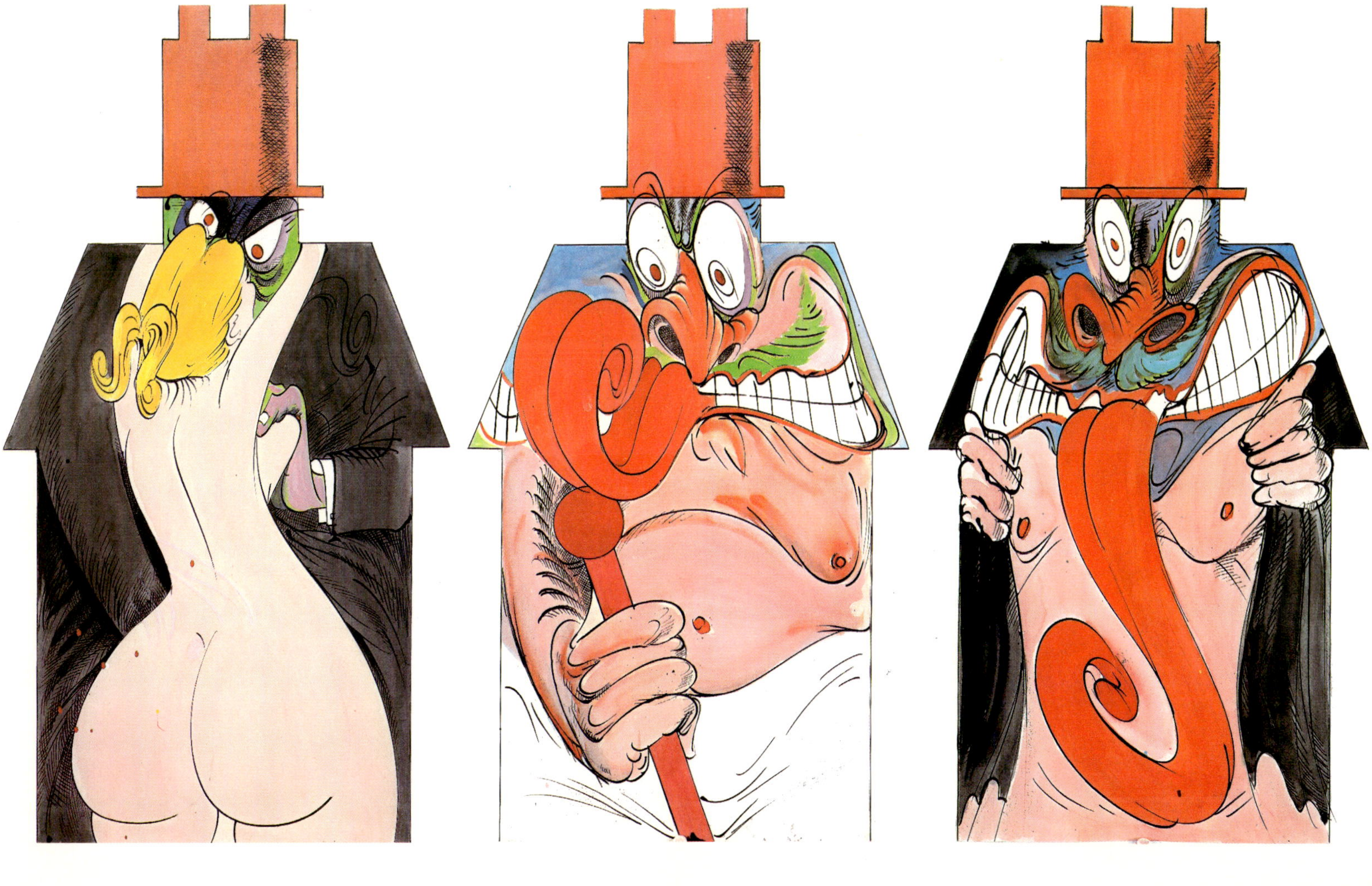

The next scene was to be the Gods rising, showering and washing. So it quickly followed that the bed should turn into a bath. I thought it would be wonderful if it transformed before our very eyes. I designed the bed so that the flat scenery flapped down and turned into a bath in five seconds flat. A bathroom with tiles and taps was let down, the chorus stripped off their nightgowns to appear naked but for towels in the bath, and a large sponge walked on followed by soap.

Those were just two scenes from this very complex show and the amount of designing work on it was enormous: the costumes alone took months of work.

Public opinion was a large figure of a woman on wheels with four singers hidden in her huge bustle.

John Styx was a fetishist in red leather corset, high heeled boots and fishnet stockings with a whip. Jupiter inflated into a spectacular fly and flew. Garden hedges were composed of people. Mercury brought the house down tap dancing in spangled running shorts and vest.

Councillors were like fat balloons, Venus was a cross between de Milo and de Mille, lambs danced, little girls in frilly knickers played violins, the Hounds of Hell sang, Mars was an apparition eight feet tall. Jupiter was psychoanalysed on a couch that looked like a naked black lady. I had girls dressed as tarts (jam and blackcurrant), girls dressed as sausage and mash, eggs and bacon, tomato sandwiches, bananas, pineapples and so on. I was involved for well over a year.

In the end it became a kind of Scarfeland and I was accused of upstaging the rest of the show.

Opposite: 'The Bathroom' set design and as it appeared on the stage of the London Coliseum, 1985.

Top of the cloud flaps down to reveal water.

Could their night shirts fly off?

Large Rubber Duck passed along 'rows!
Toothbrush?
Staggered figures. 5 rows of 8

Standing.
Sitting on shooting stick!
Sitting.
Kneeling up.
Kneeling down
All wearing towels
+ Bath caps!

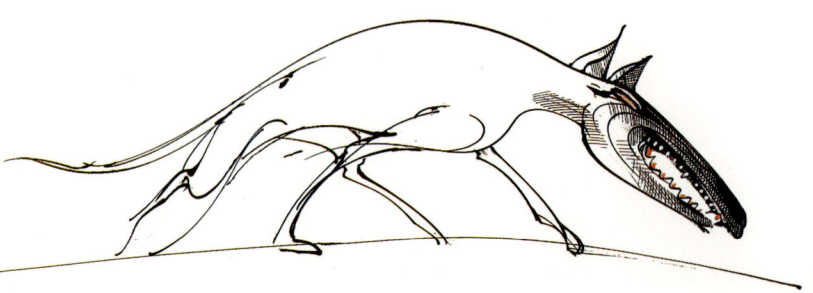

The handwritten notes on the backcloth read:

PSYCHOANALYSIS

ACT II

Metamorphosis Rondo.

PSYCHIATRIC BESTIARY

Sepia?

ALL IN WHITE COATS.
Other members don relevant masks)

CASE NO 147

JUNE 15 CRETE

Swan. Bull. Frog. Penguin. Skunk
Cock. Elephant. Snake. Zebra Chameleon
Rhino Toad Lion Giraffe
Crab Fish.

Couch.

Projector and Screen showing Jupiter perplexed
Screen as big as possible

'The Metamorphosis' backcloth. Act II. Jupiter is psychoanalysed on a couch because of his unfortunate habit of assuming animal disguises to achieve his conquests.

I enjoyed rehearsals with my props arriving daily from the workshop; my costumes being fitted in various rooms as and when we could steal the singers from rehearsals.

The first day I was introduced to the chorus they were kneeling uncomfortably, supposedly naked, in the large communal bath that I had designed. "Sorry," I said.

No one had told poor Jupiter that he was to wear elephant's trousers. In the fitting he looked bemused and worried. I explained that because of Jupiter's habit of changing into animals in order to make love to ladies (Leda and the Swan, Europa and the Bull, etc.) I had given him a dressing-up trunk full of animals' feet, tails, horns, to wear.

"Oh, I see," he smiled wanly. "It's just that I didn't understand."

Screen unfolds showing exploits.

"Don't work with children, animals and Gerald Scarfe," said the TELEGRAPH.

It played to capacity houses and brought a new audience to the Coliseum.

When the backcloths were being painted by over fifteen painters I spent weeks driving from Hammersmith to Wapping from the Elephant and Castle to West Hampstead and Watford via the Theatre Royal Drury Lane and the Old Vic, stopping only for the occasional bacon sandwich.

Rita was one of my favourite artists – she enlarged my paintings on to backcloths thirty feet by fifty in size by drawing a grid over my design and transferring what was in a one-inch square on my drawing onto a two-foot square on the back cloth.

She loved to discuss the characters in the Applause cloth. They all had names and when she went to bed at night she thought about them all.

As the first night of 'Orpheus' drew nearer I began to worry whether Rita would finish in time – so one morning I called in to see how she was getting on.

Cats of Hell.

I was met by a distressed Rita.

"Your master drawing has gone!"

"Gone where?"

"Blown away," she said. "I put it on the balcony and when I came back from lunch it had gone!"

"On the balcony?" I said. "Why?"

"Well, the light was so bad in here, I put it on this chair on the balcony to see the colour better and after lunch it had gone. The wind is so strong on these high-rise balconies I think it blew away."

I was devastated, time was short. The idea of starting the drawing all over again and matching it to the last one exhausted me. However, I went home and started.

The next day I called on Rita. "I've found it!" she said.

"How?" I said.

"Oh, a workman brought it in, he found it in a builder's skip."

"Thank goodness – what did he say?"

"Oh, he said he thought it was very good."

ACT I   THE SEND OFF FOR ORPHEUS
+ P.O.

Violin for vehicle

Flying coffin

Wheels?   Completely Black & White   Scene Flying coffin
wings beat.

LIFT OFF

Flat Sandwich board   Man Horses Head Plumes etc.

Top: 'The Maze' backcloth for Act II. The Gods search for Eurydice.
Above: 'The Send Off' backcloth. Orpheus starts his journey to heaven.
Opposite: the idea and costume design for the seven judges of Hades.

The Seven Judges
of Hades

arrive in seven
coffins on a true
coffins are closed
moments then open
to reveal painted
bandaged skeleton
forms — Bottom
of coffins le

'Orpheus' goes to Detroit in September 1986 and to Houston, Texas in November 1986. It then returns home to the Coliseum London for a further season, Easter 1987 (and then goes to Los Angeles).

I hear they have extended the intervals in Houston to allow the rich patrons to show off and admire one another's jewellery between acts.

BLOW OUT IN HADES

LE GRAND OPERA
BOUFFE

When the designs for Orpheus were completed they were roughly copied onto pieces of board, cut out and displayed as scenery on a stage about two feet wide in a model theatre like those I had as a child. As it was a co-production with Houston, the director had a model box showing. Everything went swimmingly. He didn't mind the naked Victorians in sexual clinches. He didn't mind Pluto making his entrance through a giant hellish backside. He didn't mind John Styx in a red leather corset, fishnet stockings and carrying a whip.

The last scene was six fat Victorian gourmets eating. They were composed of food themselves.

He exploded. "That's grotesque," he said. I thought it was a bit late to use the word.
"Oh, no, it's disgusting, we wouldn't tolerate that in Houston."

I did a new design. Six fat Victorians eating, not composed of food. It was painted and set upon the Coliseum stage. The night before we opened I felt I strongly wanted them to be composed of food. Jane said I should follow my instinct and, with my painters, we set about altering the fat Victorians. We gave them poached egg eyes, strawberry noses and carrot lips. We painted until about five o'clock in the morning. It was a bit rough and ready but at least I felt I had done what I wanted.

No one seemed to notice.

I was frequently painting, touching up some detail on stage shortly before the curtain went up. I thought I might get caught on stage with a paint pot and have to sing an aria.

My feelings when the overture began on the first night of 'Orpheus' were unbearable. A year's work waiting to be judged. The lights went down and my tension increased. The curtain rose to reveal the first scene. A stunned silence from the audience and then applause. Lovely, lovely applause.

These well-known characters were for a fifty-five-foot back-drop to the 'Merry Wives of Windsor' which was produced at the Guthrie Theatre, Minneapolis, USA, in July 1986.

From left to right: The Queen, The Duke of Edinburgh, Prince Charles, Andy and Fergie, Duke and Duchess of York, The Queen Mother and Princess Margaret.

*I*n 1964 I had lunch with a Welsh whizzkid publisher and the conversation turned to money. "How much do you make, then?" he said. "Three thousand a year – if you're lucky?"

It was more like one thousand a year but I nodded. "Yes, but at least I'm doing something that might last," I said, being young. "Come off it, boyo!" he said. "Do you think Hieronymus Bosch gets an erection every time someone looks at one of his paintings?"

I took his point.

Here I am, at the end of the book, in 1986. I find myself back on the pavement again, in Covent Garden, drawing in front of a crowd, as I always like it, for 'Bread not Bombs'... Spare a copper...

One Man Exhibitions

'Gerald Scarfe', Horse Shoe Wharf Club, London, 1966
'Gerald Scarfe', Tib Lane Gallery, Manchester, 4-28 Jan, 1967
'US Election '68', Waddell Gallery, New York, 15 Oct-9 Nov 1968
'Hung by Scarfe', Grosvenor Gallery, 4 Feb-1 March 1969
'Hung by Scarfe', Sears Vincent Price Gallery, Chicago, 8 July 1969
'Gerald Scarfe 60-70', Waddell Gallery, New York,
    24 Feb-27 March 1970
'Gerald Scarfe', Motif editions Gallery, London 1970
'Gerald Scarfe', Sculpture Pavilion d'Humour, Montreal, 1970-1973
'Drawings From The Sunday Times', Workshop, London, Dec 1971
'Gerald Scarfe', Art & Design Gallery, Didsbury, Oct 1974
'Gerald Scarfe', Wivenhoe Arts Club, 3 April 1974
'Gerald Scarfe', Gainsborough House, Sudbury, 1 March-28 March 1975
'Gerald Scarfe', The Polytechnic, Wolverhampton, 21 Jan-14 Feb, 1975
'Gerald Scarfe – A Retrospective', Chester Arts Centre,
    1 Sept-30 Sept 1978
'Gerald Scarfe Drawings & Lithographs', Bohun Gallery, Henley,
    15 Sept-4 Oct 1979
'Gerald Scarfe At The Festival Hall', 1983
'Encore' Royal Festival Hall, 24 April-14 May 1983
'Gerald Scarfe at Watershed', Watershed Gallery, Bristol,
    8 Oct-5 Nov 1983
'Gerald Scarfe in Swansea', Glynn-Vivian Arts Gallery, 17 Dec 1984
'Gerald Scarfe in Manchester', Manchester Gallery of Modern Art,
    8 Sept-22 Sept 1984
'Gerald Scarfe at Newport', Newport Museum & Art Gallery,
    3 Sept-1 Oct 1984
'Scarfe Draws The Arts', Royal Festival Hall, Oct 1984
'Gerald Scarfe in Bradford', Cartwrights Hall, Bradford Art Gallery,
    20 Oct-25 Nov 1984
'Gerald Scarfe in Sheffield', Graves Art Gallery, 5 Aug-25 Sept 1984
'Gerald Scarfe at Cleveland', Cleveland Gallery, 23 July-20 Aug 1984
'Gerald Scarfe in the Isle of Wight', Michael West Gallery,
    Jan 3-Jan 24, 1985
'Gerald Scarfe in Aberystwyth', Aberystwyth Arts Centre,
    28 Jan-Feb 25, 1985
'Gerald Scarfe in York', Castle Museum & Art Gallery,
    27 July-8 Sept 1985
'Gerald Scarfe', Manchester Royal Exchange, 9 Jul-10 Aug 1985
'Gerald Scarfe', MacRobert Art Gallery, Stirling,
    27 March-29 April 1984
'Gerald Scarfe in Glasgow'

Theatre

Traverse – 'Ubu Unchained', Jarry, (costumes) 1967
Oxford Playhouse – 'What the Butler Saw', Joe Orton, 1978
    (costumes & sets)
Royal Court – 'No End of Blame', Howard Barker, 1981
    (back projected sets)
Dominion – 'The Big One', Susannah York, Bill Bachle (sets) 1983
Royal Exchange Manchester – 'Who's A Lucky Boy', written by Alan
    Price, Braham Murray and Gerald Scarfe (costume & set design) 1985
Coliseum – 'Orpheus in the Underworld', Offenbach (costume & set
    design) 1985
Guthrie Theatre Minneapolis – 'The Merry Wives of Windsor',
    (set design) 1986

At the end of every exhibition, in respect to my mother, and to all the
people who have asked me over the years, "Why don't you draw
something nice?" I include this drawing of poppies. So why not end the
book the same way?

Group Exhibits

Violence in Contemporary Art, Institute of Contemporary Arts,
    19 Feb 1964
Heroes Live, Tussauds, 3 October 1967
It's Great Britain, New York, 27 Nov-1 Dec 1967
Whitechapel Upper Gallery, Oct 1967
Cartoonists of the British School, East Kent & Folkestone Arts Centre,
    16 March-20 April, 1968
Friends and Famous People, Grosvenor Gallery, Aug 1968
Cartoon Exhibit, National Portrait Gallery, May 1970
Zeichner Graphik, Kunstsalon Wolfsberg, Zurich, 23 Jul-26 Sept, 1970
Langton Gallery Dec 1973
Exposition Dessins d'Humour, Galerie Gérard Guerre, Avignon,
    July 1974
The Polytechnic, Wolverhampton, Jan-Feb 1975
Sudbury, March 1975
'Lives', Hayward Gallery, March-April 1979
'Between The Lines', City Gallery, Dec 1979
The American Institute of Graphics Arts, 29 Oct-26 Nov, 1980
'Snap', The Great Hall Gallery, Aberystwyth, 28 Aug-18 Sept 1981
Time Magazine Exhibit, Royal Festival Hall, 30 Sept-19 Oct, 1983
The Art of the Beatles, Walker Art Gallery,
    Liverpool, 4 May-30 Sept 1984
Europa Quo Vadis, Amsterdam, 1984
Royal College of Art Exhibit, 1985
The Angry Line, Plymouth Arts Centre, 14 April-12 May, 1985
The Angry Line, Association of Illustrators Gallery,
    16 May-7 June, 1985

Film

BBC – I think I see Violence All Around Me – Part writing & animation
    1968
BBC – Hogarth – Writing and Direction 1971
MGM – The Wall – Part writing. Design. Writing, Designing and
    Directing Animation 1982
BBC – Long Drawn Out Trip – Writing and Design. Directing &
    Animation 1971
Digital Dreams – Bill Wyman, Animation 1983

BBC Film Titles

This Nation Tomorrow 1963
This Nearly Man 1973
Yes Minister 1984
Yes Prime Minister 1986
Absurd Person Singular 1985

Rock and Roll

Wish You Were Here – Pink Floyd. Animation 1977
The Wall – Pink Floyd (Earls Court London, Los Angeles, New York,
    Dortmund Germany) Design, Animation, Puppets
Pros and Cons of Hitchhiking – Roger Waters (European Tour,
    American Tour) Production Design, Animation, Puppets

Books about Gerald Scarfe and work

Gerald Scarfe's People 1966 Peter Owen Ltd
Indecent Exposure 1973 Gerald Scarfe Ltd
Expletive Deleted 1974 Gerald Scarfe Ltd
Gerald Scarfe 1982 Thames & Hudson Ltd

Books illustrated

Father Kissmass & Mother Claws, Bel Mooney and Gerald Scarfe,
    Hamish Hamilton 1985
Sketches from Vietnam, Richard West and Gerald Scarfe,
    Jonathan Cape 1968
Pink Floyd The Wall, Avon Books 1982

Work has appeared in:

Daily Sketch	New Scientist
Daily Mirror	Journalist's Student Review
Sunday Telegraph	New York Times Book Review
Daily Mail	Economist
Observer	Ink
Sunday Times Magazine	Life Magazine USA
Sunday Times	Asahi Shimbun Tokyo
Evening Standard	Student
Punch	Town
Private Eye	Illustrated London News
Time Magazine USA	Die Welt
Esquire USA	Times Literary Supplement
New York Magazine USA	Jeune Afrique
Encounter	Queen Magazine
London Life	Della Stampa, Milano
About Town	Holiday Magazine USA
H.P. Mag, Holland	Rheinische Post
Penthouse USA	Fortune Magazine USA
Oui Magazine USA	New Statesman
Contact Magazine USA	

Articles about Gerald Scarfe appeared in

Isis, June 1964
Ham & High Express, 7 August 1964
Daily Express, 5 November 1965
Sunday Times, 16 January 1966
Encounter (Malcolm Muggeridge), May 1966
Women's Wear Daily, 28 March, 1966
Sunday Times Colour Magazine, 3 July 1966
Daily Mail, 7 July 1966
Time Magazine, 15 July 1966
Observer Weekend Review, 10 July 1966
Guardian, 7 July 1966
Arts Review, August 1968
International Herald Tribune, 25 February 1969
Arts Review, 15 February and 1 March 1969
Art & Artists, February 1969
Studio, February 1969
Montreal Star, 5 July 1969
Chicago Daily News, 12 July 1969
Chicago Today American, 13 July 1969
Chicago Sunday Times, 13 July 1969
Women's Wear Daily, 4 March 1970
Sunday Telegraph Magazine, 10 April 1970
Montreal Matin, 17 June 1970
The Washington Post, 2 April 1971
Radio Times, 11-17 December 1971
New York Times, 3 January 1973
Radio Times, 6-12 October 1973
Isis, 2 December 1974
Dagbladet, 9 June 1975
H.P. Magazine (Holland), 29 October 1977
Penthouse, March 1981
Observer Magazine, 11 July 1982
The Record, USA, 6 August 1982
Aquarian Arts Weekly, USA, 18 August 1982
New York Post, 23 August 1982
Los Angeles Herald Examiner, 30 August 1982
Punch, 1 September 1982
Sunday Times Magazine, September 1982
Guardian, 21 September 1982
People Magazine, 4 October 1982
WIT?, 30 October 1982
Blitz Magazine, Oct-Nov 1982
Arts Review, 1 8 March 1983
Forum, 15 May 1983
Ambiente Wohnen International, June 1983
South Wales Argus, 26 August 1983
Glasgow Herald, 19 November 1983
Target Magazine, Autumn 1984
City Life, 13 September 1984
Yorkshire Post, 20 October 1984
Leeds Other Paper, 2 November 1984
Manchester Evening News, 1 July 1985
Lancashire Life, August 1985
Sunday Express Magazine, 8 September 1985
City Life, 13 September 1985
Sunday Times Magazine, 14 June 1964
Studio International, May 1966
Life Magazine, 28 April 1969
Diese Woche
Ark 41 1966
Guardian, 4 Jan 1967 Rheinische Post
Vogue, 1 April 1971   The Studio